BLUEGRASS DAYS NEON NIGHTS

BLUEGRASS DAYS
NEON NIGHTS

High Rolling with Happy Chandler's Wayward Son, Dan Chandler

John L. Smith

STEPHENS PRESS, LLC • LAS VEGAS, NEVADA

Editor: Geoff Schumacher

Cover design: Sue Campbell

Text layout: Maria Coccaro

Jacket, author photo: Amelia Smith

ISBN-10: 1-932173-43-9

ISBN-13: 978-1-932173-43-7

Library of Congress Control Number: 2005931589

CIP Data Available

 STEPHENS PRESS, LLC
A Stephens Media Group Company

Post Office Box 1600

Las Vegas, NV 89125-1600

www.stephenspress.com

Printed in Hong Kong

Dedication . . . and an Explanation

*D*an and I were sipping Johnnie Walker at the Cabin in Versailles one night before the Kentucky Derby after Richard Crane, Duke Davis and a dozen other pals had turned in for the evening. I'd been working with him on his story, but he was struggling with his health and didn't have much energy.

Although I'd chauffeured him to various doctors, I never realized just how sick he was. His big old bulldog's body and even bigger heart were gradually breaking down.

So I changed the subject slightly and asked him, "Who would you dedicate your book to?"

Through a cloud of Cuban cigar smoke, he replied in his warm bluegrass drawl, "I've been thinking a lot about that."

Then he said "It will go like this:

> "To the coaches in my life: Roger Mudd, Paul "Bear" Bryant, Adolph Rupp, and especially Albert B. "Happy" Chandler.
>
> To my daughter, Erin, who is the angel God has allowed me to walk with the longest, and to her mother, Lynne.
>
> This is also for "Happy" Cornell and her mother, Dolores.
>
> And in memory of Chan. You'll always be my boy."

This is Dan Chandler's story, told in his voice.

He reviewed the manuscript, made corrections and suggestions, and I've done my best to render the story and voice of this undeniably unique character to the best of my ability.

— John L. Smith

Contents

A Note from Dan Chandler

General Douglas MacArthur said, "On the fields of friendly strife are sown the seeds that on another day — on another battlefield — will reap the fruits of victory."

Through the growing and nurturing years, there is no influence as important as the coaching a youngster receives. His parents, his coaches, his role models, those he selects as his heroes mold his character and create the fiber of the individual.

As ever, I am reminded of something my daddy said: "Rumors die. Facts live on." I have tried to present the facts as I know them.

I have a deep and abiding respect for the opinions expressed in this story. After all, they are my own. I'll let you decide what they're worth.

Chapter 1

Bluegrass Boy

ome men start at the bottom and work their way to the top. My daddy, the late Commissioner of Baseball and Kentucky Senator Albert B. "Happy" Chandler, was that kind of man. In one incredible lifetime he went from dirt poor to the Governor's Mansion, the halls of Congress, and baseball's Hall of Fame.

The apple of my life fell near Daddy's formidable tree, but through a twist of fate rolled hundreds of miles west and came to rest in Las Vegas. My youth held the promise of great things, but I missed the off-ramp to respectability and wound up in the heart of the wiseguy wonderland.

Which reminds me of a story. A son approaches his father for $100 because he's going on a trip. Instead of giving his boy good advice, the father says, "Here's $200, son, go twice as far."

Born the youngest son of one of the most popular men in the United States, I started at the top and have spent a lifetime working my way to the middle. Along the way, I've met scores of the famous and infamous and have played the gracious host to every one while always trying to remember the lessons my daddy taught me. I have found as often as not that there are some lessons in life that only experience can teach.

In thirty years in the Las Vegas casino business at Caesars Palace and other resorts, I've seen what the power of money can do to a man. In that time, I've befriended a Hall of Fame's worth of sports celebrities, have gotten to know on intimate terms many of the biggest names in entertainment from the latter half of the 20th century, and have bumped into everyone from Presidents to alleged associates of organized crime.

After decades away from Kentucky, I remain unindicted and seldom uninvited.

This is my story, but it begins with the man they called Happy.

Daddy was born Albert Benjamin Chandler on July 14, 1898, near Corydon, a small farming community in east-central Kentucky in Henderson County. The Chandler clan came to Kentucky from Virginia in the 1830s and were fruit farmers in Corydon. The first family member born in Kentucky was my great-grandfather, Daniel Madison Chandler, who is remembered as a "reckless and daring" man who served as a second sergeant with Confederate General John Hunt Morgan's raiders. (Although I've often been described as "reckless and daring," I've tried to make it a habit to do the best I could for my team and play for the winning side. My daddy often said his grandfather was "shot in the heel at Shiloh." At Shiloh, the Confederates were all leaving in a hurry.)

Daddy's young life was defined by hard work and heartache. I am undoubtedly biased in this area, but it's my opinion that my father's boyhood remembrance of the day his mother abandoned the family is one of the saddest passages in the language. He recounted it in his autobiography with Vance Trimble, *Heroes, Plain Folks, and Skunks:*

"Angry voices came from the bedroom. My mother and father were quarreling. She was packing her suitcase. Out at the front gate someone waited in a buggy. My mother was leaving home, abandoning us. I was just four years old. This is my earliest memory.

"'Do you want to take the children?' my father asked.

"'I'll take Robert,' she said. 'I don't want Albert — he looks too much like you.'

"My father shook his head. 'No. If you don't want both — just leave them with me.'

"I followed mother out to the buggy, crying. Dusk was beginning to settle over our little Kentucky hamlet. She gave us two boys a quick kiss, and Robert a long, long hug. The buggy wheels crunched off toward the depot. I sat down at the gate and tears rolled down my cheeks."

If that passage doesn't choke you up, read no further because nothing I have to tell you from here on out will match it. To add to Daddy's heartbreak, he lost his little brother, Robert, to a farming accident just a few years later. Then it was only him and his father, Joseph Sephus Chandler.

Daddy's rejection by his mother drove him the rest of his life and affected all his relationships. He managed to meet her years later, but they were never reconciled. "As far as a normal mother-and-son relationship goes, we just never had it," he wrote in his autobiography.

Daddy's nickname was Happy because of his ever-present smile, but beneath that smiling surface burned a fire of white-hot intensity. My father could not accept defeat in himself or his family and was especially exacting on his children despite the fact that he himself was rarely in the picture at our home in Versailles. That pressure was manifested in many ways on us, but it had tempered him like steel.

My father achieved great things in his life. Born Albert Benjamin Chandler, he became the youngest governor in America when he was elected in 1935, and he was the youngest man in the United States Senate when he entered it in 1939. He was the first man in the history of the commonwealth, which did not allow its governors to sit for consecutive four-year terms, to be re-elected. After serving as Commissioner of Baseball, he returned to the Governor's Mansion in 1955.

To say his children were proud of him doesn't begin to describe our state of mind, but his enormous success was a little intimidating. Although we didn't know it at the time, walking in those formidable shoes would be impossible — though Lord how we tried.

Each child plays a role in his family. The Chandler family got a head start, as Daddy liked to call it, when eldest sister Marcella was born. She had been the only salvageable commodity from Mama's brief first marriage and was a fine and devoted daughter. Next came Mildred, followed by Ben. I arrived late to the party as usual, October 17, 1933.

As the son of an aspiring politician, I grew up standing on the edge of big crowds of people as they listened to my father's off-the-cuff speeches and rousing renditions of "My Old Kentucky Home," "There's a Gold Mine in the Sky," "Sonny Boy," and "Happy Days Are Here Again."

By 1935 the Chandlers were in the Governor's Mansion in Frankfort. This is the atmosphere I was born into. Don't you know it was quite a disappointment when I learned that the People's House wasn't ours to keep.

As the youngest of the four Chandler offspring, I soon discovered that many of the traditional family roles were already filled. As the second-born male child, I quickly found that the job of rock-solid responsible son had been taken by big brother Ben. Almost from the start Ben appeared destined to maintain the family honor and tradition and to please my father and mother. Proof of that is his operation of the *Woodford Sun*, the only newspaper in the county. Since the 1950s Ben has been a voice of reason and a reliable provider of information for his community. Daddy bought that newspaper as a personal house organ, and when it came time to pass it on he looked to Ben, who has always been a tough act to follow in the maturity department.

There's no doubt that Ben was Daddy's shining son, for Happy was never shy about expressing the opinion. In fact, he made a point of mentioning it in his autobiography. "Ben, of course, is the favorite. Every time Mama hollers, he shows up. They get along so well together. Ben loves that paper and Mama has been writing a column for the *Woodford Sun* for thirty years."

Then there's sister Mimi, the apple of Daddy's eye. Mimi was marvelously dramatic as a child and went on to act in Hollywood as a contract player at Paramount Studios before returning to Versailles and her own people. She later served as Kentucky's Commissioner of Tourism.

One of my favorite memories of Mimi was when she and Mama would shuffle off to Keeneland to make a day of it at the races. They'd have more fun playing the horses at two dollars a race than anyone I've seen before or since. Dad, on the other hand, never placed a bet, smoked a cigarette, or had a drink of whiskey. Racetracks served one purpose for him: They gave him a captive audience so he could work the crowd.

One time Happy, seeing the girls prepare for another day at the track, decided to become a bookmaker for a day.

"I'll book all your bets today," he said.

They reluctantly agreed and made their picks hours before the first post. Then they slumped off to the track, some of the fun gone out of their naturally sunny dispositions.

Well, the first race came through a winner. Then the second one hit. Before you know it, they'd cleaned up at the track on the only day my daddy ever acted as a one-man pari-mutuel. The girls made a small fortune, their winnings all the sweeter considering the source.

Mama and Mimi were once photographed at Churchill Downs attending the races, which wouldn't have been newsworthy had Daddy as Commissioner of Baseball not been attempting to crack down on gambling. He'd even banned players from going to the track. So that photo made a good gotcha story, but Daddy chilled out the sports press by responding, "What team do they have a contract with?"

To say I tried to please my father is something of an understatement. In simplest terms, I worshipped the ground he walked on. Forget that he was almost always either headed out the door on business or headed back through the door after a trip to New York, Washington, or Chicago. Or that there were times I saw more of him in the newspapers than at the kitchen table. None of that mattered to a boy hopelessly smitten with the image of the most liked man in Kentucky and, next to Will Rogers and a few others, one of the nation's favorite sons.

As the second son of a favorite son, I accepted my role and made the best of it.

Daddy wasn't one of those sensitive types. He left the nurturing to Mama. His role was strictly disciplinary in nature, and he wasn't shy about going to the switch to get the results he desired. It was crude but effective behavior modification, but it would be a mistake to say it was a good substitute for actual fathering. In some years Daddy was around less than some comets — although he burned as brightly on a national stage. In fact, big brother Ben for a time took to calling him "Uncle Daddy" in sincere confusion over his place in the family pecking order.

Once at home, however, he was quick to assert his authority. He went to the whip faster than Willie Shoemaker. He wrote in his autobiography, "Dan was more clever. He knew the whipping would stop as soon as tears came.

"Definitely I was rough on 'em. Dan misbehaved and I ordered him upstairs. I stood by the stairs and helped boot him up. 'I'm introducing my shoemaker to your tailor,' I told him."

That's precisely accurate, and I can almost feel those punts to this day.

As Commissioner of Baseball, Daddy was focused on the issues of the day, the greatest of which was the potential — most owners called it the "threat" — of integrating the game. After World War II, it was clear to anyone with eyes that the Negro Leagues fielded players who were well qualified to play in the National or American League. Question was, how would white fans react? Because once you let them on the field, you couldn't very well deny them access to the box seats. It was a complex issue that all America hung on.

Of course, there was other business on Daddy's agenda. Near the top of the list was what to do with Brooklyn Dodgers Manager Leo Durocher. "Leo the Lip" had been a classic scrappy infielder who was transitioned into a pugnacious manager. But it wasn't his managerial skills that were controversial with Dad. It was his inability to stay away from big gamblers and bookmakers and guys who took their fedoras and overcoats very seriously. Dad suspended Leo, and years later when I was at Caesars and Leo was still hanging around the fedora-and-overcoat set as well as Frank Sinatra, he found out my lineage and maintained his grudge against my father by proxy. He made it clear he hated my guts, and I rapidly got to the point where the feeling was mutual. Nature, in my humble opinion, has made no more difficult creature to handicap than the little man.

Dad told Dodgers owner Branch Rickey, "It looks like you can't take care of him. Let me take care of him for you."

After all, Durocher had busted a heckler's jaw and had been running around with the wiseguy gambler crowd.

"If I made any error, it was on the side of being too lenient. Just suspending him for a year was no great thing. I could have put him out for life, it would have been justified. One year wasn't any big deal. I signed thirty-six death warrants as Governor, so it wasn't anything for me to get excited about."

Daddy wasn't through shaking up the game. He didn't hesitate to suspend the players who jumped to the Mexican League chasing the promise of big pesos. Unlike Durocher, who got a one-year sentence, the Mexican Leaguers were hit with five-year suspensions.

But historians remember Dad as the players' commissioner — and for good reason. He championed their first pension program and carved out a deal that helped it get funded through a contract he negotiated with the Gillette Safety Razor Company in exchange for letting them advertise during the telecast of the World Series and All-Star games.

In January 1947, Baseball's owners had a secret meeting at the Waldorf Astoria to consider Rickey's proposal to bring a little-known infielder named Jackie Robinson up from Triple-A Montreal to the Big Leagues in the coming season. Ordinarily, there'd be no need for such secrecy, but this was no ordinary infielder. This man was black, and Major League Baseball had never had a Negro player. The vote was taken and only Mr. Rickey voted for his bold idea. The ballot was 15 to 1 against integrating the great American pastime.

Rickey went from New York to Versailles on the Dodgers' Beechcraft and met Daddy there at the cabin. It was a very emotional time and its importance was not lost on us children. Race riots were predicted at the Polo Grounds, which stood in Harlem. And there was a genuine possibility that the game's many Southern players and fans would boycott. Rickey was a great man, but the fact is he saw Robinson as a sound economic move that might get his Dodgers a long-sought World Series title. "I'd play an elephant with pink horns if it could win the pennant," Rickey once said. But in those days an elephant would have been more accepted.

Daddy didn't hesitate. He easily could have gone the old racist route of his predecessor, Commissioner Landis, who'd had many opportunities to integrate the game and had managed to avoid every one, the last coming shortly before his death in 1944. Daddy never lacked a sense of purpose and understood his place in history.

In his autobiography he recalled telling Rickey: "I've already done a lot of thinking about this whole racial situation in our country. As a member of the Senate Military Affairs Committee, I got to know a lot about our casualties during the war. Plenty of Negro boys were willing to go out and fight and die for this country. Is it right when they came back to tell them they can't play the national pastime? You know, Branch, I'm going to have to meet my Maker some day and if He asks me why I didn't let this boy play and I say it's because he's black, that might not be a satisfactory answer.

"If the Lord made some people black, and some white, and some red or yellow, he must have had a pretty good reason. It isn't my job to decide which colors can play big league baseball. It is my job to see that the game is fairly played and that everybody has an equal chance. I think if I do that, I can face my Maker with a clear conscience."

And he did — to the intense anger of the fifteen owners. Jackie Robinson was brought up to the Dodgers on April 10, 1947 — one day after Daddy suspended Brooklyn manager Leo Durocher for gambling and his associations. It was all too much for the press to fathom, and somehow Rickey was credited with breaking the color line and Daddy was blamed for suspending the feisty Durocher.

Robinson's progress remained on the front of the sports page, but his success on the field went a long way toward relieving the pressure of the situation.

🐎

Daddy's seven-year term as commissioner expired in 1951. He sought to renew his contract, for he cherished the duty despite its difficulties, but Yankees owner Del Webb led a group of owners against him and prevented him from securing the 75 percent majority necessary to renew his contract. There were three votes in Sarasota, Florida, that winter to consider whether to retain Dad's contract. The votes were 9 to 7, 11 to 5, and 9 to 7 — all in favor of renewing.

It was the only election he ever won and yet lost the job.

The owners made overtures to FBI Director J. Edgar Hoover, who scoffed at them and said, "After the way you treated Governor Chandler, I wouldn't touch it with a ten-foot pole."

At a testimonial dinner held for Daddy not long after he left baseball, his friend Bob Hope chimed in, "This is the biggest crowd I've ever seen come out to honor a fellow who's just been fired!"

But Daddy could always draw a crowd. Instead of sulking, he charged right back in to Kentucky politics and by 1955 was elected to a historic second term as Governor, this time by a record-setting landslide.

Again he was called upon to do the right thing when others were shying away from their duty. Following the U.S. Supreme Court's decision that "separate but equal" was no longer acceptable in public institutions such as schools, Arkansas Governor Orval Faubus called out the troops to block the schoolyard gate. Daddy could proudly say he called out the National Guard to make sure those gates stayed open.

Daddy was not a man with a small opinion of himself or his abilities. I planned to blossom in his long shadow, which as any amateur horticulturist knows is a nearly impossible task.

Chapter

Lessons Learned

*I*f it sounds as if Daddy was preoccupied, it's true. But he was not so distant that he could not be reached through just a few words from Mama. In fact, it was she who suggested strongly that he stop shirking his familial duties and take his youngest son with him on the road. It would be good for us to be together, and it would help calm the Chandler household back in the commonwealth. Traveling with my dad was a special time for me. Dad wouldn't fly. He'd flown in World War II around the world with the U.S. Senate Military Affairs Committee. He didn't fly after that. He always took the train. Daddy said, "If you're in a hurry, leave earlier."

When we'd go to sleep he had the lower berth and I had the upper berth. I had to hustle up to go to sleep. Daddy would take Vick's salve and put it on his chest, put it up his nose, and ask the porter to get him a drink of water. He never drank alcohol, never smoked a cigarette in his life. He'd say, "You better hurry, son. I'm going to sleep." And I'd hurry and try to get to sleep first because, boom, he'd be out in no time and then here'd come the chainsaw. His snore could be heard loud and clear above the locomotive engine.

One of those father-and-son trips took me to the funeral of George Herman Ruth. Daddy loved the Babe and understood his essential place in baseball history. Most people will point to today's superstars, who regularly hit fifty or more home runs, and say they would have mopped the floor with Babe, but the truth is none of them can take his measure. They have forgotten, if they ever knew, that Babe was not only the game's first great power hitter, but he was responsible for saving baseball after the 1919 Black Sox scandal.

Babe Ruth died in August 1948, and my daddy was one of his pallbearers. It was one of the trips Mama insisted he take me on, and so I stood with him in a crowd of people at the funeral of the greatest player to ever live. The photograph taken of Daddy and me paying our respects at the coffin ran all over the world. When I look at that picture I can remember trying not to smile. There was nothing funny about the moment, of course, but as a boy I had a nervous habit that made me grin and I recall having to force myself to look grim.

The scene was overwhelmingly emotional and terribly sad. Babe, who'd been so strong for so long, couldn't beat the cancer that ravaged his body.

Taking a seat at the knee of history and great athletic celebrity was commonplace due to Daddy's status in the world of politics and sports. While other boys dreamed of meeting a big-leaguer, men the caliber of Ty Cobb and Ted Williams regularly dropped by the house. Cobb was known as an irascible racist, but he was the picture of manners around Daddy. Williams was a personal favorite not only of me, but of Mimi, for I think he had his eye on her.

Williams loved my dad, but was so uncomfortable around adults that he would disappear in the middle of a gathering to walk down to a nearby field to watch ragamuffins like me play the game. It was heady stuff that never failed to impress the neighborhood boys, and the sense that I could please a crowd depending on the company I kept must have made a lasting impression, for years later as a casino marketing host in Las Vegas I specialized in such matters.

By then, of course, I'd not only fallen in love with sports but had secretly vowed to become either a statesman like Daddy or a slugger like Ruth, Cobb, or Teddy Ballgame.

Daddy was one of Ty Cobb's trustees for his estate. Cobb stayed out in the cabin and he definitely drank. One time I took my friend Bruce Miller to meet Ty at the cabin, and the kid nervously approached the great hitter.

"Mr. Cobb, what do you think of Ted Williams as a hitter?"

Cobb snarled, "Boy, you don't know enough to ask me questions." The kid wanted to cry.

That was Cobb. Nobody got a break. Rough and raunchy and ready to brawl. But Ty loved my daddy.

Ted Williams got called away twice to serve his country, in World War II and the Korean War as a Marine Corps pilot. Ted sought Dad's advice. The South is full of real strong America Firsters. And Ted heard a lot of that kind of talk from Dad and appreciated it.

Ted Williams and Pee Wee Reese, my two heroes, were featured in pictures in my boyhood bedroom. I worshipped them and knew them because they came to the house. I never got to attend a World Series while my dad was Commissioner, but he promised that if the Dodgers ever faced the Red Sox, I'd get to go. He wasn't going to give me the total soft play. Dad was trying to make me tough, make me appreciate the privilege that was a part of my life.

If Ty Cobb and Ted Williams had had their say, my dad would have been elected to the Baseball Hall of Fame on the first ballot, but it wasn't until 1982 that Daddy was inducted. He got along with most people, but as Commissioner he couldn't get along with Red Smith, who was the leader of the New York sportswriting fraternity. Red took them all away from Daddy. He was once asked, "Why can't you get along with sportswriters from New York?" He said, "Principally because when you get across the Hudson River they think you're in

Indian Territory." All that did was incite them further. Of course, he wasn't trying to be easy on them. He wasn't easy on anybody.

He was the players' commissioner. He didn't kowtow to the owners. And he was a non-person for thirty years after he left the commissioner's job. It was Bowie Kuhn who brought baseball back to him. He was inducted that day with Henry Aaron, Frank Robinson, and Travis Jackson.

Of course, Daddy wasn't always on the road or on the stump. We shared some great moments together, but no one ever accused him of being the gentlest of men. There was one time we were playing softball with some neighbor kids and he whacked a long one to center field. The outfielder retrieved the ball and threw it home as he circled the bases. That day, I was covering home plate.

I'll let Daddy take it from here, as recollected in his autobiography:

"Instead of stopping at third, I charged on toward home, trying to stretch it into a home run. Dan, holding the ball, stood guarding home plate, waiting to tag me out.

"I barreled into Dan just like they do in the major leagues. Dan was knocked one way and the ball flew the other. And I was safe at home.

"The back screen door burst open and Mama, white-faced with anger, came rushing out. Dan was picking himself up.

"'Poor, little Dan, you've killed him!' she screamed. 'Why did you do that?'

"'Mildred, nobody else is gonna get out of his way and I want to teach him a lesson.'

"Her eyes kept flashing fire.

"'The thing is that Dan's got to hold onto the ball, and take care of himself, and tag the runner out. If he loses the ball, the fellow is not out. Nobody's ever gonna let him just win . . . not in this life.'"

I understood what he was saying, of course. But I was thirteen. If I'd been wearing a jock, the impact would have knocked it clean off.

Once the cobwebs cleared, I tried to take the lesson to heart. Years later, as if to ensure that the incident was remembered in the best possible light for his legacy, Daddy wrote in his autobiography, "Dan was impressed as a kid by what I taught him about being aggressive and competitive. To a friend he remembered: 'Growing up I had enthusiasm and intellectual curiosity, but I didn't have the killer instinct. I could get the ball down inside the ten, but I just lacked the drive to get it over. You know Daddy would take it into the end zone and right on through. If anybody ever had the killer instinct it's him!"

My early life was marked by men who specialized in the killer instinct, a trait that somehow failed to rub off on me. My father was the first. He was followed closely by Roger Mudd, my football coach at Darlington Prep School in Rome, Georgia. Darlington was a nondenominational school with a heavy Presbyterian flavor that my big brother Ben had attended, and I followed his lead. Longtime viewers of television news will remember Roger Mudd as the ramrod-straight reporter and anchor for CBS News, but he started as a teacher and coach at the private school. Dan McNall was my basketball coach, and I became an All-Conference player under his tutelage. Dan was a strong positive influence in my life, but Coach Mudd was the man with the whip hand. He went to it often. He was an apprentice Bear Bryant in the discipline and slave-driving department.

Coach Mudd later went on to become one of America's first generation of great television news reporters. Years later, I was proud to host him at Caesars Palace.

Coach Mudd was one of those kinds of guys you'd run into later in life in boot camp in the form of a drill instructor. Ironically, thanks to Daddy, Coach Mudd and Coach Rupp, when I entered the Army for two years active duty after college, boot camp was a breeze and I finished first in my company in the infiltration and obstacle courses at Fort Campbell and Fort Leonard Wood. Those men were like "New York, New York." If you could make it there, you'd make it anywhere.

I excelled on the court and playing field in high school, but I didn't match my dad's success. No one could. Compared with him, who'd overcome so many obstacles, I always felt my success was sort of artificial. He always said that I was better than him. Statistically, that may have been so in some areas, but the difference was that with me success was an option. When I'd come home with C's on my report card, Daddy would say, "Dan, you think anything over 70 is wasted." But he'd had to make good grades or he would have been stuck in the fields for the rest of his life. For him, success was a matter of survival. Jim Murray used to say that he wasn't amazed when a kid from a ghetto pulled himself up by his bootstraps and made it in the professional ranks. What choice did he have? Jim said that what was truly amazing is when some kid from a good family, who was driven to school, who was raised with a silver spoon, became a champion, because he has so many more diversions. And for the one who isn't hungry and hustling his next meal, putting in the extra effort is an option.

The difference between me and my dad as athletes is the difference between natural and artificial education. It's the difference between Robinson Crusoe and reading about Robinson Crusoe. If it hadn't been for the friendship of Dr. Carpenter way back in Dad's youth, his athletic ability would not have been discovered. He wouldn't have been awarded a football scholarship to Transylvania College, and it was that education which opened doors to the rest of his incredible life. Without a break, he would have been an amazing football and baseball player who, in all likelihood, would have remained a small-town hero. People in this generation don't realize how large the world was then and how incredibly small it is now.

I was an All-Southeast Sectional player in basketball and was good enough to land a scholarship at Colorado University, but Dad decided it would be best if I attended the University of Kentucky and played under its legendary coach, Adolph Rupp. So of course I did.

In those days, Rupp didn't recruit players but merely selected the best of the best. He was rumored to hold the franchise rights to all players east of the Mississippi and south of the Mason-Dixon. He merely had the lease option on the rest of the country.

⚞

Coach Rupp was the ultimate taskmaster and, like Paul "Bear" Bryant, the Kentucky football coach in those days before his legendary career at Alabama, didn't believe you were building character until you had collapsed from exhaustion. Surely Coach Rupp would build my character and temper it like the sword of a knight of old — if he didn't kill me in the process.

He was a decidedly unsentimental man whose ultimate and only goal was winning basketball games. Had he chosen to pursue a career on Wall Street, he surely would have become a billionaire. If he'd taken to a field of battle, that field would have run red with the enemy's blood.

As good a shape as I was in after my senior year of high school, I was still ill prepared for what Coach Rupp had in store for a freshman basketball recruit with more heart than talent. For me, it was an opportunity to play basketball on the best team in the nation. For Coach Rupp, it was a chance to fill out his roster of blue-chippers with the capable son of the most powerful man in the commonwealth. Even in those days Coach Rupp was a legend on the court and a political manipulator with few peers. Had he entered politics, he surely would have challenged Daddy's mastery of that blood sport.

His Wildcats teams were perennially among the best in the country, and he was known as the sport's toughest coach. There would be many practices interrupted by players vomiting and even collapsing, but they only came back for more because they believed in his ability to make them winners.

He gathered us in a circle on that first day of practice at the empty, silent Memorial Coliseum and held up a basketball.

"Most of you think this is something you play with, but it's not," he said. "This isn't play. This is work. This is a job. See those 12,000 seats? We don't give any of them away. We sell them. We sell them because we win. You've been hired to do a job, and that job is to win basketball games. If you don't do the job, you'll be fired and we'll get someone in here who does the job."

I grew up a little bit that afternoon with Coach Rupp's "Welcome to Kentucky" lecture.

Then we ran until our legs turned to rubber and our lungs felt like they were on fire.

Then we ran some more.

To say that Coach Rupp was all business begs the obvious. To say he'd flunked sensitivity training is an all-world understatement. With Coach, you were never confused about where you stood in the pecking order.

He divided the world into two categories: starters and turds. The starters received all his attention. The turds were relegated to the status befitting the title. They were fodder for practice drills.

I was one of Coach Rupp's turds.

He played five players, five incredibly gifted players. When they tired, which was seldom, he played one or two more.

He was loath to play more for fear of not blowing out opponents and allowing people to recall Kentucky's scandalous years past. I was the eighth man in a seven-man basketball strategy. Over the next three years, I played little but learned a lot about sports, egos, and human nature.

"Sitting the bench" for Coach Rupp was a terrible misnomer. Those who did not play but were taking up valuable scholarship space were likely to be the focus of what can politely be described as a big chill. You sat during games. The rest of the time you ran until you dropped and were drilled nonstop by Rupp's assistant, Harry Lancaster. Simply stated, Lancaster was Coach Rupp's runoff man. When a guy couldn't play as well as they wanted him to play, that got Lancaster after him. Lancaster's job was to make it so indignant, to give that man so much grief, to find that man's weak spot and then exploit it and drive him away. Lancaster tried to give those suspect players so much rejection that they finally took the hint and quit. Obviously, Harry and I weren't going to be the best of friends.

The joke was that Rupp kept Harry around to tell him the names of players beyond the seventh man.

If there was anything I was used to, it was running up against impassive taskmasters, and I made it my goal to outlast Lancaster and beat him at his own game. I took all he dished out and kept on coming. They might not put me in the game, but they sure as hell weren't going to disgrace me in front of my friends and family by calling me a quitter.

Kentucky was on probation when I joined the squad in 1952. The program didn't need me, but it sure could use the credibility associated with my dad. Time has faded this story and today the sports pages are riddled with tawdry tales from the police blotter, but back then the scandal associated with Kentucky was the most embarrassing incident in all of sports.

In 1949, a group of players at several universities was approached to affect the outcome of games by piling on the score, effectively ensuring that the point spread would be beaten. Seeing no harm in giving an opponent an extra whipping and making a few bucks on the side, Kentucky's Ralph Beard, Alex Groza and Dale Barnstable took the fixers up on their offer. They made $100 a game and Kentucky was the mostly highly regarded team in the nation.

As part of its punishment, the team was only allowed to scrimmage. But we played four intersquad games that year — all to sellout crowds at Memorial Coliseum.

I'll never forget when he took the microphone to announce to the crowd, "The two best teams in America are playing at Memorial Coliseum tonight: Our first team against our second team."

You know something? He was right.

But it was more complicated than that. Coach Rupp's pride was hurt and he vowed never to let such an embarrassment happen again. It would be many years before he would set foot in Madison Square Garden, where some of the questionable games had taken place. And he attacked the business of basketball with a vengeance.

Even for one as thick-headed as myself, it didn't take long before I realized that I held no place in Coach Rupp's heart or game plan. So I augmented my lack of playing time that year by turning out for the tennis team. It was not exactly a status symbol at Kentucky, where basketball was king and football — even with a young coach named Paul "Bear" Bryant coaching — was a distant second. There was no third.

In my sophomore season, I was a member of the only undefeated basketball team in Kentucky history. I played little, but had managed to gain the support of fans who apparently liked my effort. There was no denying I was giving my all for the team, mostly in practice.

We went 25-0 my sophomore year. The team was voted national champions by the Associated Press and United Press International coaches' polls.

But we did not go to the NCAA playoffs that year, and the reason we stayed away has rarely been put in the proper perspective. The reason was pure Coach Rupp, who practiced the maxim that there is no interest in life as attractive as self-interest.

Three of the team's best players, Cliff Hagen, Frank Ramsey and Lou Tsioropoulos, were ineligible for postseason play because they had finished their undergraduate work during the year of suspension and had started postgraduate studies. With my performance in the classroom, I would have never had this problem. It was one of the most asinine rules in a college sports system littered with them. Those three players had been drafted by the NBA, but chose to stay at Kentucky to help Coach Rupp win a championship and recover some of the esteem he'd lost due to the point-shaving scandal. Remember, these players had also been forced to sit out the penalty season the previous year even though they had nothing to do with the cheating.

CHAPTER TWO

Cliff later recalled, "We were penalized for the year we were forced to sit out and that was for something we had not been involved in. If we had taken five years to graduate we wouldn't have had a problem. So we were penalized for trying to do the right thing."

We reached a crossroads at the end of the regular season. Either we congratulate each other on a job well done and go home, or we vote to go on without some of our stars and try our luck in the NCAA Tournament. Understand, no one on the court that day believed for one second there was a team in the country that could beat us — with or without all our standouts. By a show of hands, we voted 8 to 3 to participate in the tournament.

But we had mistakenly believed that Kentucky basketball was a democracy. After the hands were counted, Coach Rupp interrupted us with a reality check. We'd wrongly assumed that it was our team, when in fact it was his.

He said he had hoped we would vote not to accept the invitation. But since we had, he had decided we weren't going. He wasn't going to let "a bunch of turds" ruin the perfect record. Forget that we knew in our hearts we could succeed. We went home without ever knowing.

The Wildcats went 23-3 my junior season, during which I had the biggest game of my career. In keeping with my career highlights, you might guess that my performance had nothing to do with putting the ball through the hoop. In fact, I didn't play a single minute in my big game.

I scored a few points that season — I like to wink and say I hold a school record for free-throw percentage, a perfect 3-for-3 — but my most memorable game came my junior year against the University of Alabama and was one in which I didn't play a minute. The game was a showdown with the Southeast Conference title in the balance.

In keeping with custom, Coach Rupp handed five basketballs to the five starters during pregame warm-ups. The key substitutes also shot around while the rest of the team was assigned to stand at the ten-second line near half court and eyeball the opposing team's players. We were supposed to study their moves, notice any flaws they showed, and generally focus on the game in case we happened to be called into it. As the Memorial Coliseum filled to capacity with 12,000 fans, we kept watching the Alabama players.

The atmosphere was one that intimidated most teams, but this game Crimson Tide Coach Johnny Dee decided he was going to give Coach Rupp a little of his own medicine. So he assigned his bench players to walk to the edge of half court and stare down the Wildcats. Dee had mistaken our pre-game warm-up and focus for an attempt at intimidation. He told several of his players to walk right up into our faces and not take any shit.

Little did he know that we were Coach Rupp's Turds. Shit was our business.

And so when 6-foot, 7-inch, 200-plus-pound forward Jim Bogan dared me to cross the ten-second line, I couldn't resist. Forget the fact I was a stretch 6-footer, or that my job was to study the opposition, not spar with it.

The crowd was looking at the two of us standing within a foot of each other. I'd try to look around him to the left, and he moved to obscure my view. I moved right, and so did he.

When he dared me to cross the line, I did. And he popped me right in the jaw. I was rattled, but I was also on the court in front of the home crowd. So I responded as best I could against the larger man, getting in my licks. In a moment, I found the fighting grew much easier after teammate Ray Mills grabbed Bogan's arms and nobody grabbed mine.

With such an edge I could have whipped Rocky Marciano, and I took full advantage. It's only in Western movies that the hero throws down his gun when a fistfight breaks out. With such an edge, I wore out poor Bogan.

The State Police eventually took the floor and restored order as "The Star Spangled Banner" played and the crowd cheered.

I took a victory lap before the adoring masses before hitting the showers, and I actually thought I saw Coach Rupp smile.

Sportswriters later noted that I won on points in an unscheduled preliminary to the Alabama game, which we also won.

My senior year I was hurt but recovered in time to try out for the baseball team. I played second base and shortstop and hit .370, but the batting average wouldn't keep me from serving a hitch in the Army.

After coaches Chandler, Mudd and Rupp, the Army was a piece of sponge cake. I was in the best shape of my life, and Fort Campbell was like a summer camp. I was finally a starter on an athletic field, but it turned out to be the infiltration and obstacle courses of the U.S. Army. I spent two years in active duty, six more in the reserves and helped coach the freshman basketball team at Kentucky while picking up my final twelve hours of classroom work to finish my degree.

Meeting and marrying Lynne Bryant, the daughter of a Lexington auto dealer and the university's most beautiful girl, was by far my greatest accomplishment. We had two great children, Erin and Chan, and although we divorced long ago, she remains the love of my life.

I had forever and always wanted to please my daddy, but like a one-legged long jumper I fell short time after time. After finishing my bachelor's degree and acting as assistant freshman basketball coach several floors under Coach Rupp, I recruited and scouted for the program for a season and applied unsuccessfully for head coach openings at the University of Nevada and Tennessee.

With no solid coaching jobs open, and not wanting to begin at the bottom of the ladder in the high school ranks, I used my gift of gab and increasing circle of contacts to sell stock and found it to my liking. There was good money in it, and it would take good money to keep my sweetheart in the lifestyle to which she'd become accustomed. At that moment, my life should have been complete, but there was something missing: recognition through public service.

I had watched Daddy politic my whole life. Meeting the people came as naturally to me as falling off a curb, and a buzz began in Democratic Party circles that I might someday make a fine Congressman.

Of course, I was not at all interested in waiting for someday to arrive.

Chapter 3

Politics and the Prodigal Son

*I*t has been said, at least by me, that politics is a disease of the blood that inflates the ego. And my daddy reveled in his political fever throughout his long life. His unprecedented success on the stump and at the ballot box — he was the only man in the 20th century to serve two terms as Governor of the Commonwealth of Kentucky, was twice elected a U.S. Senator and served as Commissioner of Baseball — gave him ample cause to believe his opinion carried great weight and insight.

He was a political phenomenon. In an era of intense political packaging, in which every hair follicle and every sound bite is groomed, it might be difficult to imagine that my daddy was a natural. He took to politics like few men in the century, rose from nowhere to the Kentucky statehouse in 1925, was in the U.S. Senate during World War II, was re-elected Governor in 1955 and was so nationally popular that year that he was seriously considered for the candidacy of the President of the United States, getting votes in seven states. My mama used to say politics was as natural to Happy "as a goose going barefoot." Epigrams and folksy sayings came naturally to him. Citizens would long remember lines like, "I'll put the jam jar on the bottom shelf so the little man can reach it," but never know that such things came to him as he went along and were not scripted by a dozen speechmakers. In fact, Daddy rarely used a note when he spoke. The man sometimes ended a speech by singing a song to his crowd of adoring fans.

And he never forgot a name. Once he met you, you were a friend of Happy Chandler.

"My skill at recalling names has helped immensely," he wrote in his autobiography. "I've been asked the secret of that. It's simple. You don't need any complicated memory code. I learned a long time ago. When you meet a fellow, you'll look him in the eye and shake his hand and hear his name. Now the average fellow doesn't hear his name and really doesn't give a damn. If you never heard his name, you've got no way to recall it again. And a lot of folks don't pay any attention . . . I always try to concentrate on the name. I have been able to astound fellows. I would say I saw you at a certain place at a certain time, and they'll say, 'My God — unbelievable!' In 1918 I met a fellow in a churchyard at Ewing, Kentucky. I never laid eyes on him again until twenty-five years or thirty years later. I called him by name and mentioned where we met. He liked to have fell over.

"Something similar happened on one of my many trips to New York. A cabbie picked me up at the railroad station. He muttered something about being from Brooklyn. I said, 'Yes, I know who you are.' And I called him by name. He almost stopped his cab. 'Commissioner, you're a bum,' he said, shaking his head, 'All Baseball Commissioners are bums, but you're the best bum of them all.'"

Daddy's political contacts knew no bounds. He was a bona fide player on the national scene. In Chicago, he was on intimate terms with the most powerful man in the state of Illinois, Mayor Richard M. Daley. In fact, it was through Daddy's old contacts that out in Las Vegas I eventually befriended House Ways and Means Chairman Dan Rostenkowski, one of the toughest political pugilists of his day. Once on a visit with Daley, Daddy encountered Bob Hope and

Prince Philip of England. When the visit broke up, Hope told the prince, "Say hello to the wife and kids for me." Daddy loved Bob, and it was through him that I later befriended the comedy king, who never failed to tell me how much he loved my dad.

Of course, Dick Daley and John Kennedy had more in common than party affiliation. The commonly circulated story in the late 1960s was that on election night in 1960, Daley and Joseph Kennedy conferred and Daley asked Kennedy, "How many votes do you need?" The would-be President's father told him, and Daley delivered. One thing is certain, John Kennedy never forgot or failed to show respect for the Boss of Chicago.

Daddy had a strong working friendship not only with future President Kennedy, but he'd also been impressed by his eldest brother, Joseph Kennedy, who'd been a Massachusetts delegate to the Democratic National Convention in the late 1930s before going off to war and dying there. Of course, Happy had also been on intimate terms with papa Joseph Kennedy, who had been Ambassador to England and was as tight with the Daley Machine and the old bootlegging crowd as any man alive. He'd sung songs late into the night with Boston Mayor "Honey Fitz" Fitzgerald the year the Boston Braves won the pennant. Daddy never drank, but he hung out with revelers of every political stripe.

My own encounters with John Fitzgerald Kennedy were unforgettable. We worked hard on his behalf in Kentucky during the election and were among those invited to the inauguration that cold January in 1961. With the snow several feet deep, we walked up the front of the portico of the White House. JFK himself let us in.

I was so excited I could hardly speak, which is saying something in my case. In many ways, my whole life's ambition had led up to that moment, and I even entertained thoughts of becoming part of his White House staff. I'd been infatuated with Washington since childhood, when as a thirteen-year-old kid I sat in the East Room of the Mayflower Hotel in Washington and listened to my dad as he ate ice cream and talked policy with great Senators of the day like Dick

Russell and Harry Byrd, Henry Cabot Lodge Jr. and James Eastland. They moved armies around and carved out policy, and I soaked up what I could. Even then I appreciated the power of those men. It wasn't movie stars that were celebrities to me. It was those strong men of that era, and I had entrée to their world through my dad. I grew up appreciating that strength.

On that cold January day, I stood with the strongest political figure in the world. My lifelong friend Buzz Nave was with me as JFK ushered us into the Oval Office for a visit. He, of course, wanted to make sure I knew how much he admired Dad. I shook his hand and introduced him to Buzz.

Buzz was even more nervous than me. As he rose and leaned across the desk to shake hands, I couldn't resist goosing Buzz. His hand jumped a foot and he nearly went sprawling across the desk.

To this day Buzz calls that his most embarrassing moment and his most thrilling moment at the same time. It's not every day you get to meet the President.

The family's contact at the White House was the President's appointment secretary, Kenny O'Donnell, the Harvard football star who was close to Bob Kennedy. We would go through him when we wanted to see the president.

Not long after he took office, JFK made a stop in Louisville, and of course we were there to greet him. He made a speech and invited my wife, Lynne, and me up to his room for breakfast at a downtown hotel.

We took the elevator up to his floor and were met by a gaggle of Secret Service agents. When we got to his suite, I was surprised to see him smoking a big Cuban cigar in his T-shirt relaxing on the couch. It sounds strange, but I never thought of him wearing a T-shirt, much less relaxing. He was the leader of the free world and here he was asking us if we'd like coffee. We of course accepted his gracious offer. He ordered room service pancakes and couldn't have been more charming. I saw then why so many were so devoted to him.

To say we were both infatuated is something of an understatement. I'd been around great athletes since childhood, but I'd rarely seen a man with as fine a physique. And he was the most handsome man I'd ever seen — good Lord, I'd swear that T-shirt was tailor-made — and Lynne couldn't keep her eyes off him.

Nor, I noticed, did his eyes stray far from hers. He had an incredibly engaging stare. She'd been the homecoming queen at the University of Kentucky and time had not diminished her stunning looks. I was used to having men stare at her, but this wasn't just any man. This was the leader of the free world, and it was obvious that he liked what he saw.

He was a consummate gentleman, of course, but if Lynne had wanted to run away with him, I wouldn't have blamed her. Even at that time I thought that if he sent out for someone, they must come on the dead run. He didn't exactly look like Grover Cleveland. He was movie star handsome with an aura of power about him that was nothing short of intoxicating. Later, when stories began to come to light about his alleged liaisons, it was not difficult to believe them. It should be remembered that in those days of Camelot, the free world was throwing itself at JFK. I couldn't condemn him for catching a few.

After Dallas, the nation mourned and we were sick with mourning. Though many years have passed, the pain of those dark days will never leave me, and I cannot fathom what that family endured. I wrote a letter of condolence to his family and brother, Bobby. I didn't know then that it was the beginning of a friendship, albeit a heart-breaking one, that I cherish to this day.

In many a conversation as a young man, when I aspired to public office in the wrongheaded notion that I could follow in my dad's formidable footsteps, I'd attempt to interject my own point of view on a topic of political importance.

Getting a word in with Happy was like trying to catch a fast-moving train, and so I'd blurt out, "Here's what I think . . ."

But before I could finish a simple sentence he'd cut me off like a Civil War amputee.

"Don't think, son, it weakens the team," he'd say, sending me to my corner with a bruised ego.

Many times he was right. Many times I would have been wiser to listen and make them wonder if I was a fool instead of opening my mouth and removing all doubt.

But there came a time in 1968 when my political ambition outraced my better judgment. As a 28-year-old stockbroker and young married man, I decided to jump in to the participatory side of politics with both feet. I challenged the heavily entrenched Congressman John Watts, who sat as the No. 2 man on the coveted House Ways and Means Committee and knew the importance of bringing home the bacon for his fellow Kentuckians. I was part of the admittedly idealistic groundswell that was sweeping Bobby Kennedy, whom I'd met and befriended when he was U.S. Attorney General, toward the replacement of President Lyndon Johnson. LBJ was mired in Vietnam and had decided not to run for a second term, and Kennedy was, in my unabashedly biased opinion, simply one of the most dynamic political figures of the century.

If Bobby could become President, then I felt I could move out the old guard and join the revolution as a member of the House. I was like a two-year-old thoroughbred who was kicking the stalls down I was so anxious to get on the track and run. It took time to penetrate my thick skull, but I eventually discovered how wrong I was.

I was on the track, but I wasn't ready to run and I knew it. But by then I'd committed and my daddy expected me to give it the blood-and-guts effort. It had worked for him, and he couldn't see why it wouldn't work for me despite the fact that we were woefully underfunded, Watts was well liked and controlled everything from thoroughbred breeding taxes to tobacco farming subsidies, and the people of Kentucky had no compelling reason to hand him his hat.

I was on my way to a drubbing, and anyone not suffering from the political fever could see it. Early in my fledgling campaign, Watts made a private proposal: Would I consider backing off in exchange for a job as a field secretary for the House Ways and Means Committee? It was prime duty, an excellent opportunity for me to learn the ropes in Washington. It might lead to a more assured future in politics, and every prominent ally we knew said I should take it.

But Dad said no. He couldn't understand that his popularity wasn't going to be handed down like a tailored suit from one generation to the next. "Now is when you establish yourself as a sellout if you give in now," he said.

To say it put me in a bind is something of an understatement. As one who lived, and quite comfortably, in his shadow much of my young life, it was crushing rhetoric. It was just my dad's mindset and he refused to listen to all his friends who said I should take the job and live to fight another day.

It was the great Kentuckian Henry Clay who said politics is a series of honorable compromises, and we all tried to convince my dad that this was an honorable compromise. But he was a combination of Bear Bryant, Adolph Rupp, Knute Rockne and Teddy Roosevelt. He refused to acknowledge the facts and made my status a question of honor.

I tried to tell him what I thought, but he'd remind me not to think, that it weakened the team. So I stopped thinking and ran straight ahead — into a scene straight out of the Little Bighorn, with me in the role of General Custer. I threw a scare into Watts, but little more. I not only didn't get the job in Washington, but I didn't impress the home folks by getting bounced by the more experienced Watts.

In my zeal to please my father I'd foolishly tried to step into his footprint. If I were deposited at the heel of that print, I'd be winded by the time I got to the big toe. His shoes were impossible to fill.

But, oh, how I loved politics. I enjoyed being a public man, but in my naivete I'd left gaping holes in my lifestyle that enabled them to run in and criticize me. It was no one's fault but mine, but I learned more from running than anyone can imagine who has not had the experience. You can learn more from life by being a participant than as a spectator, and that truth applies to any field.

One of the things I gained from the experience was what would grow into a lasting friendship with members of the indefatigable Kennedy family, not the least of which was an admitted crush on the incredible Ethel Kennedy. After I'd established myself in Las Vegas, I met her through my man Don Klosterman, who in those days appeared to own the Bel Air Country Club and would play host to Ethel when she was in Los Angeles. I joined them for some of the most delightful lunches I've ever known. The courage of some people, and I include Ethel and Don in this group, is nothing short of awe-inspiring.

I was chastened by my loss to John Watts, but that didn't chill my political fever. In 1971, I accepted a job as deputy finance chairman of Edmond Muskie's presidential campaign. Muskie was a fine, if painfully plain fellow, and I believed Richard Nixon was beatable by a mainstream Democrat who, unlike the incumbent, didn't throw a five o'clock shadow at noon. Time proved me wrong about the race but right about Nixon.

As a stockbroker, I was on friendly terms with the top guys at Lehman Brothers. My contacts in business and on Wall Street made me a logical choice to help fund-raise for Muskie, and so I took the position, flew to Washington and checked into the Mayflower Hotel, where Daddy had lived when he served in the Senate. I had barely unpacked when the wheels of politics turned back home, and I was called in to National Committeeman Jack English's office. He delivered the bad news. Kentucky Governor Wendell Ford had promised to deliver thirty votes to Muskie come the Democratic National Convention under one condition: That I be replaced as deputy finance chairman in favor of one of his allies. I later learned that someone back home was concerned that I might be plotting a return to candidacy at a high level and they had no intention of me enjoying a national spotlight. I learned that I got knocked out of the job by Wendell Ford, whom my daddy had been for and against over the years and who would later serve in the Senate. Senator Muskie wasn't about to take chances with the Governor of Kentucky when they believed that the nomination process would be close. History would note that the principled liberal George McGovern would win the nomination and rush headlong into a slaughter against Nixon.

As one who has tasted defeat, I knew something of how McGovern felt.

I was feeling especially depressed. Not only had I let myself down, I had let Happy down.

My daddy told me, "Son, sometimes it skips a generation."

It took thirty years to figure out just how right he was.

One of the lessons I had to learn the hard way was taught to me by John Y. Brown Jr., the man who took Kentucky Fried Chicken public and made it a household word and later became Governor of Kentucky — thanks to the star quality of his beautiful wife, Phyllis George.

Johnny's father, John Y. Brown Sr., was what you'd call a perennial office-seeker. The people of Kentucky didn't know it was spring unless John Sr. filed for some office. Although he eventually won a term in Congress, he must have held the record for most losses in the history of the commonwealth. While my dad was busy winning races, Johnny's dad was busy losing. That created a competitive grudge that I only learned at a high cost years later.

My dad, who went to law school with John Y. Sr., had the winningest record. He was elected to the state Senate, then lieutenant governor, then governor, then elected to the U.S. Senate. John Y. Sr. was a late entry against my dad when he ran for the Senate the second time, and my dad won 119 of 120 counties.

Johnny and I went to college at the same time. We debated each other, and Johnny got the better of me. He was a great salesman even in those days and in fact sold encyclopedias when he wasn't playing on the university golf team that was led by future PGA Tour champ Gay Brewer.

Johnny had a competitive problem with me, but it was thirty years before I knew it. He had a talent for making money and I was not much of a businessman. I'd had a couple of good years as a stockbroker, but when the market went down my portfolio took a tumble and I got in a terrible hole with my taxes, getting charged with failing to file a corporate income tax form, a misdemeanor, despite the fact that I'd overpaid my personal taxes by $1,600. I was, in fact, broke and pled no contest to the charge. It left a mark that certainly didn't help my future in Kentucky politics or business.

I couldn't make a living in Kentucky. My marriage was on the rocks. I tried to get a job through Governor Louie Nunn, the Republican who'd been elected with Dad's help, but could only land duty counting the toll roads for a few hundred a month. My friend Walter Trautman called and asked me to come to Florida and take over the tennis concession at the Jockey Club in Miami, which I did. And there I made $150,000 a year. But I wanted to return to Kentucky and resume my previous life. I didn't know at the time that trying to turn back the clock is a fool's errand.

Meanwhile, Johnny wanted to buy Lum's restaurants and he knew that I knew Cliff Perlman, who was a member of the Jockey Club and led a group that controlled the chain. I got Cliff interested in selling the Lum's restaurants in Dayton and Broward counties, and so put together a willing buyer with a willing seller. Then I called a friend from Lehman Brothers, Bill Kempton, to come in and square away my end of the deal, which I promised to split with him. Bill received $285,000 cash for his effort, but when it came my turn to be paid, Johnny implored me to stick with him. He said he'd put my half into stock in a company called Restaurant Franchise Industries, and within a year it would be worth a million dollars.

Johnny was fresh out of taking Kentucky Fried Chicken national when he cut a deal with a fellow named Ollie Glitchenhaus to acquire the rights to franchise his popular Ollie's Trolley burger stands in parts of the South. A friend of mine, Atlanta businessman Charlie Barton, wanted to buy a piece of the franchises, and I wanted to sell my stock and get on with my life. I told Charlie I would sell my shares to him, but when I went to close the deal he said that he'd discussed it with Johnny and Johnny thought it best that he bought his shares instead.

"Just let Dan keep his," Johnny told Charlie. "I'll sell you some of mine."

With no one else to buy the stock, I was forced to sit on my shares. Needless to say, they did not hatch into gold.

Little did I know that Johnny would take Restaurant Franchise Industries into bankruptcy a few months later and my end of the deal would turn to nothing. It kicked me so hard that I then knew there was no way I could go home again.

Johnny was on a roll. While I had believed him a man of his word, he had avenged his father's failure in a game I never knew was being played. I could never forget what he'd done because it may have had the effect of shoving my marriage over the edge.

(My luck with chicken franchises got no better a little later when I briefly entered an agreement to purchase a string of Daniel Boone Fried Chicken stores with Sammy Davis Jr. It had the makings of a genuine score and a breakthrough in the business department for yours truly. Instead, it was more gristle and bones. Sammy wasn't used to losing money on business deals he was associated with, so it took him a while to mend, but years later at Caesars we ran into each other and maintained a friendship.)

It was about that time Cliff Perlman offered me a job at Caesars Palace in Las Vegas for $40,000 a year. Addled by the turn of events, I accepted his offer even when it was reduced to $25,000. Lynne refused to move from familiar country and asked for a separation. I told her there was no way I wanted to practice getting a divorce and so we split up for good.

On January 3, 1974, I landed at McCarran Airport in Las Vegas and went to Caesars Palace, where I was met by Cliff and his main man, George England, who at that time was married to Cloris Leachman. I met the President of Caesars, W. S. Weinberger, that day and believed my interview was going well.

During a break, I walked around Caesars Palace and was impressed with the place. Who wouldn't be? With its enormous fountains and dozens of statues, it was an impressive sight. The casino was jumping and I went outside to get a little air by the fountains.

A car pulled up beside me and the attractive woman behind the wheel lowered the electric window. She motioned me to come closer, and I did.

"Would you like a blowjob?" she asked.

I smiled and thought, "Dan, you're not in Versailles anymore. I think I'm gonna like this town."

To say Daddy was underwhelmed with my misstep and life choices in general skirts the truth. There was a time he was almost ready to change my name or his. As they say, he was with me "win or tie." But to fail in a marriage, in politics, or business was hard for him to accept.

In his autobiography, he was exceptionally noncommittal. Whereas he described sisters Marcella and Mimi and brother Ben in the most glowing terms, he was somewhat more reserved with his depiction of your humble servant.

"There's no argument that Dan turned out to be our most unusual offspring," he writes. "Certainly the most peripatetic, and he's every bit as gregarious as I am. He attended the University of Kentucky and played basketball on Rupp's team that had five All-Americans. He became a stockbroker in Lexington and married a girl he knew at the university. They had a boy and a girl. They are now divorced. It's terribly ironic that part of my main duty as Baseball Commissioner was to protect the major leagues from gamblers and now my youngest son is a well-known executive in casino operations."

Well, he was right, of course. I was the family's most unusual offspring.

A week after I arrived in Las Vegas with my clothes and golf clubs, I was sitting with Cliff Perlman in the gourmet room of the Frontier and naturally we shared a mutual distrust for Johnny Brown, who was ascending the world of Kentucky politics.

"It's all right with me if I never see the guy again," I said in an offhand way.

Cliff looked at me surprised.

"If that's the way you feel, Dan, you need to give me your resignation," Cliff said.

It wasn't until then that I realized how close Johnny was to the Caesars crowd. He was not only good at making all that money, some of which I believed was ethically mine, but he was even better at spending it in the casino.

I overcame my astonishment and learned a lesson about human nature and men who are hopelessly bitten by the gambling bug.

It was no small solace that over the next few years, even while living in the Kentucky Governor's Mansion, John Y. Brown quietly lost many millions at Caesars Palace. Some people would call that revenge on my part, but I wouldn't dream of laughing at his losses.

After all, by then I'd found my niche and while to the rest of the world he might have looked like a sucker, to me he was simply a good customer.

Chapter 4

Bugsy, Benny, Moe . . . and Me

The history of gambling is inseparable from America's own look at itself. Although it has sometimes been accused of corrupting the impressionable, the fact is gambling has been around since the beginning of time. Americans like to be known as Puritans in their early history, but they were gambling back when John Smith came to Jamestown.

But the image of gambling is changing. When Nevada legalized the activity in 1931 (it had been tolerated for decades before that), there were newspapers across the nation that editorialized about the prospect of revoking its statehood!

Most folks don't realize that a generation earlier another notorious activity, baseball, received the same treatment because of its supposed ruinous effects on young men. Supposedly, it encouraged them to smoke and drink and gamble and corrupt their morals generally.

Today, of course, baseball is the great American pastime. I'm not proposing that one day gambling will replace the old ballgame for supremacy, but it appears to be gaining ground in states across this great land.

Another lesson from history that will add to your perspective on the supposed evils of gambling concerns the game called bingo.

Today, you know bingo as that fun, entertaining game played largely by the AARP set but more recently by college kids seeking a good time. You can play bingo and drink margaritas almost as easily as you can play bingo and drink a glass of milk. The competition gets fast and furious, but the game ain't rocket science.

Anyway, these days we know bingo as such a wholesome game that it is played with regularity at church fundraisers and other charitable events as well as in state-of-the-art halls in Las Vegas. But did you know about its naughty past?

It's true. Bingo was once influenced by shadowy figures linked to organized crime. It was once the subject of major investigations and all manner of police scrutiny from Long Beach to Long Island. Atlantic City is known as the East Coast gambling capital, but in the 1920s it was a den of shameless bingo play.

In fact, many members of the casino hall of fame got their start operating bingo halls in out-of-the-way places. Bill Harrah, one of the great innovators, got his start in a humble bingo hall and opened another in Reno just after World War II. Steve Wynn's daddy was a bingo operator in as many as seven states. Steve was raised calling the numbers.

It's a safe bet that a majority of the operators in the pre-corporate era got their starts in bingo halls, backroom sports books, or illegal casinos. Their dreams came true when they moved to Las Vegas, where they no longer had to look over their shoulders.

Perhaps all you really need to know about Las Vegas is that it's only a century old, but gambling has been going on in the valley for several thousand years. Long before Bugsy Siegel popped his head up in the Mojave, Anasazi, Paiute, and Shoshone Indian tribes all had their games of chance. I'd be willing to swear that the gambling urge is in the water around here. How else do you explain the choice of early Las Vegas as a place to roll out the green felt?

Here's how it happened.

Although Spanish explorers and trapper Jed Smith had crisscrossed the region earlier in the 1800s, Captain John C. Fremont and his party were the first to map the area that became known as Las Vegas, or The Meadows. Las Vegas was an oasis with plentiful water.

It was plentiful water that attracted the San Pedro, Los Angeles and Salt Lake Railroad to cut tracks through the valley in 1905, and that May thirty-two lots were sold in the original Las Vegas townsite (today known as downtown.)

But it was the Depression-era construction of Hoover Dam that really put Las Vegas on the map. The presence of thousands of construction workers, combined with a slump in the state's mining industry, helped give Legislators the idea that it might be wise to legalize gambling — especially considering it was already being practiced openly around Block 16, Las Vegas' red light district in those days.

But just because Las Vegas legalized cards and dice, it by no means meant that gambling's practitioners were men of savory repute. Just the opposite, in fact.

But some put up a better front than others.

Guy McAfee, for instance, was a Los Angeles vice cop who managed to amass enough money crime fighting and no doubt shaking down the street element to open the Pair-o-Dice Club on U.S. Highway 91 and later front the Golden Nugget downtown. McAfee is credited with calling the ribbon of asphalt between his joint and downtown "The Strip," after Hollywood's Sunset Strip.

Tony Cornero was a classic old-school Italian character who'd run a gambling ship out of Long Beach before going ashore in Las Vegas. He opened the Meadows, which burned, and years later was the driving force behind the creation of the Stardust. He died before it was finished.

Motel chain owner Thomas Hull opened the El Rancho Vegas in 1941. Movie theater mogul R.E. Griffith built the Last Frontier Hotel and a collection of guys put together the El Cortez that same year. Among the percentage owners of the El Cortez: Meyer Lansky and Benjamin Siegel.

Las Vegas bustled along, but it wasn't until *Hollywood Reporter* publisher Billy Wilkerson ran out of money for his dream project that Siegel emerged as a player in Las Vegas. His contacts with the Syndicate financed the completion, millions over budget, of the fabulous Flamingo at Christmas 1946. It was a legendary flop, and six months later — even though the casino had recovered nicely, house odds being what they are — Siegel was murdered at Virginia Hill's place in Beverly Hills.

Talk about a tough retirement plan. And I thought my 401(k) was hurting me.

Las Vegas has always been dominated by larger-than-life characters, men who were ballsy enough to practice the casino craft and still fade the heat from society, the government, and the strong-arm types.

Society was simple. As long as the gamblers kept to Nevada, only it would be stained and respectable states could go about their moralizing business — even though it was their citizens who flocked to Las Vegas every year to heat up the dice and cards!

The government was a tougher nut to crack, but fortunately, politics being what it is, the high moralizing and finger-pointing was usually limited to a few months every four years — by no small coincidence, about the time Congressmen and Senators were running for re-election. They might gamble, drink, and carouse in Sin City on the sly, but that didn't mean they couldn't threaten fire and brimstone from the pulpit of hypocrisy.

The first federal official to take a big swing at the gamblers was U.S. Senator Estes Kefauver of Tennessee. Kefauver is the man who dreamed of using the Senate Rackets Committee he chaired as a launching pad for the presidency. Although he received the equivalent to prime air time on a national stage, the rail-skinny moralizer's message went flat after a fashion. Like the police chief in *Casablanca*, Kefauver was "shocked, shocked" to find gambling going on all over the United States. And that gambling was being run by, you guessed it, racketeers, mobsters and ne'er-do-wells of every stripe and station. Except that, in Nevada, where gambling was legal, all those illegal racket boys got religion and practiced the games in the open. They were undergoing slight but increasing licensing scrutiny (the Gaming Control Board era wouldn't kick in for a few years yet) and most importantly they were paying their taxes.

If they skimmed a mother lode off the top, well, that was for them to know and the FBI to find out.

The impact of the Kefauver Committee on Las Vegas was twofold: It put enough heat on gamblers in other regions to drive them to Nevada, and it was a helluva advertisement for Las Vegas.

At the time, Morris Barney "Moe" Dalitz was one of those transplanted liquor and gambling racket kings who had decided there was less heat in Las Vegas in July than there was in Cleveland in February. Moe and his boys combined with Wilbur Clark to open the Desert Inn, and I'm proud to say that in later years Moe was a friend of mine. On that account I cannot claim exclusivity, of course, for Moe was a friend of every man and woman who set foot in Las Vegas. Old John C. Fremont might have been the first to map Las Vegas, but men like Moe were the real pioneers who put the town on the map with their investment and innovation. Moe created the Tournament of Champions golf tournament and used his connections with the folks who ran the Teamsters Central States Pension Fund to generate many loans that built, among other things, the first for-profit hospital in Las Vegas. Those loans might have been considered suspicious in origin, but they sure were good for the town.

From the standpoint of traditional casino ownership, it's hard to top Moe for color and success. He is known as the former Cleveland bootlegger who made Kefauver look like such a mope during those infamous Senate subcommittee hearings in 1951. But Moe was far more important to the development of Las Vegas than as a mere casino boss. He had the Teamsters Central States Pension Fund connections with President Jimmy Hoffa, who he'd known since they were both young men in Detroit and later Cleveland. At a time when no civilized white glove lending institution would dream of touching Las Vegas, the Teamsters ponied up a couple hundred million in pension fund loans, most of which were paid back with interest and without incident.

In that regard, you might call Moe the godfather of Las Vegas in the best sense of the term. He not only built the Desert Inn and ushered the Stardust and Sundance (now Fitzgeralds) into existence, but his connections and association with Paradise Development resulted in Southern Nevada's first for-profit hospital (Sunrise), first major shopping mall (Boulevard), country club (Las Vegas Country Club), and numerous other developments. In terms of physical stature, Moe was a small man, but he was a giant who cast his shadow across the valley.

In his later years, I had the pleasure of spending time with Moe. We traveled a bit in his specially designed motorhome and always in the company of pretty women. He knew how to live, all right.

But I loved to talk to Moe about his start in Las Vegas. It wasn't always an industry he was running. Old Estes Kefauver and his Senate boys swore it was a racket tied to the Syndicate. Although during those Senate hearings Kefauver got in a few digs with others when he brought his traveling circus to town, he got nothing over on Moe. Moe was smart as a whip and wise enough to hire Kefauver's old law school chum as his lawyer. Moe turned the committee upside down and reminded the esteemed Senators, many of whom had been born into wealth, that he "didn't inherit any money."

Nor did my man Benny Binion, a dirt-poor Texas boy who went from horse-trading to liquor running to dice dealing to Las Vegas, arriving shortly after World War II with a couple million in cash in suitcases and his brood piled into a Cadillac, high-tailing it out of the Lone Star State ahead of the sheriff. In his salad days, Benny was known as a man who could, as he once put it, "do his own killins." But that was the nature of the liquor and dice business in Dallas. In the modern era, competition is a bit healthier, but when Benny was in action the competition could get a little rough.

Although the heat didn't fade from Benny for several years — he took a brief vacation for a tax beef — he quickly became one of gaming's major players and easily its most colorful operator. His Horseshoe Club downtown was known for its great food, cheap whiskey, and high-stakes gambling. Until the day he died in 1989 Benny would fade any bet a man had guts enough to place in cash on the table. "If you can bring it, you can bet it," Benny used to say.

Benny was also an all-world character with a horse sense deserving of a Ph.D.

Benny used to say, "Aren't we brilliant out here sitting on a mound of cash?"

He would also remind casino experts he encountered that "In the land of blind, the one-eyed man is king."

Benny lived by a rule he liked to repeat to friends and acquaintances alike. "I believe in the Golden Rule," he'd say. "The man who has the gold makes the rule."

Benny would also say, "It's easy to be honorable when you got plenty of cash. But it's not so easy to be honorable when you're broke."

In other words, he knew it's easy to have character when you're on top. You can look like a superstar, but that's the shallow end of it. But it's like the poet says, "What tests your mettle and proves your worth; it's not the blows you deal, but the blows you take on this good old Earth that shows if your stuff is real."

Not long after I arrived in Las Vegas, I befriended Benny Binion, whose Horseshoe Club was not only one of the hottest casinos in the city, but was a center of political activity. Benny might have had trouble ciphering, but he could read the writing on the wall and the political landscape like few men in Nevada.

One day he called and asked me to visit him in his office, which was in the casino coffee shop. Passers-by would commonly see him having breakfast with judges and lunch with the sheriff. I was honored to be called to his table, for I knew this was where careers rose and fell.

"Son, you come from good stock," he said. "I want you to run for state Senate. I think you'd win, and I'd be willing to bankroll it."

I was flattered. Here was one of the men who made the wheels turn in Las Vegas. But I couldn't mislead him. I'd had a dustup in Kentucky in that misdemeanor tax case and had had a belly full of the participatory end of the political stick. I told him about my tax troubles, and he just laughed.

"I know something about that myself," he said. Benny had had an extended stay at Leavenworth courtesy of the IRS many years earlier. It had done nothing to dampen his country sense of humor.

But if I no longer wanted to command the spotlight in politics, it didn't mean I was done with the ultimate American blood sport. Far from it. In fact, I've had more fun working on the periphery of the game than I probably ever would have had being in the middle of it. Along the way, I've met and befriended many leaders of national significance and am proud to say I even helped a new generation of Chandlers succeed where I had not.

And there was Jackie Gaughan, who teamed up with Mel Exber to buy up downtown like spaces on a Monopoly board. If I had an ounce of their business sense I would have been a millionaire decades ago. Jackie and Mel got into the business booking bets, but when they came to Las Vegas their horizons expanded. Jackie had a small piece of the El Cortez and eventually bought the whole show. He and Mel owned the Las Vegas Club, with its great baseball theme that Mel loved so much, and Jackie later created the Plaza. Between Jackie and Mel and J. Kell Houssels, downtown was a going concern and an essential part of the city's and state's economy.

But that didn't prevent the government from poking around for scandal and secret ownership.

The second push by the federal government to get to the bottom of the gambling phenomenon and its murky relationship with organized crime came nearly a decade later when my friend and political ally Bobby Kennedy was Attorney General. The impact of those hearings further pushed the gambling set from the back rooms of Covington and Queens to Las Vegas, where the games were straight and the action was legal.

Las Vegas had no shortage of gamblers, but with the exception of Moe Dalitz, there was only one man who qualified as a visionary. His name was Jay Sarno.

You won't find him ranked among the city's top gamblers or casino operators. He wasn't even a successful businessman in a city that helped give rise to Kirk Kerkorian and Steve Wynn. But Sarno, I'll say, was easily as important as both of those innovators.

In short, Jay was a big-idea man. It was his vision, with heavy Teamsters financing and mob influence, that in 1966 became Caesars Palace. From the start, Caesars was the finest casino in Las Vegas. It was the ultimate carpet joint with plush accommodations, high-limit gambling, exotic restaurants, Roman-themed statues throughout, and palatial fountains marking the entrance. It was a place apart, Sarno's Caesars.

The fact that "the boys" owned it lock, stock, and dice table was beside the point.

Jay got his start in the motel business in California and grew wealthy building his cabana-style motor hotels.

Like a lot of men who wound up in Las Vegas, the story of how he got there is a curious one. He used to say he was going from Texas to San Francisco on a packed flight that stopped off in Las Vegas. When that plane took off again it was almost empty. It was then Jay knew there was something going on in Sin City.

But Jay also had some one-in-a-million Miami Beach connections, and through those he landed Melvin Grossman as the architect for Caesars Palace and More Mason Construction along with the Las Vegas company, R.C. Johnson. Combine that expertise with enough Teamsters Pension Fund loan money to get the job done, and Caesars rose as the first casino built in Las Vegas in nine years when it opened August 5, 1966. Jay's mark was all over the building metaphorically and physically, for one of the building components was an "S"-shaped brick that became known as Sarno block.

Jay knew that every male visitor to Las Vegas fantasized about being treated like a Caesar of old: the booze, the food, the female companionship. And so he designed an entire resort around that concept. The cocktail waitresses at Caesars wore togas. The Bacchanal restaurant became instantly famous because of its wine goddesses and complimentary neck massages. Once Jay stepped aside and let the gamblers do their thing, Caesars was a smashing success.

The hype of the new Las Vegas is so great that people forget Jay first had the idea of adorning his resort with works of art. But his choices were in keeping with Caesars' Roman Empire theme.

He loved statues and fountains and so he filled the place with remarkable replicas of famous works, some cut from the same Carrera marble from the same Italian quarries that had produced great works by Michelangelo. When visitors saw the enormous "David" and incredible "Rape of the Sabines" statues, they were seeing as close to the real thing as they'd ever likely lay eyes on.

He wasn't finished yet. In 1968, again with help from the boys, Jay built Circus Circus, the most innovative casino concept in the world. On the main floor was an ocean of gambling, on the second floor was a sprawling arcade for young people and families. High above were trapeze artists, and on stage were other circus acts. Although initially unsuccessful — Jay opened without building a single hotel room and initially tried to charge admission to the arcade — once Bill Bennett took it over, Circus Circus became the most profitable major casino in Las Vegas. And it set records without granting credit or catering to the gourmet-grinding high-roller set. Jay's big idea had been enough.

Sarno died before he could bring his plan for a super-sized, 6,000-room resort, the Grandissimo, to life. Of course, no one at the MGM Grand would probably admit it's more than a coincidence, but that 5,000-room resort bears a general resemblance to Jay's dream.

A lot of men can take a bow for their role in helping to create Las Vegas, but no one had wilder ideas than Jay Sarno. Steve Wynn sometimes receives credit for "inventing" the new Las Vegas, and he did an incredible job with the Mirage, Treasure Island and Bellagio, but in reality the man who was the star in that arena was Sarno.

On the casino floor, the games were not run by Phi Beta Kappa key holders, but by guys with checkered pedigrees and a world of street experience. Back when I arrived in Las Vegas, the day-to-day operations were run by men who talked out of the sides of their mouths in exotic accents and hailed from other places. Finding a local-born pit boss was harder than finding gold in the street.

For years a visitor to Las Vegas would be forgiven if he mistakenly believed that Youngstown, Steubenville, Wheeling, Covington, Cleveland, Miami Beach, Brooklyn, the North End, and the South Side were all suburbs of the Las Vegas Strip, for that's where the dealers came from.

And that is the world I walked into as I crossed the threshold at Caesars Palace, the ultimate carpet joint.

The Lord made few men more colorful than Jay. Everything he did was big and bigger. He gambled like a fiend and threw away millions across the tables. His table manners were, in a word, unique. He would eat two ice cream cones at once and he was known to eat spaghetti and meatballs — with his hands.

But with that eccentricity came the mind of a true genius. And he was not without a sense of humor. When Circus Circus opened, he brought in a trained elephant not only to entertain the guests but to stand in the craps pit and throw dice. With its trunk, the animal could pitch a pair of dice a country mile.

To put it politely, the elephant gave a new definition to the term "craps pit." Its birthday cake-sized tips were not appreciated by the other players.

Jay Sarno died in 1984 without ever seeing his Grandissimo dream come true, but without him it's safe to say Las Vegas wouldn't be the same.

🐎

There have been a lot of eccentric human beings in the Las Vegas casino business — there's something about the scent of money that encourages the behavior, I'd bet — but none was stranger than Howard Hughes. He was a playboy billionaire when the world had darn few billionaires. He'd been around the gambling racket boys from World War II and had bedded most of the starlets in Hollywood. In fact, he owned a cabin mansion at Lake Tahoe with a guest house right on the water that was especially designed for the objects of his affection. He even used some of his chiefs of security to procure the best talent.

But he was an increasingly strange cat when he arrived in Las Vegas by train in the middle of the night on Thanksgiving weekend in 1966. He set up shop on the top floor of the Desert Inn, and eventually bought that property and half a dozen others.

Hughes was entering the final stage of a wild life, and he was doing so with sufficient means in his pocket. Just six months before he moved to Las Vegas, he sold his majority stake in Trans World Airlines. Cash-out: $547 million. And, as I say, in those days that $547 million stretched a little further than today.

Hughes had money, but if you're inclined to believe recorded events he didn't have a permanent place to stay. He'd arranged to stay at the Desert Inn just a month, for after Christmas the New Year's holiday traffic brought real gamblers and Hughes no longer gambled. (On his original forays to Las Vegas after World War II, he was a high-roller and gambled as he serenaded the senoritas.)

When Dalitz finally ordered Hughes to leave to make way for gambling guests, Hughes decided he liked the place well enough that he bought it for $13.2 million.

That is a great story, one that has been repeated in every history ever written about Las Vegas. And there's some truth in it. But don't forget that Hughes was no hotel operator. Nor was he a casino operator. In truth, the hotel and casino men who'd run the Desert Inn for Moe Dalitz largely continued to operate it once Team Hughes took the reins. Hughes added his Mormon mafia crew of loyalists, and as always the proof of his competence rested at the bottom line. The Desert Inn, then one of the hottest spots in Las Vegas and a well-oiled resort machine, lost money. Which meant only one thing: Someone was going south with the greenbacks.

Robert Maheu had been with the FBI before it went by those initials, and he knew the ins and outs of investigation and law enforcement like few men. He worked as a special vice president for Hughes and was paid $500,000 a year — more than most casino presidents. Maheu has remained active in the Las Vegas community since those early days and has outlasted by several decades the man who made him rich. Maheu is a one-in-a-million character.

Hughes was supposedly so irritated by the gaudy lights and rotating namesake of the Silver Slipper casino located across the street from the Desert Inn that he was compelled to buy the joint for $5.4 million. A good set of blackout curtains would have been cheaper, but the Silver Slipper story goes with the legend of a man so smart that he cashed out a half-billion from Trans World Airlines but so simple that he paid twice what the Desert Inn was worth and let it be siphoned, then paid too much for the Silver Slipper, Sands, Castaways, Frontier, and Landmark. To my knowledge, he paid too much for all of them. If that Silver Slipper story were actually true, don't you think that Hughes would have taken the time to remove that sign? He didn't. But that's part of the Hughes legend that won't die.

Another great story is the one about how he became the owner of a local television station, KLAS-TV. Hughes was a night-owl and in those early days KLAS shut down its signal around midnight and Hughes wanted to watch the late, late shows — shows of his choosing. So he paid $3.6 million and bought the station from *Las Vegas Sun* owner Hank Greenspun and others. Hank loved to tell that story, and he understood better than most just how eccentric Hughes really was.

Hughes was known as a sharp businessman, but the truth is he was plucked like a barnyard chicken by men like Moe Dalitz. His places turned poor profits due to some unreliable management, and he never built a single resort. He was no innovator; he was a landlord. One operator once told me, 'How would you like to work at a place where you knew beyond a shadow of a doubt that the boss was *not* going to come in?"

Hughes is known as the man who helped clean up Las Vegas, but that view is only partly accurate. If anything, his operation just brought a new level of layering to the casino business. His presence gave rise to the creation of the corporate era.

Hughes was important, though. His ownership calmed down the feds at a time of increasing scrutiny of the casino boys, who hadn't changed much from the racket days chronicled by the Kefauver Commission.

Lest you think I fail to appreciate Hughes' contributions to Las Vegas, I'll tell you something he did do that changed the shape of the valley forever. It was so forward-thinking that the man behind it deserves a statue. When most other Southern Nevadans were looking at the valley and seeing a bustling but dusty little boomtown, Hughes studied the plot maps and saw a great metropolis rising from the Mojave sands. So he went and bought many thousands of acres of raw desert real estate for pennies on the dollar. His great legacy in Las Vegas isn't all those casinos he overpaid for; it's the desert land he underpaid for. Today, that land is covered by some of the most incredible housing developments in the West. The development is known as Summerlin, and the Howard Hughes Corporation is responsible for the creation that even the eccentric billionaire would be tickled by.

Along with that land for development, in keeping with a long Nevada tradition, Hughes also was suckered into buying millions of dollars worth of mining claims that weren't worth the paper they were printed on. The only gold and silver to be found in those claims was in the pockets of the speculators who sold them to Mr. Hughes.

Of all the stories I've heard about Howard Hughes, what strikes me as genuinely sad is that with all his money he stayed cooped up in his hotel room. There are no stories of his donning disguises and walking out among the people. He had a wide range of phobias — his germ phobia is the most well known — and he lived in fear of being poisoned.

But to write him off as a candidate for the nuthouse is to sell him short, for even in his diminished capacity — a sanity addled by drug abuse, if various published reports are accurate — Hughes was also a man of substantial vision who saw the potential of Southern Nevada. He saw the threat of the Nevada Test Site and all things nuclear on the image of Las Vegas, in his way predicting the fight forty years later over the Yucca Mountain nuclear waste project. And he kept his hand in politics at a high level, giving controversial cash donations in the 1968 Presidential campaign that would echo with scandal years later.

About the only fun I've ever heard that Howard Hughes had in his stay in Las Vegas had to do with his obsession with banana ripple ice cream. The man couldn't get enough of it. In fact, casino man Burton Cohen recalls the time the folks at Baskin Robbins stopped making banana ripple and the stuff had to be special-ordered in a lot large enough to feed an army.

In the end, Hughes left Las Vegas in December 1970 the way he arrived — in secret. The era that historians talk about to this day had lasted just over four years. Hughes had dumped tens of millions of dollars in Las Vegas and by my count hadn't had much fun — and left a whole lot of banana ripple behind.

Chapter 5

Vegas Kings

*H*oward Hughes' exit coincided with the establishment of hands-down the biggest and most successful casino developer in Las Vegas history, Kirk Kerkorian. Like Hughes, Kerkorian made some of his early money in the airplane business. Unlike Hughes, who was a silver spoon kid, Kerkorian made a few thousand bucks buying and selling airplanes after World War II. Stories about of how he would fly from Hawaii all the way to Los Angeles — and land on fumes or by gliding the multi-prop monsters in for a landing — still raise the hair on the back of the neck to this day. Kerkorian was the son of an Armenian immigrant (Kirk still gives handsomely to Armenian relief and charity efforts) and teamed with his brother Nish Kerkorian to make a go of it in the fight game. But Kirk had too much between his ears to risk getting his brains beaten to mush, and he parlayed those airplane deals into real development.

Kerkorian bought the Flamingo in 1968 from a group of Miami Beach hotel men who had Meyer Lansky's number memorized. Morris Lansburgh and Sam Cohen had owned hotels in Florida and were the subjects of a lengthy federal investigation into suspected skimming at the Flamingo.

His timing was perfect. Kerkorian flipped the Flamingo and bankrolled an even bigger and far more controversial project. He decided to build the largest hotel-casino in the world, the International, and he was determined to construct it off the Strip!

The building went up on Paradise Road next to the convention center, nearly a mile from Las Vegas Boulevard. Some critics called him foolish. Howard Hughes was jealous — he'd just bought the architecturally flawed Landmark and didn't want the competition — and the conventional wisdom was that a hotel that size could not earn back its investment. Just too many rooms.

Conventional wisdom was, as usual, worthless. Kerkorian had a winner. And he was only getting started.

Kerkorian sold the International to Barron Hilton, who renamed the place the Las Vegas Hilton. Then Kerkorian embarked on a plan to combine his love and influence of the movies (he owned MGM Grand Studios in those days) with his obsession with building an even larger palace than his International. In 1974, the MGM Grand was born. It was again the largest hotel in the world.

And it offered something for everyone. More than the usual gourmet rooms and showrooms, the MGM had a jai alai fronton and one of the greatest movie theaters ever created. It featured plush couches and cocktail service while MGM movies were screened. (One of those films was the resort's namesake, the MGM classic *Grand Hotel*.) It was a great idea that came a generation before its time.

Tragically, the MGM Grand burned on November 21, 1980, and 82 people perished. I'll never forget the way the smoke hung in the air above the Strip. It was a death shroud that hung metaphorically speaking for many months afterward. Privately, Kerkorian was devastated. He knew he'd not scrimped on any building materials and his contractors had followed codes. The fire, I think, nearly knocked the guy into retirement. He rebuilt the hotel and sold it to the Bally's Corporation. Today, it goes by their name.

Kerkorian went off to Hollywood again. He bought and sold a studio, became wealthy with super-sized stock deals, and terrorized other heavyweights on Wall Street.

But I think the man still felt he had something to prove back in his adopted hometown, Las Vegas. He kept the rights to the name of the MGM Grand, and by the late 1980s made good on a personal promise to create something bigger and better than ever.

Tom Wiesner and I were playing golf in Vail and he told me that Kirk had just purchased the Tropicana Golf Course. "You know what's next, don't you?" Tom asked. I am so smart I answered "Yes," but of course I didn't have a clue.

"Kirk has a big, big project planned. It's going to include the Marina. It will be the biggest casino in the world."

I was stunned, then smiled. Tom, of course, was a majority owner of the Marina at that time. My old pal Wiesner, who'd been a star fullback at the University of Wisconsin and was a self-made man in the tire and bar business, had hit the jackpot. It was another touchdown for Tom.

And the new MGM Grand Hotel and Casino was born. When it was completed, it had 5,005 rooms and was easily the largest hotel on the Strip. Kerkorian's legacy was complete — but that didn't mean he was planning to retire.

In fact, those of us who saw him one night dining at Piero's with Barron Hilton figured there was something in the wind. Kerkorian is the most active 80-year-old since my daddy. With the amazing Armenian, anything is possible.

After all, this is the same man who, like a prizefighter looking for a knockout opportunity, waited for the precise moment in March 2000 to land one square on the chin of my friend Steve Wynn. Wynn's Mirage Resorts for a time had been an industry leader in innovation, but Wynn had overspent on the Bellagio and in creating a palatial resort with a lake out front and had drawn business from his marvelously successful Mirage. The name of the game in Vegas is growing the market, not vulturing the business, and Wynn's bottom line began to suffer. His stock drooped like an old showgirl's assets, and that made him vulnerable to Kerkorian's left hook. With Kerkorian as head coach, Terry Lanni emerged like Joe Namath, and a new league was about to be created in Las Vegas. A buyout ensued, and before you know it Kerkorian had cut a check for Mirage Resorts, turning it into MGM Mirage and creating the most powerful gaming company in the world. With a previous buying spree, the Wynn buyout gave Kerkorian and his stockholders a portfolio that included the MGM Grand, New York-New York, Primm Valley properties, half the Monte Carlo (in association with Mandalay Resorts), Bellagio, Mirage, Treasure Island, Golden Nugget, and Golden Nugget in Laughlin. That's a lot of gambling.

The business today has its share of self-made men. When I started, it still had a number of made men as well.

I encountered the hoodlum element from the front office to the baccarat pit, but that was the water everyone swam in back then. I got into some difficulties in the course of my duties as casino host that former Organized Crime Strike Force prosecutor Dick Crane managed to clarify to the federal authorities. It's my job to talk to gamblers, and from time to time I've conversed with them while they were being wiretapped. That can lead to confusion on the part of law enforcement, and Dick is an expert at making matters perfectly clear. Dick and I argue a little every day, but he's the best friend I've known, a man possessed of a brilliant mind, a wicked sense of humor, and a rare trait in Las Vegas, true loyalty.

In Kentucky, I enjoyed many advantages as a young man growing up in the Chandler household, but an association with casino gambling was not one of them. In Las Vegas, I would have much to learn and none of it would come easy.

Occasionally, you'll meet a man who was born into the business and made the most of his opportunity. Michael Gaughan is one such man.

Gaughan came from the same circumstances where opportunity was dovetailed with ability. He had the ability to tack on the few friends that Jackie Gaughan wanted him to include, like Dick Crane and Jerry Herbst, but Michael also had the talent to make operationally strong what is now Coast Resorts. That string of mid-sized moneymakers includes the Barbary Coast, Gold Coast, Orleans, and Suncoast. These places, though not rivaling the MGM Grand for size, combine casino value with the food and entertainment that locals and weekend travelers demand but haven't always been able to find on the Strip in recent years.

Michael Gaughan was always cognizant that he was dealing with other people's money. That weighed on him and that made him different from, say, Steve Wynn, who is far more flamboyant. The fact that Steve Wynn had other people's money seemed of no concern to Steve.

That attitude resulted in the creation of some wonderful casino resorts: the Mirage, Treasure Island and Bellagio. And only a fool would doubt Steve's ability to create properties that tickle the public's fancy. But it's also true that Bellagio, for all its plush accommodations and incredible conservatory and art gallery, didn't earn sufficiently for stockholders, who generally are the last people on Steve's mind. Wynn's lavish, corporate-fueled lifestyle was something to envy, but it eventually led to him leaving the company he built after Kirk Kerkorian cut the $4.2 billion check.

Steve was always a better salesman than operator. And don't misunderstand, salesmanship is important in the casino business. It takes constant marketing and promotion to create the magic and atmosphere capable of attracting 35 million visitors a year to Las Vegas. That magic has to include all the ingredients: the risk and reward possibilities inherent with gambling; the sweet perfumed scent of the opposite sex — and with increasing numbers of women coming to Las Vegas to gamble and let down their hair it's not just a man's world out there anymore; the nonstop Mardi Gras-style partying of a place fueled by intoxicating beverages; great food, not only in the gourmet rooms but in the coffee shops as well, and entertainment for every taste.

But at some point you have to mind the store and make a score, and in today's business at the top end there's no one better at that than MGM Grand President Terry Lanni.

I think Terry knows he's in a very simple business. He's a financial man. Lanni doesn't complicate things. He knows what he wants: He wants things done his way. He doesn't want a lot of independent thinkers. As my daddy liked to say, "All in favor, signify by saying 'aye.' Those opposed, say 'bye.'"

He'd rather have a guy to take what he asks of him and, like a fullback, drive on that way. Let Terry do the thinking. Lanni is able to create a succesful employee — as long as the employee is one who listens and does his will effectively. If certain employees are given to independent thought, it's possible they won't last with Lanni.

Lanni is probably the best major operator, the best new Las Vegas operator. While he didn't learn the business by sitting on a ladder in a back alley, he does understand the mind and feelings of the player. That's in part because he is a player. He likes to gamble and is very involved in thoroughbred horseracing as an owner. That atmosphere is also a good place to find players for your casinos.

🐎

Over the years I've learned that Las Vegas wasn't built for a landlord. Truth is, the nature of the business makes it a certainty that the city will forever be reinventing itself in order to put a new spin on an age-old house percentage. If they just hung out a sign that screamed "Gamble Here," the magic of the experience would wear off for all but those hopelessly hooked on the action. So what the old bosses understood, and the new bosses have raised to a science, is the marketing of themes and images of the place. It's the same place it ever was, but depending on who's doing the pitching in recent years, Las Vegas has become known as "the Entertainment Capital of the World," as well as the capital of the convention market, tour and travel market, families market, "Cocktail Nation" party market, Hollywood stars and starlets get-away market, and, of course the best place to gamble on the planet.

The city is aided in its marketing strategy by a willing national and international press and by arranging for a series of cable and major network television programs to air from the Strip.

When I walked into Caesars Palace on January 3, 1974, a million miles from Versailles, little did I know I was setting foot in a cross between a Damon Runyon short story and the heart of the American dream.

Chapter

The Glory of Caesars

Team play had always been a big part of my life, and when I arrived at Caesars Palace I suffered from the delusion that we were all part of the same team. How wrong I was.

It soon became clear even to my neophyte eyes that the casino was not one big happy family, but an intricate tangle of many families and factions under one roof. While I had not believed my arrival in 1974 would be accompanied by rose petals at my feet, I was not prepared to have so many colleagues standing by ready to trip me up and send me packing. There were many good people at Caesars, but there also were those who, because they felt their turf being threatened, were more than happy to dig gopher holes deep enough for me to fall into and never be seen again.

My first assignment was to stand near the front desk and greet customers. As it turned out, other people's customers. I was so naïve that I did not fully realize that maintaining a list of good customers who contributed to the house's bottom line was the marketing executive's sole reason for living. Without those customers, he was a glorified gas pump jockey in a dry-cleaned shirt.

I quickly learned that the more people who enjoy your company, the more value you are to the casino.

So I imagine some of my colleagues got a little upset when I handed my brand new burnt-edged "Rome is burning" business cards to other men's customers. And many of those customers immediately responded to the fact that I was not only gregarious and friendly, but had been raised by the former Commissioner of Baseball and not the dice den wolves of Steubenville. I talked funny and had a gift of gab, and many of the new customers liked the fact that I didn't talk out of the side of my mouth like some B-movie gangster. In short, I was the flavor of the month and my Rolodex began to expand immediately.

If someone were to ask me whether Caesars Palace in those days was secretly run by the mob, in retrospect I'd have to say of course that's true. But if called before a grand jury to explain specifically how I know it, I'd be hard-pressed to present more than a few facts. Truth be told, there was a little bit of mob in many of the upper-floor personnel and casino executives. We heard tales of one fellow being connected to "Jimmy Blue Eyes" Alo and "Fat Tony" Salerno and other guys connected to Meyer Lansky and a long list of other nefarious characters. But if you want to know the truth, there was no gunplay on the casino floor and only a couple of guys got rubbed out in the total of seven times I was employed at the Palace.

I soon learned a truth about the casino business that is as true today as it was in 1974. The biggest difference at most resorts is the people package. The food is good in all the places. The beds and suites are comfortable, the rates are competitive, and the casino traps are all the same. The only difference is the care and handling of the customers. If they're treated well, customers become drawn not only to the action, but to the friendships they develop.

This business is very simple. It is a people business. The object is to get the man with the disposable income and the gaming instinct to come to your campus.

There were, however, some of the most irrepressible characters the world has ever known bouncing and bopping under that big top.

CHAPTER SIX

The casino was run by a classic old-schooler named Albert Faccinto, who was better known as Mokie. Mokie was capable of hiring and firing and he ran a tight ship in the era before accountants took over the business. He was capable of doing everything from resolving a police beef to negotiating an end to the threat of a major union organizing the casino's dealers. For the most part, dealers in Las Vegas remain nonunion to this day.

Then there was Bert Grober, whom everyone called Wingy. If you met him once, you'd know where he got his nickname. Due to a birth defect, his left arm was a miniature of his right. He not only stuck out in crowds, but it made buying suits off the rack an impossibility.

Wingy's last stop before coming to Las Vegas had been the Cal-Neva Lodge at Lake Tahoe, Miami Beach before that. In Florida, he'd run the Park Avenue nightclub and had been a wealthy man. He was so well off and well connected, in fact, that he came west as a major owner of the Cal-Neva casino at Lake Tahoe back when it was tight with names like Sinatra and Sam Giancana, Blue Eyes Alo, and the boys whom the government referred to as the Genovese crime family. At one time, Wingy had owned fifty-two percent of the Cal-Neva, but his voracious gambling habit had whittled that stake down to nineteen percent. In the casino racket, his story was not unique, for many of the men who stood close to the fire on the floor of those gambling dens were severely burned.

Wingy liked to say, "There are many roads, but only one ending." That is, if given an opportunity the player will eventually end up donating his last dollar to the casino. And Wingy was a player. And Wingy was right.

When I met Wingy he was an executive host and hated the title with a passion because he'd once been an owner. He was perpetually in a bad mood and was given to fits of yelling. Everything made him mad, even the fact that when he stayed at the hotel he couldn't answer the phone in bed because the phone in his room was on the short-arm side of the bed.

Wingy yelled at people and got away with it. Not because he was charming, but because it was pretty obvious he was a big earner who was connected. He was a strange sight even by Las Vegas standards. His shriveled-up left arm hung about a foot from his shoulder. He'd light his cigarette with his long arm and smoke it with his short arm. The old expression "Deep pockets, short arms" applied literally to Wingy.

He hated being called a host. He fancied himself as more important than that. He'd managed and perhaps at one time owned a piece of the Park Avenue nightclub in Miami Beach on Lincoln Boulevard. Everybody went there.

Wingy's physical condition necessitated him keeping in close contact with a tailor, and he'd had the same one for decades. In fact, when he ordered suits, he called New York.

So imagine how mad he got the day a new shipment of suits showed up at Caesars and he found that the wrong arm had been shortened. He was livid, and naturally it was all we could do to stifle our laughter. Visions of Wingy's short sleeve on his regulation arm, and the long sleeve covering his flipper brought tears to our eyes. He was so angry he got on the phone long distance and shouted epithets at the poor suit-maker sitting 3,000 miles away.

"You've been my tailor forty years. How many times do I have to tell you, it's the left sleeve, the left sleeve!" he shouted.

Wingy taught me plenty about human nature, much of it bad. One day, I approached a player who'd been hitting the "21" tables and was out of credit. He said, "I want to get a little more money."

I went to Wingy and he immediately raised his voice. He'd loan the man the money, but not from the casino cage. He yelled it so loud that everyone in the pit could hear him. Then he peeled off $5,000 and handed it to the gambler. A week later, that $5,000 was returned as $10,000.

Wingy wasn't the only one-man, in-house savings and loan at Caesars Palace in those days, but he was one of the more active and he wasn't afraid to advertise. Those grifters were little shops inside the shops.

By then I realized that men like Wingy had connections that ran deeper than management.

🐎

I have a great old photo of Eddie DeBartolo Jr., then owner of the San Francisco 49ers, and Leonard Tose, then owner of the Philadelphia Eagles, with Clifford Perlman and Harold Berkowitz. It was taken at the celebration we gave when the 49ers won their first Super Bowl in Pontiac, Michigan. The flags out front proclaimed, "On the Track to Pontiac." It was a grand casino event that drew a lot of customers. We won over $3 million in the casino, which was far more than any of the players in the Super Bowl. O.J. Simpson and Coach Bill Walsh were players, with Eddie DeBartolo funneling them money at the baccarat table.

During the ceremony, as I was introducing my boss Cliff, who was an alumnus of the University of Miami. I cracked the joke that I'd wanted to attend the University of Miami, but couldn't because my folks were both married. The crowd roared, but Cliff was not amused. He came up to me after the program ended.

"That joke you told wasn't funny," he said.

"Cliff, it was a joke," I said. "That's why everybody laughed. They thought it was funny."

I had one brain cell that was alive and kicking. I knew he was the chairman of the board of the company, and I saw the look of distress in his eyes. I was having a great time, but I was beginning to understand why my corporate fortunes were not soaring.

🐎

The business is so easy that it leaves plenty of time for Machiavellian infighting and petty jealousies.

Here's one example. I first met Jeffrey Katzenberg long before he was a big player in Hollywood. He was a bright young man who'd stopped at the Aladdin on his way to Los Angeles to become an assistant to the president of Paramount Studios. We had in common certain New York acquaintances. He wanted $5,000 to gamble during his overnight stay. Ash Resnick turned him down at a time when Katzenberg was on his way to becoming an administrative assistant to the president of Paramount. I was at the Aladdin at the time after the first of many partings with the mercurial Caesars.

When Perlman approached I said, "Don't sweat it, Cliff, I'm not taking players from you. I'm bringing you one."

I'd gotten a call from that mutual friend in New York, who said Katzenberg was good for the $5,000 marker he'd requested. And so I obliged. It was little enough, and our friend's judgment was rock solid.

Of course, the credit was played and soon repaid. An inconsequential tale, perhaps, but out of that chance meeting and treating a young man with a little respect came other opportunities. A few years later, when Disney executive Frank Wells was looking for a friend in Las Vegas, Katzenberg sent him my way and I helped him with a few basic accommodations at Caesars Palace. It was a good contact to make, but it went noticed by the fretting management of the resort, which then was run by Henry Gluck, the overrated CEO of that era, who asked me incredulously, "How come Frank Wells went through you?"

He was my boss. Since the concept appeared hopelessly foreign to the man, I decided not to tell him that getting to know such people was my business. I'd met him through Jeff Katzenberg, but instead I said, "Why, I don't know, Mr. Chairman, why don't you ask Frank?"

Gluck, of course, wouldn't dream of actually admitting a shortcoming.

Gluck was one of those very bright men who never should have been involved with a casino. He lacked the temperament and personality for the job, and it showed in Caesars' sagging performance.

I am a man whose life has had few epiphanies, but early on at Caesars Palace it became crystal clear that one reason so many people in the casino business are so protective of their turf is because the business is so damn simple that a manicured chimp can do it. There's a language that must be learned and a subculture that must be navigated, but the games themselves are child's play from the house standpoint.

When I wasn't standing at the front desk handing out business cards and glad-handing strangers, I stood in the "21" pit with my arms crossed watching the games. I had no authority and assumed none. I was there to observe the games, the moves of the floormen, and actions of the pit boss, and doing my best not to get in anybody's way. It was there I learned how simple the business was, and after six months there was little in the basic day-to-day operations that I failed to grasp.

What took longer to understand is that the casino's mathematic simplicity and the endless flow of cash and everything that money buys are what make the casino such a snake pit. After you learn 9 beats 8 in baccarat and 22 is one too many in blackjack, it leaves plenty of time to scheme and scam. You don't have to have a grift sense to be successful in the gambling business, but it sure helps. The fine hotel schools at Cornell and UNLV will teach you to properly place the mint on the pillow, but they won't do a damn thing to help you learn about the gaming instinct. It's that instinct that catches players and keeps them. The accountant knows what's in the bank account, but it's the grifter, or at least that grift sense, that helps you read a player's character.

One of the great hosts at Caesars was Murray Gennis, a man who had the grift sense and understood the gambling instinct of the player. Preston Feinberg, who in youth had been a batboy for the Chicago White Sox, was another of the original characters who graced Caesars Palace in the early years.

Murray said I was lucky because at Caesars we didn't really have to recruit players. We selected the best and let the others have the rest. It was an enviable position to be in for a number of years. In that atmosphere, Murray developed a theory that we would not call players. Instead, we would remind them of our fountains and fun and especially our special events and parties, and the customers beat a path to our door.

Times have changed somewhat, but it's still important to sell the services and provide value — whether the player is a nickel slot little guy or a $200,000-a-bacarrat-hand whale.

I used to say that only the United States Government had a stronger foreign policy than Caesars Palace. If you give me a man with enough money and the gaming instinct anywhere in the world, I'll charter a 747 for him. In those halcyon days before the corporate straitjacket came into fashion, it was all about customer service and making the bottom line look good.

And we were allowed to sprinkle good customers with gifts in order to let them know they were valued. Room, food and beverage comps, commonly called "RFB" in the trade, were only the start. From there, players were upgraded to free airline tickets. Above that, we provided private jet service for the substantial players, men who kept active $100,000 credit lines.

And there was any excuse for a party, which I'm proud to say was a specialty of mine. I exploited my longtime association with the Kentucky Derby and year after year brought in big players for a day at the races. There were Super Bowl tickets, World Series tickets, and tickets to the NCAA Basketball Tournament. Almost anything a man could desire was made available — as long as it was a man of means.

And what about the women?

Well, now we get to a somewhat dicey part of our story, because prostitution is not legal in Las Vegas. It is, however, a big part of the tourist attraction. At Caesars back then, players who were interested in companionship generally learned — though by whom I cannot recall — that the bell desk was the gateway to the land of earthly delights.

Of course, there were also plenty of extremely attractive penthouse-level working girls who frequented Caesars Palace. As long as they hooked up quickly with a player there was no problem. What consenting adults do in private is their business, in my humble opinion. And many of these women were professional models, escorts, and actresses. We're not talking about streetwalkers here. We're talking *Playboy* centerfolds.

Outgoing fellow that I am, I was constantly handing out my business card to players of all sizes and one evening encountered a group at a table in the lounge. I sent over drinks and then dropped by to say hello, and in the process handed my card to a fine young thing. She was a breathtaking beauty. In truth, I had no idea what her profession was and thought it rude to ask. I mean, you don't walk up to the most beautiful woman in the most popular casino in the world and inquire, "Hey, are you a hooker?"

A few hours later, Metro Vice Detective Dave Hanson stopped me on property and questioned me. It seems one of the working girls had been stopped by one of Metro's crack undercover cops, and in her struggle to avoid arrest had produced my business card as proof that it was with the blessing of management that she roamed on campus. A short explanation cleared up the matter, and Detective Hanson and I later laughed about the incident.

At Caesars we learned a golden rule about Sheriff Ralph Lamb and the men and women of his department. They were good for business. And I took care of the officers whenever I could and gave them my business cards. After all, they enforced the law and protected the work force from its own indiscretions.

I knew I wasn't purchasing a get-out-of-jail free card, but I learned a long time ago that it never hurts to have the police on your side or at least familiar with you. I would tell the younger hosts, "Remember, when you get pulled over, you will not want justice. You will want mercy." Don't misunderstand. I wasn't buying influence. I was just improving the odds that the cops would be in a good mood when they saw me.

It was at Caesars that I met one of the industry's top rising stars, J. Terrence Lanni, whom everyone calls Terry. Terry was an executive at Caesars when he reached a crossroads that told me a lot about the man. He'd climbed through the company with the help of Cliff Perlman, but when Caesars tried to open a casino in Atlantic City, Cliff's past began to haunt him. And Terry made a decision that illustrated just how tough he could be.

Terry refused to go to Atlantic City to testify on behalf of Perlman, whose background was kosher in Las Vegas, but whose long ties to Meyer Lansky's man Alvin Malnik were what New Jersey gaming commissioners refer to as "problematic." Cliff was calling in all his markers to win licensure, but Terry refused to go back and testify for him. It was a bold move at the time, and it set the stage for Henry Gluck to become the new boss. Terry, meanwhile, was also working behind the scenes to buy out Perlman.

It's impossible to tell whether Terry or some other casino industry executive used their contacts with the Casino Commission to actually turn up the heat on Cliff, but in the end his licensing difficulty had the desired effect: his ouster from the company he'd helped build.

By rights and ability Terry should have moved into the chairman's office right then, but Gluck managed to block him and become the man. That left Terry in a difficult position: He could walk away and, no doubt, be picked up by any number of rival companies.

Terry had helped put Gluck on the board and thought he would become chairman. But he celebrated too early. Perlman's replacement on the board sided with Gluck instead. But Terry made it costly on Gluck. Terry had read all the books that said you're supposed to check in daily with the chairman. Gluck gambled whether Terry would knuckle under. But Henry didn't know Terry. Terry Lanni is as keen a judge of talent as any man I've ever met.

Henry got to run the company, which was good for Henry but not necessarily good for the company. Under his guidance, Caesars cut back on comps for players and cut out some of the finishing touches that helped make it a unique and memorable place. Those distinctive burnt-edge business cards were one thing to go. The giveaways to players were others. Henry didn't appear to realize that the gambling customer doesn't react the same as other customers. There's more psychology to it than accounting.

Terry was on his way elsewhere, and by the time he joined Kirk Kerkorian he'd found the path to the top. Kerkorian is one of the most amazing businessmen not just in Las Vegas history, but in American history. And he can spot talent from a distance in a heavy fog.

Today, Terry oversees the whole MGM Mirage Las Vegas empire, including the MGM Grand, Bellagio, New York-New York, Mirage, Treasure Island, and more.

And Henry Gluck? His limitations eventually were revealed for all to see. Caesars Palace in the 21st century is still recovering from those who operated it with plenty of knowledge of business but insufficient knowledge of the leisure industry.

Chapter 7

The Ultimate Vegas Guys

*I*rving "Ash" Resnick was undoubtedly the most colorful character I met in all my years at Caesars Palace. You will notice I did not say he was the nicest, kindest, friendliest, most honest, most accountable, or otherwise best person I encountered. But he led all leagues in the color department.

Ash never earned a buck he wouldn't rather have lifted. A one-time Boston Celtic, he never met a basketball game whose outcome he wouldn't have liked to fix. His old pal Lem Banker likes to say Ash led the NBA three years in most games fixed. And Lem was his friend.

His enemies were less kind. They sometimes tried to kill him. As they say, Ash would steal a hot stove and move so fast he wouldn't get a blister. His reputation for self-improvement around the casino was legendary.

Ash liked to stay on property. All the better to act as puppet-master. He kept his fingernails manicured and his libido massaged at company expense.

There were times Ash was quite generous. Of course, he was spending the house's money, so perhaps we should put generous in quotes, but he was very sharing nonetheless. At the time, I happened to be in need of a car and had found a used Cadillac for $3,000. At the time I didn't have two shiny nickels, so I asked Ash for a little cash. He gladly obliged, but didn't reach into his pocket.

"Go over to the cage and pick it up," he said. "Just tell them I said to put it in the 'Items' account."

Somewhat skeptically, I went to the cage and made my request. Permission was granted so fast that I barely had to sign a marker. The marker, I later found out, was no more than a formality. The money from Ash's "Items" account was never-ending and nonreturnable.

I took the $3,000 and bought the car and thought, "Man, I'm used to country banking, but this beats that."

Ash was one of those one-in-a-million guys who was made with balls of brass the size of Brunswicks. Ash had a couple of bookmaking convictions, had decided that discretion was the better part of valor when he declined to testify before the Securities and Exchange Commission. His tax conviction was overturned.

Ash was luckier than most cats. In his time around Caesars, he'd survived a car bombing and an attempt to kill him with a pistol. Ash was fast to play but slow to pay, and not everyone appreciated his familiarity with the casino count room.

Which reminds me of a story. One of the great Las Vegas characters I had the pleasure of meeting at Caesars in the early years was one of the casino's original owners, Dean Shendal. In a town riddled with wannabe tough guys, Dean is the genuine article. Although physically not a big man, he was no one to bet against in any forum. I would put Dean up against any of the National Football League Hall of Famers or champion boxers in the ferocity department. But like a lot of real tough guys, Dean has a great sense of humor and is a hail-fellow-well-met as long as he's not provoked.

Dean came to Las Vegas from St. Louis after World War II. He was a rodeo cowboy and middleweight boxer by trade, and of course there have been rumors of his ability to perform heavier duties for the local casino crowd over the years. Although the baseball record books note that Ted Williams is the last man to hit .400 with a baseball bat, there are those who estimate Dean hit even more than that without ever donning a uniform.

To give you an idea of Dean's place in local lore, he was a reliable man at the Sands during the time Jack Entratter was the owner of record but Meyer Lansky and Frank Costello also managed to maintain their influence. Dean later on also owned a piece of the Rose Bowl Sports Book, then the greatest legal sports parlor in the world. Dean had come to Las Vegas with the blessing of Sid Wyman, a St. Louis bookmaker and Strip casino innovator, most notably at the Dunes. He was also mentored by Carl Cohen, who was a double-tough old-schooler most remembered these days for knocking out Frank Sinatra's front teeth after the crooner got out of line at the Sands.

Dean was once charged federally with possession of a pistol and silencer. At the time he was represented by a young criminal defense attorney named Oscar Goodman, who would represent a hall-of-fame of Mafia types before going on to become mayor of Las Vegas. Dean was asked why he would need such a weapon in his possession. He said he liked to hunt ducks and was a good shot.

But why the silencer?

He wanted to get all the ducks.

With Goodman's help, he beat the rap.

At Caesars Palace, Dean's relationship with Sheriff Ralph Lamb was well known. The first time I saw Dean with the sheriff, they were strolling through the casino toward the count room. I decided then they must have been the best of friends, for only a precious few employees were given access to that area.

Dean knew everyone in Las Vegas and commanded respect. Those who got out of line paid the price. Take the time he played doubles tennis against Steve Wynn back in 1967. Wynn was a young, well-connected kid from Maryland's bingo country who would go on to develop some of the best resorts in Las Vegas history. But in 1967 he was a 3 percent owner of the Frontier Hotel and made no secret that he was a man with a future in the city.

The tennis match was going along without incident until Wynn slammed the ball at Dean's doubles partner, who just happened to be an 8-year-old kid. Dean approached the net and asked to talk to Steve, then dropped him with a left hook.

"If you want to slam the ball, slam it at me next time," Dean said.

To his credit, the shaken Wynn got up, brushed himself off and apologized.

Given Dean's reputation, that was probably the wisest decision of his young life.

(Later on, the two became better acquainted. After Steve's eyes started to go bad due to retinitis pigmentosa, he enlisted Dean's help with an intense, high-altitude weight-loss expedition in the Rockies. They were strapped arm in arm as they busted through the boulders and up the trails at 10,000 feet.)

Dean was trusted implicitly at Caesars, not only because legend had it he knew his way to the inner sanctums of Meyer Lansky in Miami Beach and the Genovese family of New York, a group that included such respected old-schoolers as Anthony "Fat Tony" Salerno and "Jimmy Blue Eyes" Alo. Fact is, he was an honest man in a slippery racket.

My man Ash kept Dean busy all by himself.

Now Irving Resnick was a good friend and I learned a wealth of information about life from him, but there was no percentage in trying to imitate him. He was one of a kind.

Ash was a man of action who would bet on anything that moved. He was no stranger to cruising the chorus line, and he survived more than one assassination attempt. But bullets, bombs and even the FBI didn't manage to stop Ash, who had connections with a variety of mob guys, Anthony Salerno and the Patriarcas of New England included.

What bombs could not do, Dean nearly did one night in the count room. Dean looked away from the first count, and when his eyes refocused there seemed to be a problem with the cash on hand. Where $15,000 had been, a mere $3,000 now stood.

"Ash," Dean said with that dead-serious understatement of his. "Drop your drawers."

"What are you, queer?" Resnick asked, but he saw the look that meant his cooperation was required.

And so he did. The $12,000 in cash fell out.

Ash was only slightly embarrassed. He was not a man to let a little thing like getting caught robbing a joint stop him from enjoying himself.

Ash was not subtle. After my slight Kentucky lilt one day, he nicknamed me Beauregard and took me under his soiled wing for a time. The nickname was used only in small part out of affection. It was also a reminder that I was a rookie, a stranger to the world of Jewish and Italian wiseguys.

Time spent with Ash was a learning experience, to say the least, and what I learned most was to watch out for Ash. The man could get an apprentice hurt or worse.

The Hawaiian people, God bless them, are great gamblers and very fun-loving. That makes them ideal Las Vegas visitors, and each year hundreds of thousands of Hawaiians make their pilgrimage to the Mainland to party Las Vegas style. Over the years I've met and befriended many wonderful gamblers from the islands, but occasionally the players can't settle up on the premises and must be politely pursued for collection purposes back to their home turf.

Having collected gambling debts from here to Buffalo in the dead of winter, I much prefer Waikiki in February to the subzero East Coast.

I accompanied Ash on a collection trip and we were chauffeured through the city and made stop after stop. Ash rode shotgun and would cavalierly toss envelopes with up to $50,000 inside to me in the back seat.

When we returned to the hotel, it was party time. We entertained high-rollers in their hometown, and Ash made certain I signed for everything while he managed the cash. I dutifully complied.

At one point the phone rang in my suite. I answered and listened to the sound of a very upset Islander's voice as he asked me to put Ash on the phone. My room was about the size of the closet in Ash's suite, and I mentioned to the caller that he was unavailable at that time.

"Tell him he is going back to the Mainland in a box!" he said.

I decided not to ask who was calling, and, breaking out in a sweat, immediately informed Ash of the pertinent part of the message.

Instead of showing fear, he shrugged and went to play golf. All during the match I just knew we were going to be plugged from persons unknown at any moment. I imagined hitting a long birdie putt, then taking one between the eyes before having a chance to savor it.

We managed to leave the island in one piece, but it wasn't long after that that Ash experienced a murder attempt. In those days, it was not uncommon for casino bosses and their underlings to wind up dead.

Not everyone associated with Caesars Palace was as lucky.

Edward "Marty" Buccieri was a helluva nice guy who'd been in the racket his whole life when I met him in 1974. Born in Steubenville, he was cut from genuine green felt and was as connected as the Las Vegas sun is hot. Officially, Marty was a floorman at Caesars who had been there since the beginning.

His run ended in May 1975 when someone shot him in the head as he sat in the front seat of his car, which was parked in the rear of the hotel. Mokey Faccinto, Butch Goldstein and Toby DeCaesar were among his pallbearers, and there wasn't a person in town who believed the cops' theory that he was the victim of a robbery gone bad.

Anyone who ended up with three .22-caliber bullets in the head in Las Vegas in those days was the victim of a mob hit. And, sure enough, years later it came out in a Kansas City mob trial that Marty had been hit on approval from a Chicago mob boss named Joseph Aiuppa, who'd also approved the elimination of a Stardust Hotel executive named Jay Vandermark. When Marty died, police found a business card in his wallet tying him to Stardust frontman Allen Glick.

Although Marty's murder has never been solved, and his family still lives in Las Vegas, those who understand such things know that it wasn't a robber, but none other than Tony Spilotro who was responsible for killing him. Spilotro, the subject of the 1995 Martin Scorsese movie *Casino*, was allegedly responsible for more than 20 murders in and around Las Vegas but was never convicted in his lifetime. His lawyer was none other than my man Oscar Goodman.

Tony's lifetime ended in June 1986. He died of heart failure after being beaten to pieces and dumped with brother Michael in a shallow grave in an Indiana cornfield.

Marty's death taught me a couple of valuable lessons about Las Vegas. First, that people are not always who they seem and even the nicest guy you know could be living a double life. And second, it never pays to know too much. My experience was teaching me that Vegas guys who knew a lot were usually the ones next in line for indictment or liquidation.

I soon learned that the job was not for the weak of heart or constitution, but in the early years I had little difficulty hanging out until dawn's early light. If you're seeking a career with steady hours and emotionally stable supervisors, player marketing is not for you. If you're successful, and I've had my share of success, then you're on property at all hours — especially late — playing chaperone to the near-rich, rich, and super-rich.

Although I was divorced and lived a long distance from Erin and Chan, I tried to maintain a relationship with them as well as possible given my crazy job choice. Lynne was kind enough to send them to Las Vegas for a few weeks each summer and we had some grand times together.

They often stayed on property with me, ordered from room service and played by the pool. At night when they got a little older, they sometimes accompanied me to shows and went backstage. I think Erin might have received the spark that led her to pursue a career in acting after one of the trips backstage. After all, it's not every kid who gets to hang out with Sinatra after a show.

There were also times the job forced me to leave them in restaurants like the Bacchanal for far longer than I would have liked, or overnight with my dear friend Marti Scholl. I regret the moments I fell short as a father and let my children down, but I cherish our good times together.

Chapter 8

Old Blue Eyes & Company

*N*ot long after unpacking my bags, it dawned on me that I had not only entered a new world on the casino floor, but was in uncharted territory when it came to the universe of Las Vegas entertainment. The lounges were jammed with comedians who would become household names. The showrooms were filled by the greatest names in the business.

The names on those mammoth marquees were a direct reflection of the desires and tastes of a majority of gamblers. Being at Caesars Palace was a ticket to backstage and entrée into the working lives of the greatest of the great.

None was greater than the man we called "the Noblest Roman of them all," Frank Sinatra.

Sinatra has achieved a deserved super-icon status in death. In Las Vegas, a street bears his name as well as a Sinatra family-sponsored slot machine. But the Sinatra I met in those days was a once and future king who was making a comeback in a town that had seen the best and worst of the man.

When you worked in the casino in those days, it didn't take long to figure out that the bellmen had the best jobs in the house. They were fountains of knowledge and infinitely resourceful. At Caesars,

Dominic, John, Nick, and Gary served as early guides to the inner workings of the place.

They were also not above pulling my leg. Three months into my job, I was called to meet Mickey Rudin, who'd just checked in. I did not know, but shortly learned, that Rudin was Frank Sinatra's attorney, agent, and dear friend. I was cordial to him, but the bell desk boys just snickered when I attempted to give him the two-minute speech on the wonders of Caesars Palace. Hell, Frank and his pals had practically built the place, and Mickey could have told me plenty I didn't know about the joint. And of course Mickey knew all the right people at Caesars — Billy Weinberger, Jerry Gordon, Stu Alleman, and Sid Gathrid, among many.

Mickey and I hit it off and he couldn't resist introducing me to none other than Leo Durocher, whom my father had suspended from baseball for gambling years earlier. To say he was unimpressed with the fact that he was being hosted by Happy Chandler's son is an understatement.

Mickey said, "Leo, this is Dan Chandler. His father is the one who kicked you out of baseball."

We didn't hit it off, but that was fine with me. Leo Durocher was a creep and a sponge who lived for the table scraps thrown his way by Frank Sinatra. The day I met him he was waiting for Sinatra to come into the casino so he could sit down beside him and swipe a few black chips. That was Leo: all class. He was the reason they put locks on lockers after he'd swiped Babe Ruth's wristwatch during an All-Star game.

The press was really knocking Frank in those days, and I was among many who sought to shield him from those seeking to sully him further. Columnist Rex Reed captured the prevailing theme in the media when it came to him: "Somebody ought to do something about Frank Sinatra. His public image is uglier than a first-degree burn, his appearance is sloppier than Porky Pig, his manners more appalling than a subway sandhog's and his ego is bigger than the

Sahara (the desert, not the hotel in Las Vegas, although either comparison applies.)"

Now that's ugly.

Sinatra was never one to take jabs from the press without returning fire. Not long after Reed's catty swipe at him, he responded with a stinger of his own: "I was going to sing 'God Save the Queen' tonight, but I won't out of deference to Rex Reed."

One of the best Sinatra stories to come out of Las Vegas just happens to be one of the worst stories about the man. He was so used to being pampered at the Sands that he couldn't fathom having his credit cut off at the tables. He'd broken up with Mia Farrow and was hitting the juice pretty hard — and wouldn't we all if we'd broken up with Mia Farrow — when he crossed the line with double-tough old-school casino manager Carl Cohen.

Now, Carl came over on the Las Vegas equivalent of the Mayflower. He was not one of the sons of the pioneers, but a pioneer himself. And although Sinatra was the biggest star in the country, headlined at the Sands and owned a piece of the action in the casino, Cohen's bosses were not ones who accepted excuses for failing to maintain order in the house. And so when Sinatra blew another few thousand, Cohen told him there'd be no more.

He was apoplectic. Friends who watched him that night still shake their heads decades later at a guy who was so out of his head that he was looking to fight anyone and anything. Well, Carl was no stranger to the fight game, so he gave Sinatra a match that ended after two hits: Carl hit Frank, and Frank hit the floor. Sinatra's front teeth were loosened, but it was reported by columnist Don Digilio that the choppers were missing in action. "Singer Tony Bennett left his heart in San Francisco, but Frank Sinatra left his teeth — at least two of them — in Las Vegas," Digilio wrote.

Sinatra was thoroughly scalded and left the Sands for Caesars Palace, where I later became acquainted with him.

Of course, it wasn't all hearts and flowers for Frank at Caesars. He gambled high, drank heavily, could be terribly demanding, and fancied himself a close friend of upper management. How far up is a matter of speculation, for if you believe Caesars was influenced by owners whose names weren't on the books, that puts him in the notorious company of men like Sam Giancana, Anthony Salerno, Raymond Patriarca, and Meyer Lansky.

But whatever his contacts, Frank wasn't afraid to flex his muscles. He did just that one night while playing high with his friend and Palm Springs neighbor Danny Schwartz, who had his own interesting circle of contacts. The long and short of it is, when Sinatra and Schwartz won a big score, perhaps a million or more, they cashed out and made the money disappear. But on the night in question at Caesars, they were down $400,000 and suddenly got amnesia. When his credit was cut off, he roared.

Sandy Waterman said, "Frank, you and Danny won two million. You took it with you. Now you owe us. The boys want their money."

But Sinatra was Sinatra, and Sinatra wasn't paying a man he saw as a flunky. He threw his remaining chips in Waterman's face and slapped him on the forehead. It was nothing like assault, just another Sinatra outburst, but Waterman was livid. He went and got a gun.

When he returned, Frank said, "Aw, come off it. That gun stuff went out with Humphrey Bogart."

Waterman's career went south, but Sinatra's barely skipped a beat.

If an average punk had tried to pull the stunt, he'd have been hauled off in handcuffs, but Frank Sinatra was no average punk. With him there was always special treatment and a delicate hand. The responsibility fell to Caesars Vice President Sandy Waterman to collect the money owed without blowing himself to bits in the process.

Sinatra is known for his outbursts and arrogance, and there must have been plenty of it because the press sure wrote enough about it. The man I saw was an icon after hours, a king who had a chance to take off the damn crown and relax a while. It was an enlightening experience.

Sinatra was a man who welcomed kids backstage and gave them his time while all the high-rollers and hangers-on waited impatiently. He was the kind of guy who, if you could keep the ass-kissers at bay long enough, had a real sense of humor about himself and the larger-than-life image he projected. He would talk about his early days in the business, crossing the Hudson on a four-cent ferry ride from his hometown of Hoboken, New Jersey. He'd sometimes tell audiences that story when he was in a particularly good mood, and they loved it because it was true.

People who saw him in the casino, if they mustered the courage to say anything, sometimes called him "Ol' Blue Eyes" or "The Chairman of the Board." When he was starting out as a crooner to the bobby sox set, New Yorkers called him "Bones" because he was so damn skinny. I mean, this guy was a drink of water. They sometimes called him 'Hoe Handle' and "No Hips" because he was so thin.

But man could he craft a tune. I heard Sinatra sing a thousand songs, and I never once recall hearing one get away from him. He could blow a lyric and pull it off like Olivier. He was a master showman who was one of those rare entertainers who sent vibes that turned on the women and the men. I mean, after a show you'd see farmers from Iowa walking through the casino imitating Sinatra's stance and accent. One show and everyone was from Hoboken. He had that kind of charisma.

And, of course, he carried a reputation for arrogance and pushiness that he'd earned through the years. It's hard to give celebrities a little slack, but the fact is everything Sinatra did in his life was blown into a Technicolor production. So if he tipped a cocktail waitress twenty bucks just for smiling, some were pleased with the toke and others wondered why it wasn't a hundred. And there's no question that dealers visibly shook in his presence due in no small part to his propensity for disregarding the rules and getting carried away with the cards. His most notorious episode came in the company of Dean Martin at the Golden Nugget in Atlantic City. The two had taken over a blackjack game in violation of New Jersey's rules and had been abusive to a dealer. It was an incident so widely reported that it even appeared in a week's worth of "Doonesbury" cartoons. Sinatra did nothing in a small way.

Maybe that's why I cherish our time together after the shows. They weren't complex arrangements. I'd rope off an area in the lounge and arrange the chairs. You know, play the maitre 'd. Instead of having drinks run in, I'd just grab a bottle of his favorite Jack Daniel's No. 7, and he'd pour his own whiskey and chat about a million things, many of them beginning and ending with his opinion. He was not shy when it came to expressing himself and had an incredible grasp of politics and people.

The Sinatra I met was a proud grandfather. His daughter Nancy had had the family's first grandchild, a daughter, in May 1974.

In those days, Sinatra was taking a beating in the press for things that for the most part had nothing to do with his performance on stage. Columnists attacked him for his alleged associations with the underworld and his latest flings with Hollywood's hot numbers. In other words, I never saw him read any reviews after his shows. He did, however, have a locker room sense of humor and wasn't shy about applying it. He was notorious for throwing ice cubes at friends and associates and feigning anger about some made-up issue just to see whether you would take the bait.

He loved running into Joe Namath, Ken Stabler, Billy Kilmer, Sonny Jergensen and other pals from the NFL. He admired men's men and men who knew their way around contact sports.

Frank was like a grown-up leader of the pack with his man Jilly Rizzo in tow catering to his every mood. (A few words about Jilly. His whole life was making sure no one spoke with Frank unless they checked it through Jilly first. He was like a maitre 'd for a restaurant with one table. The best line I ever heard about the Jilly-Frank pecking order comes from Pat Henry, who said, "It's not true that I kiss Frank's ass. I only know Jilly's ass. I haven't met Frank's ass yet.")

And Sinatra wasn't shy about expressing his opinion to politicians, either. His dislike and distrust of his former friends in the Kennedy family has been widely chronicled, but he also editorialized about Las Vegas politics. His brawl with Clark County District Attorney George Franklin made the papers after Franklin put heat on him for getting out of line at the Sands. Rather than change his behavior, Sinatra was determined to change district attorneys.

So he gladly agreed to publicly support and even fund-raise for a local boy named Roy Woofter. When Woofter beat Franklin, Sinatra sent the loser messages in the form of telegrams. The last one said, "I am running out of money sending you goodbye wires. Suggest you settle down in a new business like maybe opening a penny-candy store. Goodbye."

This from the same man who my friend Sheriff Ralph Lamb had given notice that continued outbursts such as the ones at the Sands and Caesars Palace wouldn't be tolerated. And when the sheriff spoke, everyone listened and no one was confused. Not even Sinatra.

Here's the kicker. When Woofter lost his re-election, Franklin reportedly sent a telegram to Sinatra with the message: "For sale, one slightly used penny-candy store."

Oh how I love this town.

Sinatra's comebacks at Caesars are legendary. I'm not a professional music critic, but you couldn't beat the man for stage presence and that ability to hold an audience in the palm of his hand from the moment the lights went up.

But what I have more knowledge of is the impact of an entertainer on the cash flow in the casino. That is, when it's all said and done, the point of the exercise of signing singers to multimillion-dollar contracts and hoping they don't come down with a case of Vegas Throat: whether the wealthy are sufficiently intrigued by the prospect of seeing and hearing them that they'll accept the casino's offer and fly out to Las Vegas for a few days and bring their bankrolls with them.

Despite all the controversy, much of it deserved, Sinatra could be funny. One of his favorite lines came after he'd done a world tour. He complained about the fans in Germany and said, "I say screw the Germans. And I'd like to start with Elke Sommer."

Working at Caesars Palace enabled me not only to see the best entertainers in the world, but to get to know the rising stars. One night, I went across the street to check out Kenny Rogers and the First Edition in the lounge at the Flamingo. I was with a couple of friends and sat down and between sets Kenny came up and took a booth next to us. I piled in the booth with him and he was there with another guy. I introduced myself to Kenny and he was as nice a guy as you'd ever want to meet. Of course I'd heard of him. He was a popular guy and was headed places, and so he was someone I thought I needed to know.

We became instant friends. I told him I'd just gotten a divorce and had come west from Kentucky, and Kenny was always getting a divorce and had given his wife everything. He told me later, "I've got prospects with a real good manager by the name of Kenny Kragin, who thinks that I've got a strong future. I've kept this one song. It starts, 'You picked a fine time to leave me, Lucille.' I think it'll be really well received, and it's all I took from that marriage. She got everything else."

Connie Stevens came in and sat down with Kenny and was as close to him as a coat of paint. I saw right then that the mourning time for his failed marriage was going to be brief for my new friend, The Gambler.

Chapter 9

Wine and Roses

*W*hen I got on a schedule at Caesars Palace as a casino executive, I would work twenty-one days and be off four. During those four days I was off, I would go up to Vail or Aspen or some of the fun spots, or over to L.A. to visit with my friend former Strike Force chief Dick Crane. In Aspen, I'd hook up with Eddie Podolak and we would meet with John Denver and Jimmy Buffett, who lived there.

At that time, John and Jimmy were both having trouble with their wives. John was having trouble with Annie. He was so philosophical about it, kind of in a dream world. Jimmy Buffett was having trouble with his wife, but his was more of a go-to-hell attitude. Jimmy thought, if you don't feel like you're living with a genius, the reflection is not on me, it's on you. Jimmy thought the problems were his wife's fault while John Denver thought it was his fault. It was a case of one man punishing himself and the other man punishing the other person. But it was clear that their songs were reflecting their state of affairs.

During those trips I met several ladies, who never failed to be impressed by the fact that I arrived with Cliff Perlman, who had a home in Aspen, on the Caesars Palace jet. I became a genuine charmer when I approached a lady and said, "Let's go to Vail. The jet's on the runway, the Dom Perignon is chilled. Let's have a real good time."

I looked like and talked like and acted like I was one of the owners of Caesars Palace. One time in Aspen I met this incredibly attractive lady from Philadelphia named Dolores, who knew all the lyrics of those great songwriters. We stayed together about three years and made our share of sweet music. By the end of that time I was well-versed in the poetry of not only Denver and Buffett, but Billy Joel, Jim Croce, Glenn Frey and Don Henley of the Eagles, and many more. She convinced me that that was where American literature lived, in rock 'n' roll.

Later on, when I hired the musicians and got to know them well, I understood that Jimmy Buffett was crazy to be accepted as an intellectual. And he was a very bright and gifted businessman.

Glenn Frey was just a regular guy in touch with himself and everybody else. He loved golf and we played every chance we got. He loved other sports and appreciated the skills of the great athletes. As Shakespeare says, he had strutted his hour on the stage. While Glenn thought that one day that strutting would be diminished and his career would run its course like one of those athletes, little did he realize that maybe the most profitable and productive years of his life were after he turned 50 and had a reunion with the Eagles. The world was waiting for the Eagles to get back together. And as Don Henley said, "We didn't fall out. We just took a fourteen-year vacation."

Believe me, the world was in the waiting room when they came off that vacation. The tours put together by Irving Azoff, one of the great managers of all time, were so professionally packaged that the boys made so much money that they wouldn't live long enough to spend it.

Then there's Willie Nelson.

Willie not only remains one of the great singer-songwriters in the history of popular music, but when I met him in the 1970s he was one hard-charging party animal. We hit it hard and often in the company of a casino executive or two who will remain nameless, but we all lived through those years and can laugh about it nowadays, if only in private.

Willie was one of those old souls. He was a country boy at heart, but at the same time had a wisdom that transcended geography. When I hear him sing "On the Road Again," I'd bet he's singing on behalf of every good ol' boy and city slicker who ever had the itch to stretch out on life's highway and see where its endless interstate takes them. The great songwriters I've known, John Denver, Glenn Frey, and Jimmy Buffett included, all had one thing in common in addition to their amazing way with words and music: Each one was a free spirit who had a unique way of looking at the world and describing his view out the window as he traveled life's road.

Whoever said poetry is dead has never heard those bards tell it like it is.

Absolutely the best person I've ever seen when it came to dealing with people was Bill Cosby, who I got to know at Caesars. Bill did his own show. He was a headliner at the Hilton and Caesars and was a huge star.

But if we called him and said we had a customer who wanted to meet him, he was more than gracious. The man was only on the payroll to tell jokes, but when he was in the house he was our best marketing resource. He'd say, "We've got to take care of these people because they're the ones that make this all possible."

When Bill got up on stage, it was like he was visiting with two or three people in his living room instead of the 1,100 sitting in the showroom. He was that comfortable, that smooth, that at home making people laugh. The Circus Maximus was always sold out two shows a night. His wit made everyone in the place his friend and extended family member.

Bill didn't make money; he bailed it. He made more money than I can imagine on television, but it hasn't changed him a bit. He's all class and could give lessons to scores of other entertainers.

Bill made me look so good when I would take high-end players backstage. I told those players then and will tell anyone within earshot: Bill Cosby is a man who walked with kings and never lost the common touch.

In those days, almost everyone had a charity golf tournament going, and one year I buckled down and won the Lennon Sisters tournament. It was good to win, but even better to make the acquaintance of those classy and talented sisters, Deedee, Peggy, Kathy, and Janet. They were at Caesars in those days and made other stops, including at the Las Vegas Hilton.

I was especially fond of Deedee, who married Bill Gass, a phone company executive. Bill and Deedee lived in Santa Monica, and they made a great couple. In a town filled with celebrity egos the size of the Hindenberg, the Lennon Sisters were very down-to-earth and Deedee was a sweetheart. When the sisters weren't headlining at Caesars, I'd visit Deedee and Bill at their house in Santa Monica. We'd play basketball with their friend, Celtics great Bill Sharman, who in those days ran the Lakers for Dr. Jerry Buss. Sharman was still deadly with his one-handed push shot. Later I met Lakers great Jerry West, who was the best golfer at the Bel Air Country Club. He was a man untouched by ego, the genuine "Zeke from Cabin Creek" and always "Mr. Clutch." What a guy.

Deedee was really a family person. So was Petula Clark. She'd come with her husband and children and just do her shows and not play the Vegas game. Helen Reddy was much the same way. These women had their lives together.

Deedee and her sisters in my book were class acts, but I've encountered plenty of headliners who were just a plain pain in the neck. It's amazing how the most demanding women were married to the nicest guys. Take Steve and Edye, for instance. Steve Lawrence is one of the classiest, coolest singers in Strip history, but Edye could make life difficult for a saint.

Sonny Bono was such a nice guy, but Cher was a monster with people she deemed hired help. Cher and Edye run a close race for most demanding divas on the Strip. They complained over the least little thing, would call up and say the apple from the fruit basket wasn't ripe or the bananas were a little green.

After Cher divorced Sonny, she married Greg Allman of the Allman Brothers Band in a ceremony in July 1975 at Caesars Palace. My man Jim Brennan, a District Court judge, married them but of course gave them no guarantees. And I sent no wedding gift to the former Mrs. Bono. I recall the bride and groom wore blue jeans, though. Their industry inside friend Joe DeCarlo was the best man.

Jane Fonda only came to the Strip to shoot *The Electric Horseman* with Robert Redford, and that was enough for me. She was unbelievably picayunish and petty with people. Las Vegas definitely wasn't good enough for her.

The three of them would have made a dozen men miserable. Those women define the word difficult. They're either quietly difficult or excruciatingly difficult. They don't suffer in silence and don't suffer alone. Of course, I couldn't argue with them. The staff just had to act like glorified house boys. The star system was in full flower, and those in power loved the stars because of what they meant to the casino's bottom line.

One diva with a reputation that I think is undeserved is Diana Ross. The amazing Miss Ross packed the house twice a night, then spent the rest of the evening hitting the tables. She played high and hard and was a good player, but she was also a nice person who tipped generously. And everyone loved seeing her in the casino. All she would do was smile while we got ready for her to play 21. Truth is, she gambled sizable chunks of her pay every night, which of course management didn't mind one bit.

Just as many of those divas have reputations for being difficult, all the comedians I met were just aces. From Jackie Gale to Tom Dreesen and dozens of lesser-known guys. Although Foster Brooks, the "Lovable Lush," headlined at the Frontier, he was from Louisville and had worked at station WHAS before he mastered his drunk act. We hit it off, him with his phony routine and me working on my genuine one.

Freddy Roman would tease me for always showing up with a flight attendant hanging on my arm. I'd bring Joe Namath and Billy Kilmer with me for the show, and he used us as material, cracking that if we boys were ever cremated, the fire would burn for five years!

There was certainly plenty of whiskey consumed between the three of us. Joe Namath used to say he liked his women blond and his Johnny Walker Red. My man Snake Stabler liked to say, "There's nothing wrong with reading the playbook by the light of the jukebox."

I know of few other men as popular in their time as Joe Namath, and yet he never required the star treatment. He was great with people, and he did get overwhelmed in public by fans. What has always made me laugh is how hard some celebrities try to disguise themselves in public, so much so that they draw more attention to themselves.

Take a couple guys I know and like, Nick Nolte and Lee Majors. They'd wear the dark glasses and an Indian scout headdress, and of course people would notice them. But Namath knew that attention came with the territory, and being a ladies man Joe understood that a high profile brought with it fringe benefits. Joe was actually a very private man, but when it came to treating people, he and O.J. Simpson were the best. And nobody likes people more than Billy Kilmer. He and Paul Hornung were naturals in the marketing game. And "Snake" Stabler had a "people touch" personality that was truly unmatched.

Of course, not all the stars in Las Vegas took the stage. A few added their star power merely by hanging out there.

One was Sylvester Stallone, who when I met him was fresh from his first *Rocky* success and was considered a Hollywood phenomenon. Catering to a celebrity can be challenging, and plenty aren't satisfied no matter what lengths you go to in order to please them. There are some exceptions, though. Sly was one.

The year *Rocky* came out, Stallone could have run for president that year, and I might have voted for him. So when he came to Las Vegas, he wasn't looking for more exposure. Just the opposite, in fact.

Stallone wasn't much of a gambler, but he certainly had a sharp eye for the ladies, and at that time there weren't many better looking or more talented than Susan Anton. The tall, leggy blonde had a great voice, but most guys wouldn't have cared if she had a laugh like a busted air-conditioner. She was one hot baby doll, and Stallone had her in his sights.

"Ben Scotti gave me your name," Sly said. "I'm staying at the Flamingo, but I need a place to be for an out-of-the-way dinner. I have a friend with me, and we'd like a little privacy."

Which wasn't easy, since most of the free world was humming "Gotta Fly Now" and screaming "Adrian!" and "Cut me, Doc." Millions of people knew Stallone's lines better than he did, but I told him I'd be glad to accommodate him.

For a superb, discreet dining experience, few places rivaled the Ah So. It was not only a fabulous Asian restaurant, but it was dark enough to hide even the brightest star on the planet.

In those days, my man Al Faccinto Jr. collected celebrity photos, and he couldn't resist introducing himself to Stallone and bringing in Morgan Cashman's photographer for a quick grip-and-grin. Sly apparently has a great nose for ingratiating himself to those who can make life infinitely comfortable, for he gave Faccinto a bear hug as if they were pals from the old neighborhood. Stallone could turn on the charm faster than a penthouse call girl.

A word about my man Al. Al turned the bear hug into a recruiting tool. Players love Al. Against conventional wisdom, he was even successful with Asian players, who are known not to like hosts who are taller than they are. (Just as, for instance, Arabs are not known for wanting to deal with female casino hosts. Just the opposite, in fact.) Al's definitely one of the marketing game's front-line players.

I'd met Joe DiMaggio as a boy, but got to know him much better in Las Vegas. The Yankee Clipper was a sports icon, a hero to a generation and the envy of every man who ever set eyes on Marilyn Monroe. But Joe was an introverted man in the extreme. He was paid to make appearances in Las Vegas for celebrity tennis tournaments and appeared as a guest of the house at Caesars Palace, the Riviera, and the Dunes, among other resorts. In those days he was close to my friend Harry Vogel, who helped Joe land his immensely lucrative Mr. Coffee endorsement deal.

Mr. Coffee would appear at the Ross Miller Memorial Golf Tournament at the request of Big Julie Weintraub. Everyone called him the Clipper, and he was a lot of things to a lot of people, but the Clipper was no tipper. Believe me, he had no reach. The old expression "deep pockets, short arms" applied in spades to DiMaggio, but the truth is no one said a word.

The Yankee Clipper was a great American icon, a star among stars, and icons have special privileges in our society and especially in Las Vegas.

Chapter 10

Here Lies a Gambler

*W*ingy Grober was right when he said, "There are many roads, but only one destination." He meant, of course, that almost any player taking on almost any casino game eventually winds up tapped out at the end of the road. And he was right . . . the last check is always bad.

Gamblers who become regular customers seldom have the staying power to remain so for long. Good players go broke. Millionaires go broke. Rare is the fellow who navigates the green felt sea and reaches shore safely.

In more than three decades spent catering to the rich and near-rich, I've encountered gamblers of every shape, size, stripe, strategy, and philosophy. And over the long haul almost all of them left town lighter than the day they arrived.

Some left only for the summer or the year in order to replenish their reserves and mount another assault against the house odds. Others left never to return.

One of my favorites was an uncommonly cordial fellow named Eduardo Sabal.

Sabal was the son-in-law of the president of Peru. His mother and father were prominent in the textile business in that country and to my knowledge he was the first man in Las Vegas history to put one million dollars on deposit at Caesars Palace. Given the complex world we live in, when people are not always what they seem, Sabal's family business ties and foreign-born status probably made him an intriguing subject for officials who will never understand how a man could gamble so much money and not lose sleep or even break a sweat. All I know is, in all my years dealing with Sabal he was the consummate gentleman businessman.

By its nature gambling attracts high-rollers whose source of income is suspect. I am a strict believer in the philosophy that it's none of my business where a man gets his funds or how he gets his kicks. In Las Vegas, the first question a casino host learns not to ask is "Where'd you get your money?" Closely followed by "How do you make your living?" And "Is that your wife with you?"

For many years Sabal appeared to have an inexhaustible source of income. He played the tables for the most part, but at one point bet $1 million on the Super Bowl in 1974. Although he placed the bet at Caesars, it wasn't with a traditional sports book. In those days, the only operations capable of handling a bet that big were connected with the Chicago Outfit or one of the other Syndicate families. Sabal made a contact in Chicago and put up the money. When the Steelers won, Sabal doubled his money.

Paying him off was a challenge, but the bet was paid. He was met at the casino and accompanied to the Noshorium coffee shop. The delivery was made in grocery bags. In a moment, Sabal had sacks of cash.

Two hours later, he'd lost all that money playing blackjack.

Eduardo always said that when he died he wants to be buried beneath a headstone that says, "Here Lies a Gambler."

And a helluva gambler he was.

As happens so often with high-rollers, Sabal attracted hangers-on, and the biggest of the bunch was former dancer Johnny Brascia of the Brascia and Tybee dance team. Brascia picked the right friend. Johnny hung around Eduardo for a living, I think. It was his means of employment after he stopped dancing. Eduardo would slip him chips and bet for him.

Before he became known as the most notorious drug trafficker of the late 1970s and early 1980s, Jamiel "Jimmy" Chagra was arguably the best customer Caesars Palace had. He came to town with more suitcases full of cash than bags full of clothes.

And Jimmy would gamble on just about anything, including his own golf game. The sharps at the Las Vegas Country Club loved to see him coming and rarely allowed him to leave without being lighter in the pockets.

But Jimmy didn't care. From the looks of his lifestyle, there was an endless supply of cash to play with. I handled Jimmy's account and although all cash players nowadays arouse suspicion, fellows of his breeding weren't uncommon in those days. Jimmy rubbed some people the wrong way, but I never had a problem with him.

I even went to Florida once to collect a large debt he owed Caesars Palace. When he got in trouble with the law, I also had some explaining to do, but thankfully Dick Crane explained the facts of my job and nothing came of the government's inquiry.

Jimmy and his brother, El Paso attorney Lee Chagra, were such big customers that they were given just about anything they desired. When they insisted on using the company jet, they were given access. In time, they made use of Chris Karamanos' JetAvia fleet, which later became controversial because of the Chagra family trafficking business. If the Chagras wanted to use one of the Caesars jets to see a football game, we didn't hesitate to send it. After all, they were spending more at Caesars than some other casinos were able to drive to their bottom lines.

Years later, when he was accused of conspiring to murder a federal judge named John H. Wood, Chagra's true colors began to show. I, of course, was called in and questioned about my knowledge of this kingpin trafficker, but all I could say was he played high and played in cash and always paid his debts.

I believe Chagra wasn't interested in laundering his money. That is, in taking those off-the-record millions and trying to clean them up for use in legitimate society. A. Alvarez wrote in *The Biggest Game in Town*, "Chagra's money was as black as pitch, but he wasn't interested in cleaning it up — only in enjoying it while he had time." That's an accurate assessment, in my humble opinion. The way Jimmy gambled, it was clear he was a man on a mission to enjoy himself. And he appeared to do just that in the years I knew him.

Although he was aacquitted of the murder charges of the judge they called "Maximum John" thanks in large part to the courtroom magic of Las Vegas attorney Oscar Goodman, Jimmy Chagra spent a long stretch in prison and wasn't due to get out until 2010. With help from lawyer David Chesnoff, Jimmy did the next-to impossible: He won his freedom years early.

One of my favorite customers at Caesars Tahoe was Larry Lawrence, the owner of the Hotel Del Coronado on Coronado Island near San Diego and a future ambassador to Switzerland. Larry was an incredible guy, very intelligent and very gifted, and a big fund-raiser in Democratic Party circles. Larry had a great life and was also a good customer of ours at Caesars Tahoe. Larry forged a life that didn't exist and when he died was buried in Arlington National Cemetery because of a military career that he always said he had, but didn't.

After he died and was buried, a friend revealed his military background had been faked. When it came to light, so did Larry. He was dug up from Arlington and re-planted somewhere in California.

For several years Sukamto Sia was one of the world's great high-rollers, gambling vast fortunes without batting an eye. It's estimated that at the height of his play he wagered and lost more than $100 million.

He was fond of expensive wine, which of course was comped at up to $13,000 a bottle. It's like Wingy used to say, "No favor too great, no hour too late" and no hill too steep for a good customer.

When time and circumstance finally caught up with Sia, a native of Indonesia who lived in Hawaii, he became the subject of a federal investigation into the source of all the cash he gambled. He'd secured a more than $100 million bank loan and, more importantly for our story, owed the Rio $6 million and Caesars $2 million. He'd written checks that failed to clear, and after many years of being considered the ultimate good customer, Sia found himself being called a deadbeat.

Having known Sia for most of his Las Vegas time, I knew him to be an honorable man who would have paid his debts if he had the ability. The debt-collection push by the casinos was unprecedented, for traditionally such debts were not collectible. In the corporate era, though, the rules had changed and the house enjoyed a bigger advantage than ever before. They made no mistake on the side of compassion.

When attempting to collect a particularly tough debt, my favorite line has always been, "I'm the last friendly face you're going to see." The greater meaning is unspoken, and in reality the casinos use the law, not muscle, to collect debts. But it never hurts to leave a little lingering doubt in the debtor's mind.

I've always believed it was bad business to treat former good customers, who might become good customers again, as outlaws just because they lost their bankrolls. Sia's attorney, Dick Crane, represented him with passion. Another of his lawyers, David Chesnoff, was right on when he argued, "Mr. Sukamto is a longtime customer and a very good one. He's one of the most reputable guys in the world of gambling."

Then District Attorney Stewart Bell countered, "The Legislature has made it a crime to write a check without sufficient funds to cash that check. As long as that crime is on the books, we'll enforce it."

But the district attorney wasn't being entirely candid. The fact is, tens of thousands of checks are written with insufficient funds each year in Las Vegas, and most businessmen can't get the police or the DA to do a damn thing about it. But the casino boys aren't just any businessmen. Their contributions and political influence can make or break a candidate for sheriff or district attorney. If you guessed that their cases are given the highest priority, you'd be right.

In his 30s, Sia had been an international banker and one of the biggest players in all of Asia.

To give you an idea of just how strangely he was treated by the Las Vegas casino culture, at a time the Rio and Caesars Palace were pursuing criminal charges against him, Sia was being courted by none other than gambling mogul Steve Wynn, who flew him out and put him up in a suite at the Bellagio. Talk about a contradiction!

Hostile debt collection from established customers is just plain bad business that sends a terrible message to a world that already looks at Las Vegas with a jaundiced eye.

For a while, a man named Mr. Kim was one of the biggest players in Las Vegas. He also was a major player back home in South Korea, where I'd heard he was the head of that country's equivalent of the CIA. That was fine with me. It was clear from the amount he played that the spy business paid handsomely, and I considered him a good customer who paid his debts without incident.

It was a short while later that Kim was apprehended and taken back to Seoul, where he was executed. We heard that the president was so offended by his transgressions that he shot him himself. This, of course, precluded us from collecting any debts he might have owed.

Australian media magnate Kerry Packer is undoubtedly the greatest gambler of the past decade in Las Vegas. He is a man for whom hyperbole seems impossible when it comes to a willingness to wager vast fortunes on the turn of a card. What makes Packer special, in many local opinions, is his incredible generosity with the hired help. Tales of Packer's largess proliferate throughout the industry and especially inside the MGM Grand, where he's been known to tip the dealers $1 million and more.

Tips, or tokes as the locals call them, are split up evenly on a 24-hour basis. In that way, the swing shift and the graveyard shift make the same amount. Years ago the tips were separated into small envelopes and dealers received cash each night. Today, the corporate structure and tax scrutiny have changed the game and dealers receive checks just like traditional wage earners.

Everyone knows when Packer is in the house. He has a greater impact on the lives of the floor personnel than would the second coming of Elvis. The only people who aren't elated to see him tip are the members of upper management, for they look at those huge gratuities as money they might win if he'd only held onto it a little longer and not been as generous. Frankly, I like his style.

He once tipped a cocktail waitress he took a liking to six figures to accompany him on a trip. The money, I hear, changed her life and enabled her to start her own business. His largess has put the children of some dealers through school, remodeled the kitchens of other lucky stiffs. When he's hot and spreading it around, I swear Packer could get elected mayor. He's that popular.

My man Ed Podolak was a helluva fullback in his day and could run through walls as a member of the Kansas City Chiefs, but he had a deft touch when it came to human relations. Ed and I spent much of our spare time in Vail for some years and it was there that we introduced a girl he knew to Packer. She was an exceptionally attractive woman who appeared to have everything going for her. There's no doubt she benefited from the relationship with one of the wealthiest, most generous men in the world. Her shortcoming was one common to snow bunnies in those days: She had a propensity for something more than martinis. In a few weeks her problem became obvious and she was bounced from Packer's inner circle. It was too bad for her. She'd live the rest of her life and not find a man of that financial caliber.

Packer is a big man with an eye for the ladies and a weakness for, of all things, polo. He keeps a string of boys around just for that purpose: to mount the horses and play polo. Now, as I say, Kerry is a big man. He might weigh 260 pounds. He might weigh more than that. I have always wanted to see the size of his horse.

He liked to golf and I remember a time he wanted to play Shadow Creek, what was then Steve Wynn's private golf course. Trouble was, Kerry was a Caesars Palace customer, and Steve said he was welcome at Shadow Creek on one condition: that he move down the street to the Mirage. Packer was insulted and stayed put.

Someone who knows both men told me Packer told Wynn, "No, I won't move to play Shadow Creek, but don't you even think of coming to Australia with an eye toward doing any business."

Personally, I would have come out and put the tee in the ground for him just to get him in close. The Mirage was a fabulous resort with any number of reasons for a man of Packer's stature to change addresses. That was one time Steve's personality got the better of him and cost him a few million.

🐎

If you've been in Las Vegas long enough, you have a Bob Stupak story. The former Vegas World and Stratosphere Tower casino creator defines flamboyant in a city of overstatement. He's a chain-smoking, angle-hustling kamikaze poker player who is to common etiquette what Hitler was to travel agents. If Bob hasn't hit on your wife or attempted to talk you into a bet where you're sure to get the worst of it, stick around five minutes.

I remember when Bob first came to town. He was going to create what was called Vegas World. He was the son of a Pittsburgh gambling boss named Chester Stupak, but for some reason Bob had to bring his money in from Australia, which the last time I checked was not a suburb of Pittsburgh. But such are the mysteries of Las Vegas. Australia was his source.

After he put together the Vegas World operation following a fire and controversial insurance claim at his World Famous Gambling Casino and Museum, Bob started going after business in a fascinating way. He started hanging around Caesars, drinking and gambling and looking to cut in on high-end players.

There was a big-time New Jersey gambler named Roth who was the biggest player on our campus at the time. I was new to the game and listened closely to Murray Gennis when he told me, "Don't let anybody come in and cut in on this player."

Times weren't the best economically and it was important not to let a cash cow wander off the farm.

That's how I met Bob. He was angling toward Roth and it was my job to keep him from distracting our man from Hoboken. It was about like a chainsaw to a sycamore log. That is to say, not smooth or comfortable at all. It simply did not compute with him that he wasn't welcome around our big player, and I had a hard time turning him. There's one in every herd the sheepdog has a hard time turning, and I had Bob. It wasn't easy. Fortunately, in those days security paid attention to a request from the casino.

Undaunted, Bob rounded up enough players and attracted legions of suckers with his coupon giveaways and funky versions of "21" and craps to become a legend among low-rollers everywhere. (He was also asked not to market his Vegas World vacation packages in a state or two by attorneys general who obviously didn't appreciate his flare for promotion.) His big bets at the poker table and on the Super Bowl — he once bet $1 million on the football game and played high-stakes cards against a computer as publicity stunts — got him worldwide attention. And attention is second only to money on Bob's list of priorities.

But even those skeptical of his good sense were amazed when he managed to get on the Stratosphere Tower.

Around the poker room, Bob was something of a card. He's always gravitated toward the best players and was himself a very good one, but he's as well known for pulling stunts as aces from the deck. Bob is the kind of guy who will bet you $1,000 that he can "do between two and three hundred pushups." Now, for the record, Bob Stupak is a fellow slight of frame who might smoke 200 cigarettes a day.

If you go for it, he drops to the ground and pumps out one, two, three pushups.

"I said I'd do between two and three hundred," he would say. "Three is more than two. I win the bet."

Bob Stupak, you're one of a kind.

Chapter 11

The International Language

One of the biggest players of the decade of the 1980s was a former Japanese League baseball star named Ken Mizuno, who played and lost many millions at Caesars and at Steve Wynn's Mirage. Mizuno was so close to Wynn that the two shared adjacent lockers at the casino man's Shadow Creek golf course. That was before Mizuno ran afoul of Japanese law in a billion-dollar golf course membership scam that sent him to prison.

Before that, however, he was on an amazing run. He was such a big player that some authorities believed he wasn't gambling, but was investing in the hotels where he played.

Mizuno also owned a fine-dining restaurant at the Tropicana that bore his name and for a time also owned a local golf course. While Las Vegas police suspected Mr. M. had ties to the Yakuza, the Japanese organized crime group, he was a very good customer at the Aladdin, Tropicana, Caesars, and Mirage — and that meant he was good for Las Vegas.

🐎

One of the most incredible high-rollers to ever crash the party in Las Vegas was a man we called "The Warrior." His name was Akio

Kashiwagi, and he was a Tokyo-based developer with an incredible appetite for the tables. He bet $100,000 a hand at baccarat and was known for his aggressive play.

It's exceedingly rare that any gambler has a run of good fortune so great that he breaks the bank of even a small casino. But before making his first foray to Las Vegas, Kashiwagi beat an Australian gambling hall for $19 million and literally put it out of business.

From such fierce play are legends made.

In New Jersey, Kashiwagi gave Donald Trump palpitations when he took Trump Plaza for $6 million in a single weekend. Of course, they were feeling much better after he donated twice that much back.

By the time the mid-1980s rolled around, he was on the West Coast in Los Angeles and decided to try Las Vegas after hooking up with one of the wily old foxes of the casino marketing trade, Clifford Choi. Choi lined up Kashiwagi for a $5 million round at the Dunes, which then was owned by Japanese billionaire Masao Nangaku and run by Dennis Gomes. A jet was sent and the high-roller arrived with fire in his eyes.

Gomes was trying to put the Dunes back on the map after many years of rough going, and he figured Kashiwagi was just the man to help get him there. Anyone as aggressive as The Warrior was potentially very good for business.

Of course, it was also possible that he would be very, very bad for business.

When he started playing, it was Gomes's worst nightmare come to life. Kashiwagi kept winning, and winning, and winning. In a few hours, he'd won the house's $5 million and was about to slip out the door.

Gomes had to think fast, and what followed has become a casino industry legend.

Instead of panicking, he enlisted Choi to keep Kashiwagi from flying back to Los Angeles. A story was invented on the spot. The jet would need to be refueled and wouldn't be ready for several hours. So why not enjoy a gourmet meal and a bottle of wine while he waited? He didn't have to gamble. In fact, no one asked him to play a single dollar. Kashiwagi was persuaded to spend the night in Las Vegas.

Gomes and Choi knew the spirit of the player is extremely strong, and they rightly guessed that Kashiwagi couldn't resist the temptation. He said he would play only $10,000 a hand, but as the story goes he won the first hand and wondered why he hadn't bet his usual $100,000.

So he did.

A few hours later, Kashiwagi's fortunes reversed and he not only had lost the $5 million he won from the Dunes but had pushed his $5 million across the table, too.

That was the way of the Warrior.

But as with so many stories of the great gamblers, the Warrior's road ended brutally. In 1992, deep in debt to the Yakuza with no ability to repay the $10 million he owed the infamous Japanese mob, Kashiwagi went into hiding. He returned to his heavily secured mansion at the foot of Mount Fuji and waited.

He didn't have to wait long. Somehow, assassins slipped past Kashiwagi's security measures and exacted their revenge. The Warrior's body was found in the kitchen hacked to pieces by a Samurai sword.

Some who knew Kashiwagi speculated that he might have hired his own killers in a desperate face-saving measure. Others believed the Yakuza boys had ten million reasons to put an end to Kashiwagi's borrowing spree.

One time a high-roller from Hong Kong went on a run and was up $4 million when he decided he was going to quit because he was hungry. He'd been playing for hours and hadn't complained, but suddenly he wanted out. Even Caesars in its heyday would have been temporarily stung by a $4 million dent in the bottom line.

Management went into overdrive, offering him a bold array of food brought right to the table. I mean everything. The best caviar, shark fin soup, lobster, Kobe beef, and Dom Perignon to wash it down.

No, nothing like that, he said. He was hungry, but not for the usual gourmet bill of fare. He wanted a "hot and juicy" Wendy's hamburger.

If the baccarat boss had had his way, he would have ordered a Wendy's franchise to open at Caesars that very minute just to satisfy Mr. T.

On that night, Caesars needed a baccarat boss named Dave Thomas.

New York publisher and gambling aficionado Lyle Stuart tells the story of gambling next to Mr. T, one of the richest men in the world and the owner of a number of Macao casinos before the Portugese gave up the island in 2000. Mr. T lost hand after hand and didn't appear to have a bit of fun playing the game that, on the occasion in question, had cost him more than $2 million in 1980. So Lyle asked Caesars Palace baccarat supervisor Gene Ficke if he had any answers to this Oriental mystery.

"It used to puzzle me, too," Gene said. "What I've come to believe is that he has conquered everything he's ever challenged, and he's just not going to let this game beat him."

Barney Vinson remembers a time when Tony Cook was dealing in the baccarat pit at Caesars Palace and his boss came by and asked how he was doing with the Asian high-roller. Tony smiled and said he was up more than a million.

Half an hour later, the boss floated back through and asked for an update.

"Now we're stuck about $800,000," Tony said.

"How can you be stuck $800,000?" the suit asked. "You were just ahead $1.2 million."

Tony replied, "Well, we're gambling here. We're not selling bread."

That's true. But sometimes it seems certain players have an endless source of "bread" themselves.

At the highest end of the casino trade, money takes on an almost surreal meaning. For example, I remember a time a group of Japanese TV and appliance importers were playing at Caesars. They played poorly and were losing badly. They might have been down two or three million in a short time. I thought they might be reaching the end of their bankroll before they'd even had a chance to enjoy the resort, which can leave a bitter taste in a player's mouth. So I asked one of the bosses in the baccarat pit how they were faring.

He leaned over to me and said, "What do they care? All they have to do is fill another ship full of TVs and they'll make it back."

And he was right. It was all relative.

Although it was hard to top the two-fisted play of Diana Ross, Andy Williams, or Colonel Tom Parker in the celebrity category, one of the most memorable entertainers at the tables was actor Telly "Kojak" Savalas. It wasn't because he played high, though. It was because he led everyone to believe he played high.

Telly was one of the great tough guy actors and he was a good casino customer all his life. But he was even better for the house. When he'd sit at a table, especially when his popular "Kojak" series was on the air, he'd draw a crowd by playing with stacks of chips. He'd pile them up and move them around and needed a shovel to pick them up.

Most casino customers didn't realize all those chips were worth $5 apiece. He looked like a bigger player than Khashoggi.

That's Khashoggi, as in Adnan Mohamed Khashoggi. International businessman, world arms dealer, endless pursuer of blond female companionship, and excellent casino customer.

Khashoggi's parade in Las Vegas was the talk of the casino industry for many years. He played at the highest level and managed to surround himself with centerfold-quality companions as well as a number of big stars, who surely must have liked him for his personality but certainly weren't repulsed by the fact he was widely known as "the Richest Man in the World." The actress Melissa Prophet, a former Miss California, was no stranger to Khashoggi's company.

Khashoggi had a man servant in his inner circle named Abdo Khawagi, who had connections with some of the most beautiful women in the world through Madam Mimi and the Select Models Agency. Khashoggi was also familiar with a number of *Playboy* Playmates.

That is the way it is for those who have big money. Some can afford the real thing; the rest are relegated to buying the magazine.

As you can see from Khashoggi's background and from those of many other high-rollers who've come and gone, a place in the Sunday choir is not a prerequisite for entering a casino. But it's important to note that there have been legions of good customers who weren't in the least notorious and who didn't stay too long.

⚘

There's a strange but funny side to the casino crowd, too. Gamblers are an endlessly interesting study in the human condition.

One story I know and believe involves a handicapped man who approached a dice table while hobbling on crutches. He shot one pass after another and walked away perhaps $50,000 richer.

He walked away without a limp and without the aid of his crutches. And they say the age of miracles is past.

Although experience has taught me that the real god inside the casino is Probability, not Chance, and that the odds always and forever will favor the house, it hasn't stopped the people who believe that luck is on their side. They come in with lucky key chains, lucky hats, lucky shirts, and lucky dolls. They cross their legs, their arms, and their fingers. They stand in the same place at the dice table or sit in the same chair at the blackjack table. They seek out a lucky dealer or lucky cocktail waitress.

And you know? It's all good fun, in my opinion. And who am I to tell them otherwise?

I've seen my share of good luck charms over the years. Folks with key chains loaded with everything from medallions to bass lures. Plenty of rosary beads and crucifixes, rabbits' feet, whistles, hats, ties. Even a guy who claimed the hooker he'd met and set a place for at the table was his good luck charm.

But I've only seen one good luck rodent.

I was strolling through the casino one night when there was a commotion at a jammed blackjack table. I walked close enough to hear the dealer say, "That's a nice rat, sir, but we don't allow animals in the casino."

"It's not a rat, young man," the guy replied. "It's a mouse, and it's my partner. He brings me luck."

The dealer, perhaps wondering whether to call security, the floor boss, or the local mental hospital, just nodded and invoked his Fifth Amendment right against self-incrimination.

"Just keep it out of sight, or I'll have to call security," the dealer said.

The man complied, storing the little fellow in his shirt pocket.

Apparently, the mouse was having an off night. The dealer went on a streak and busted the man and his mouse in just a few minutes.

The man was as surprised to find he'd lost as he would have been if a piano had fallen on his head with Liberace playing it. He got up slowly from the table and staggered away, talking to his shirt pocket.

Of course, when the odds are against you and your favorite lucky charm won't come through, it's always good to have the house on your side.

To give you an example of how much times have changed, there's a famous Las Vegas gambling story that occurred only a few years after World War II when the dusty town was visited almost accidentally by First Lady Eleanor Roosevelt. She'd been so close to our family when I was a boy. Eleanor was supposed to come to Nevada to praise the Boulder Dam, which by then had been renamed Hoover Dam. Instead, she got sidetracked in Las Vegas and was implored to put a quarter in a slot machine at the old El Rancho Vegas on U.S. Highway 91, which we now call the Strip.

Like so many players before her, she lost.

Here's where the story gets good. The El Rancho's management, which I believe was headed in those days by Beldon Katleman, "adjusted" a machine to make it more easily seduced. In no time the thing started ringing and rattling like a cheap brass band, and the first lady grinned in approval. She walked away several hundred dollars richer and the casino's investment was returned many times over in the form of free advertising.

If you didn't know better, you might think that the 35 million or more people who travel to Las Vegas each year to try their luck at cards and dice were gamblers. They're not — at least not according to the Book of Chandler.

The vast majority of those people are not gamblers at all, but customers and players. People falsely assume Las Vegas was built on gamblers. In reality, Las Vegas was built on players.

What distinguishes a real gambler from a player?

It's simple, really.

Players play to play.

Gamblers play to win.

Sound confusing?

Read on.

Even the best players, ones with great sense of the nuances of the games, underneath it all are in it for the thrill of playing and eventually will lose their bankrolls. A true gambler, on the other hand, sizes a game the way a cheetah picks the most vulnerable spring buck out of a herd. He leaves little to chance.

There have been some great casino men who have gambled their way out of sizable fortunes. Men I've worked with, Wingy Grober and Ash Resnick, for instance, played every day. They couldn't get up in the morning without the prospect of the day's action. Ash has the distinct advantage of being able to arrange interest-free loans to himself at many of the places he plied the trade. Wingy once held 52 percent of the CalNeva casino at Lake Tahoe and played his way down to 16 percent.

Billy Weinberger was a fine fellow, but after he left Caesars Palace for Bally's and the Mirage each time he returned for a haircut from Caesars barber Jose Trujillo, he couldn't resist hitting the tables. And they hit right back.

A shave and a haircut might have cost Billy Weinberger upward of $60,000 per trip.

Then there's Bobby "The Owl" Baldwin. Here's one of the best gamblers in history when it comes to a deck of cards. He's a master, a man with few peers. He's the first winner of the Horseshoe Hall of Fame poker tournament and was known as a killer card player throughout Oklahoma and the Midwest before reinventing himself as a casino man in Las Vegas.

He's also an excellent pool player, but his losses at that game to a diminutive gambler known as Archie the Greek are legendary. The stories of his nonsuccess with a cue stick range from $5 million to $10 million. That buys a lot of chalk and rosin.

Bobby is living proof that a great gambler in one arena is a mere player in another.

A fellow cut from the same cloth is Eric Drache, who was once the Mirage poker room manager and now is partnered with *Hustler* magazine publisher Larry Flynt in a California gaming venture. Eric is by many measures one of the most well-liked men in the industry. He later went to work for the new owners of the Golden Nugget.

He's also one of the best poker players to ever cut a deck. Tales of his high-stakes wins are legion. Trouble was, Eric also liked to bet sports with both fists. He lost a fortune and ran up heavy debts, but amazingly managed to pay them off.

Eric Drache is proof that Durocher was wrong. Sometimes, nice guys finish first.

Stu "The Kid" Unger was another great gambler who lived for the action and died pursuing it. Stu grew up in New York and was considered a card phenom by the time he was eight years old. He was staked to big-money gin rummy games and beat the pants off the best players in the city. In no time his reputation grew.

When Stu moved out to Las Vegas in the late 1970s, he found a paradise, but not for a gin rummy champion. He quickly adapted his amazing skill to poker and won the game's biggest event, Binion's World Series of Poker, in 1980. To show it was no fluke, he won again in 1981 and was recognized as the best player in the world.

"The only time I'm not gambling is when I'm eating or sleeping," Stu once said.

As great as Stu was with cards, he spent money faster than he earned it and at one point was so deep in debt to loansharks that some people believed his life was in jeopardy. But let me tell you something about loansharks: If they're owed five hundred or five thousand, the one who owes might be in trouble. But if they're owed half a million or more, the one who owes is their partner. And so Stuey had several partners over the years along with legitimate gamblers like Billy Walters, who staked him in tournaments.

But Stuey couldn't stand success. The fast lane of the poker world wasn't fast enough, and he started using drugs. He went through rehabilitation, but slipped back time and time again. It was a great sadness and a tremendous waste of talent, but addiction can be a terrible thing.

The First Family of the Commonwealth of Kentucky

Daddy and me with American League President Will Harridge at Babe Ruth's funeral.

NATION MOURNS RUTH
Game's Most Famous Star Dies at 53

Started Life as Waif on Waterfront

Placed in Industrial School at Age of 7, Remained There Until 19

Babe's Last Bow in Yankee Uniform

His Homers Created New Era in Play

Bam's Big Earnings Also Helped Raise Pay Level for All Players

GEORGE HERMAN RUTH . . . February 6, 1895 — August 16, 1948

CERTIFICATE OF AUTHENTICITY

This certifies that this reprint of the August 28, 1948, Babe Ruth Special Section is from an authentic limited edition produced under the supervision of The Sporting News*

DATE: *January 28, 1993*   NUMBER: 222/5000

STEVE GIETSCHIER
ARCHIVIST

I was there the day the baseball world stood still.

At Kentucky, with one of the great college basketball teams of all time.

That's me in my homecoming days.   *With Lynne, I was out of my league.*

I was awe-struck by President Kennedy.

Bob Hope doesn't look impressed by Happy's son.

Talking turkey with Tip O'Neil, Howard Cosell, and Freddie Roman.

Mugging it up with Clint Eastwood and Rosie Greer.

Joe Dimaggio wasn't as sour as he looked.

Erin and Chan, the best things that ever happened to me.

The kids and I loved the Bacchanal Room.

Who could blame me for thinking I owned Caesars?

It wasn't all work and no play.

Here I am with the Greatest.

Waylon Jennings was just about wild enough.

Here I am with Billy Martin and Judge Eddie Sapir.

The Lennon sisters are a class act.

That's Paul Hornung and me at a Caesars roast.

Lee Majors was the $6 Million Man, but Preston and Anita Madden (left) had more money.

Former roommate Jimmy Connors with his lady love.

Daddy and Mama on their special night at Caesars.

Coach Jerry Tarkanian was one of the best in the business.

Flirting with my casino sweetheart Claudine Williams.

Coach Rick Pitino is a great friend.

⇊ **DANTHEBLUEGRASSMAN** ⬜4⬜
CHURCHILL DOWNS   Heleringer/Helringer Family Re-Union   4 FOUR FOOTED FOTOS
1 & 1/16 m $66,000   1:43.47

464   Churchill Downs   6/28/03   Michael E Pegram...Owner
X COUNTRY....................................Second   Bob Baffert...Trainer
HORRIBLE EVENING...........Third   Pat Day..Jockey

It's not every day yours truly finds himself in the winner's circle at Churchill Downs.

Danthebluegrassman was a winner at heart.

My man, Bobby Baffert, trainer par excellence.

Pat Day made my day when he rode Danthebluegrassman to victory.

With a good cigar and an even better view of the Derby.

My man Dick Crane (left) is a dear friend and a great attorney.

With Erin and her husband, Dan Gilboy, at the Kentucky Derby.

With Ken Stabler, Jimmy Buffett and friends.

At the Cabin in Versailles.

Yours truly looking for the next big casino customer.

When sober, Stu remained the best player in the world. When addled by booze or drugs, he was still one of the best.

When he won an incredible third Binion's World Series of Poker title in May 1997, we all figured he had finally gotten over the hump and was back on top for good. He'd been staked in the tournament by Billy Baxter, and so had partners who shared in his profits, but that $1.1 million in prize money should have lasted him a good long time.

But within weeks he was broke again, and in 1998 "the Polish Maverick" Bob Stupak was taking care of him. Bob tried to clean him up and get him off the crack cocaine he'd been using out of friendship and in an effort to stake him in some big tournaments, but Stu was too damaged.

On November 23, 1998, The Kid's body was found in a room at the Oasis Motel on Las Vegas Boulevard. He was 45.

Stu Ungar was hardly the only man who got lost on the way to the pot of gold.

Las Vegas history is brimming with similar tales. Billy Wilkerson, the man who created the Fabulous Flamingo, the *Hollywood Reporter* newspaper, and some of the best nightclubs ever seen on the Sunset Strip, played his way to the brink of bankruptcy and beyond. What fortunes he might have amassed if he'd only played a little less.

So who is the best in the business, in my humble opinion? That's easy: William Thurman Walters, known to the world as Billy. He's unquestionably the man to beat when it comes to all-around gambling.

Born in Kentucky, he has emerged as a prominent golf course developer and philanthropist in Las Vegas, where his million-dollar donations to the wonderful people at Opportunity Village are unsurpassed. Opportunity Village provides work and other assistance to Southern Nevada's mentally challenged adults. It's one of the great Las Vegas success stories, and so is my man Billy.

The gaming world knows him as the man behind the Computer Group sports betting operation that was so successful at knocking off the bookmakers during the NFL season in the 1980s that it attracted federal scrutiny. The whole group, including Billy's beautiful wife, Susan, wound up getting indicted on gambling charges.

Why? For the most part, because they were successful and everyone knows sports bettors can't consistently beat the books, right?

Wrong. The Computer Group combined advanced handicapping skills with the ability to move its bets faster than the bookmakers could move their betting lines. Billy treated the games like stocks and himself likened the activity to a form of legal arbitrage.

The group was eventually acquitted of all charges and Walters returned to work, along the way reinventing himself as a golf course developer and substantial political player.

The government took another shot at him in 1996 when New York authorities discovered that Billy's Sierra Sports operation was maintaining daily contact with several big-time Big Apple bookmakers. They encouraged local Metro Police to raid his place and seized $2.5 million in cash.

The hassle was enormous. Billy was indicted three times on state money laundering charges — charges that to my knowledge had never been brought once against a gambler — even though he could account for every nickel of the cash and had paid taxes on every item in his life.

Six years later, he had the money returned with interest after every charge was thrown out.

That's what makes him controversial, but what makes him the greatest gambler? Having ice in the veins helps. Billy has no choke point that I know of.

And brother does he know how to set up the bet. He'll invest the time and effort required if the pot's right. If you're a sucker, he's the most dangerous man you've ever met. If you're a friend and colleague, he's the best in the business. You want him shooting free throw for you if there's a tenth of a second left and you're one point behind.

I never saw anybody his equal at showing his gratitude toward his adopted hometown of Las Vegas. The Opportunity Village program and several other charities have benefited to the tune of millions. I believe he's genuinely tried to share the wealth. He's not on his deathbed trying to play catch-up to St. Peter.

My friend Pittsburgh Jack Franzi likes to say Billy came to town busted and he'll leave busted. Pittsburgh is 50 percent right. He did come to town busted.

Along the way, Billy also got smarter. He stopped drinking, which adds a step to your game. He hasn't had a drink in more than 10 years.

Billy has about as good a grift sense as there ever was. By that I mean he can smell an opportunity, size it up, weigh all options, and get the best of it in the time the rest of us are lacing up our shoes.

Billy is not only arguably the world's most successful sports bettor, he's prevailed at high-stakes poker, won $400,000 and more on a single game of pool, played a round of golf for half a million and won, played roulette and blackjack at Steve Wynn's Golden Nuggets in Las Vegas and Atlantic City and knocked out the house.

That's noteworthy. As most players know, roulette is not the best game in the house in terms of percentage. It's a beautiful game to watch, but it's hell on the pocketbook in the long run.

Unless you're Billy Walters.

As the story goes, he had heard through the grapevine that there was something slightly out of sync with a roulette wheel at the Golden Nugget in Atlantic City. And so he went there to see for himself. Now, a wheel that's slightly out of balance will, on average, hit some numbers more than others. Of course, a wheel that's slightly out of tilt is taken off the casino floor as soon as it's noticed by management. The wheel in question, however, showed no outward sign of a problem.

But Billy noticed something — something he's kept a secret to this day — about that certain wheel. He didn't touch it, nor did he have a friendly dealer trying to assist him. And yet he saw the score and played it.

And played it. And played it until whatever minute advantage he perceived in playing it paid off. Man, did it ever. By the time he stopped playing, Billy Walters had won $4 million at roulette.

Nobody playing that long wins that much at that game. Nobody but Billy Walters.

To say Steve Wynn was livid greatly understates the situation. Wynn not only vowed to get even with Walters, but as the story goes he hired a NASA scientist to analyze that wheel. But no matter which way they looked, they couldn't see what Billy Walters saw.

For the real gambler, it's essential to know your competition's strengths and weaknesses as well as your own. Most men can talk all day about their strengths, but can't recall a single weakness. Billy always knows the strengths and weaknesses of the field.

Gamblers are competitive by nature or they wouldn't be in the racket, but too much competitiveness can kill. You can't let your competitiveness override your brainwaves. If you're the underdog in a game, you have to play it differently than if you're a favorite. Billy Walters is better at making the proper adjustments in order to prevail in a match than anyone I've ever seen.

Billy's grift sense is impeccable. While I don't go back to the days of Titanic Thompson, I believe if the greatest of the great old-timers knew Billy, they would back up what I'm saying. So would Steve Wynn, at least in a private moment.

🐎

Truth is, even today's biggest names in the casino business have been known to play in big bunches. Kirk Kerkorian came to Las Vegas as a gambler before creating the largest hotel-casino in the world on three different occasions. Steve Wynn was a fair player, and Terry Lanni of MGM Mirage is a substantial player and a real risk-taker.

He owns thoroughbred horses.

12 Chapter

Days at the Races

*a*s with everything else in my life, the entry of my namesake thoroughbred Danthebluegrassman in the 128th Kentucky Derby field was not without controversy.

Danthebluegrassman had an impressive bloodline, but was listed as a 50-to-1 shot. In the end, he pulled out and watched the race from the sidelines.

I knew something of how he felt.

Long before that first Saturday in May, he'd proved he belonged among the greatest horses of the year when he won the Golden Gate Derby. He loved to lead, but most of the experts had him down as a longshot due to his lack of consistency and the exhausting mile-and-a-quarter length of the race. At 50-to-1 in the opening line, he was even money in my heart.

His stakes victories qualified him, no question, but the decision of my dear friends and running mates super-trainer Bob Baffert and owner Mike Pegram to enter the animal meant that another qualified horse, Windward Passage, would be bumped out. This no doubt disappointed Barry Irwin, the leader of the syndicate of investors who own Windward Passage, but it was perfectly legal.

What made it a problem for Baffert is the fact that it gave some of the press a chance to take a shot at him. Those who know Bob Baffert love him, but those who have the wrong impression of him love to criticize him. Bob fades this sort of nonsense with aplomb, but the ignorance of some writers really irritated me.

Churchill officials didn't help matters when they announced Baffert's decision just a few minutes before the Derby draw was set to go on national television. Fortunately the good folks behind Windward Passage were informed just in time and saved themselves some embarrassment.

What happened next was a pure pleasure for me. Pegram and Baffert allowed me to make the draw.

I was in heaven. My feet barely touched the ground.

Two days later, reality smacked me upside the head when I awoke on the morning of the Derby and watched on the big screen at my cabin in Versailles as the ESPN announcers informed the world that my longshot had been scratched by his trainer due to a muscle pull. I'd received a phone call just a few minutes before and felt a genuine sense of loss. Such things happen every day in horse racing. You just hope they don't happen a few hours before the biggest race in the sport.

I knew Baffert and Pegram were disappointed. Truth is, only one man in Kentucky was more disappointed than they were: yours truly.

Bob had no time to waste. He still had a horse in the Run for the Roses. His name is War Emblem, and his story is one for the books.

War Emblem was the winner of the Illinois Derby and had an Andy Beyer speed rating of 112, easily the highest in the field. But he'd have to be more than fast to win the Kentucky Derby. He'd have to break quickly and get room to use that incredible speed.

Without Bob Baffert's amazing eye for horseflesh, and the ready millions of his benefactor and friend, Prince Ahmed bin Salman of

Dubai, War Emblem would never have made history. But Bob saw the horse and believed in it, and the prince trusted his judgment implicitly. A check for $900,000 was cut and War Emblem quietly joined the Thoroughbred Company stable of champion horses.

It was almost an afterthought. On race day War Emblem, with Victor Espinoza aboard, was a 15-to-1 shot. *Racing Form* handicappers listed the horse only as high as fourth — and then only once among all their dozens of combined selections — on the day of the race. Even Andy Beyer, whose amazing speed ratings are the respected standard in the sport, didn't think War Emblem could win over the distance.

But then came what they call "the most famous two minutes in racing" and the rest is Derby history. The prince had finally won a Kentucky Derby. Which is a good thing for him, because he suffered a fatal heart attack just a few weeks later.

It was at my annual Sunday chicken picnic after the Derby — and nowhere on television or anywhere in print — that Bob admitted the prince, bless his now-departed soul, hadn't seen the horse until the morning of the race.

But he died a happy man thanks to my man Bob Baffert.

I was born in the heart of thoroughbred country and had been a regular visitor to Churchill Downs and the Kentucky Derby since childhood. Mama and my sister Mimi loved to bet the ponies, and were regulars at Keeneland for many years. Thanks to Daddy's immense success, the family was introduced to just about every major player in the business and moved easily among the swells, oil millionaires and trust fund crowd that fills the penthouse of the sport.

But it wasn't until I met Mike Pegram and Bob Baffert that I fell in love with the Sport of Kings. In an activity known for its bluebloods, royalty, pomp, and pretentiousness, here are two self-made men who've risen to the pinnacle of the sport without affecting airs.

Mike is a Kentucky native who grew up in Evansville, Indiana, at his daddy's pool hall. He owns a string of McDonald's franchises and many other successful businesses and he's a straight-ahead man's man who'll do anything for a friend and punch the lights out of an enemy. He is what my daddy called a horny-handed son of toil.

With his white hair and handsome bride, Jill, at his side, Bob Baffert is a funny, outspoken and gifted trainer — the best in the business in your humble servant's opinion — who still wears jeans and cowboy boots in this world of spats and top hats. He's from Nogales, Arizona, and, as he says, he took "The Dirt Road to the Derby," but remains as plain as the folks back home even after earning millions and bringing three horses to the winner's circle at the Kentucky Derby since 1997. In a sport known for its class structure, pecking order, and painfully conservative commentary, my man Bobby is a gale force of fresh air.

And, for the record, all he does is win. In fact, among major trainers Bob had the most victories from 1998 through 2001, ending a streak of thirteen straight years registered by D. Wayne Lukas.

I met Mike in the early '80s when I was in casino marketing at Caesars Tahoe. He had some McDonald's franchises in Sacramento and would come up and play. Him being from Kentucky, we hit it off immediately.

As one destined to start at the top and work his way to the middle, I haven't had to worry often about managing my fortune. That puts me at a distinct disadvantage in the world of horse racing, where the services of top studs are sold for $150,000 and some owners spend more to board and groom a single animal than an inner-city neighborhood earns in a year.

But I discovered early that one of the secrets, if you're not going to be wealthy, is to have wealthy friends. In the positions I've held in the casino world, with access to corporate jets and yachts and suites, meeting wealthy players is a lot of fun. They come to gamble, and I get to summon the air force and the navy and provide them with all the toys that go with their wealth.

That makes for a lot of great times and some good acquaintances, but a man's a fool if he thinks he has more than a few friends in his life. I consider Mike and Bob two of my best. Not because they have status and wealth, but because of who they are. I've always admired men of character, and they've got it.

Pegram says of Baffert, "I hooked my wagon to the right star when I hooked up with Bobby." I feel the same way about them. Frankly, I've been able to live the life of a thoroughbred racing player through them, and they've been very gracious. It's been a wild ride that's taken me from Del Mar to Dubai.

Although my own attempt at thoroughbred ownership was short-lived and unsuccessful, I've enjoyed having my name associated with their animals. The first was a horse named Chandler the Handler, who won at Santa Anita with Gary Stevens aboard. The horse had a promising career, but like his namesake, he broke down and had to be put out to stud. Who says winning is everything?

But following Chandler the Handler enabled me to make the acquaintance of Gary Stevens, who is undoubtedly the best of the best riders in the West. He's a West Coast legend whose name deserves to be mentioned in league with Chris McCarron. It's no wonder Mike and Bob are fans of Gary. Not only is he a winner, he's a kid from Boise, Idaho, who is as plain as the state's famous potatoes.

Gary is a racing hall-of-famer with nearly 5,000 wins to his credit. He's also a winner in life, having overcome a debilitating degenerative hip ailment as a boy that threatened to cripple him and leave him in a leg brace. He didn't let that or any of life's other obstacles stop him from getting to the winner's circle time after time.

One of the least appreciated aspects of horse racing is the fiery competitiveness of the jockeys. Because of their diminutive size, there is a misconception that they are less than courageous athletes. This couldn't be further from the truth. In fact, I believe many are as tough and gutsy as any of the NFL stars I've known. These men in the saddle endure more broken bones in a career than a league of linebackers.

And if you want to talk about competitive, look no further than the rivalry between my man Gary Stevens and a very good rider, Pat Valenzuela. To say they don't exchange Christmas cards is an understatement in the extreme. Fact is, their hatred of one another many times spilled over into knockdown, drag-out fistfights that one time resulted in Valenzuela suffering a broken wrist that put him out of action for six weeks. He broke it on Gary's head.

And I thought I had a hard head.

Gary explains it this way in his book, *The Perfect Ride*:

"As a child, I fought hard with my brothers, although I loved them both, and also fought a lot at school . . . Early in my riding career, I fought continually in the jockeys' quarters and was fined a lot for doing so. At one point, I was actually on probation in Oregon for fighting in the jocks' room. If anyone crowded me on the racetrack or did anything I felt was wrong, I would just come back and beat him up. I felt like I had to establish the fact that I would not be messed with when I rode.

"Sometimes peace is impossible in the jocks' room, particularly among young riders. Feuds start, and often the only way they can end is with jockeys exchanging fists. Angel Cordero Jr., used to keep a set of boxing gloves in the sauna. If there was going to be an altercation, the fighters were locked in the hot box, told to put on the gloves, and punch the anger out of their systems."

Bob Baffert is my man for many reasons, not the least of which is the fact that success hasn't changed him. It's controversial to say it, and there are many challengers to the throne, but he is the sport of horseracing's best trainer. This is a man who has remained true to himself throughout his meteoric rise through the ranks. This is a man who quite literally walks with princes and royalty of every stripe and remains their equal and better.

Good lord, even his horses love him.

Bob Baffert is the best because he's not afraid to get his hands dirty. In other words, he works at it. He's a keen judge of horseflesh, has a memory for the minutest details about animals the way my daddy remembered the names of voters, and he knows how to get an animal ready to make the run of its life. He gets the best out of the horse and brings out the best in everyone around him.

In a sport full of elitists and bluebloods, Bobby comes from quarter-horse country and is proud of it.

He writes in his autobiography, *Dirt Road to the Derby*, "Although I always wanted to be the best, I never dreamed of getting where I am now. I was just some kid from Arizona who couldn't even put a halter on a horse. To dream of attaining what I have would be like someone dreaming of becoming president."

Bobby is classy in victory, classy in defeat, and there have been many more of the former than the latter over the years. But for me, one of Baffert's defining moments came in 1996 when he brought the gutsy gelding Cavonnier to the edge of greatness at the Kentucky Derby. As I say, Bobby's had many big wins, but it was his photo-finish loss to the D. Wayne Lukas-trained Grindstone that tempered his steel and helped him make the transition from the kid from quarter-horse country to the best trainer in the business. He was happy and excited to get to the Derby, but the tough loss made him even hungrier to succeed at the top of his profession. And man has he ever done that.

Although he once feared he'd never make it back to the Run for the Roses and hear "My Old Kentucky Home" played in the traditional style, Baffert is making Churchill Downs a second home. In 1997, Baffert guided Robert and Beverly Lewis' Silver Charm from the San Vincente Stakes to victory in the Kentucky Derby and the Preakness Stakes. Bob's fear of failure drove him like a man possessed, but somehow he kept his blue jeans perspective and sense of humor.

By 1998, he not only returned to the Kentucky Derby, this time with Mike Pegram's Real Quiet, but he won at Churchill and then took the Preakness Stakes, coming close to the Triple Crown and cementing his reputation as the sport's trainer of the future. True to his nature, Bobby generally gives all the credit for his success to his daddy and his man, Pegram.

Television cameras and newspaper reporters are like moths to his flame come Derby time, and they haven't always appreciated his sense of humor. Don't forget, the Sport of Kings traditionally has been ruled by a class of rather humor-impaired characters.

Take the time he and Pegram bought a crooked horse in El Paso and wound up in a hot tub in Las Vegas.

Now I love Texans, they're great people, but El Paso is what they call a good place to be from. And Pegram, who had his own money and plenty of it thanks to his purchase of a string of McDonald's franchises, said, "I might end up in Dallas, or I might end up in Chicago. I might have to go the wrong way to get where I want to go, but I sure as hell ain't staying here."

Well, all roads lead to Las Vegas, and pretty soon Baffert was watching something he'd never seen: a certified high-roller gambling at the tables with more money riding on a roll of the dice than he'd spent on some of his quarter horses.

He writes, "They put us in this suite, and I had never seen anything like it. It had this huge living room and a baby grand piano and a Jacuzzi. Mike had some friends he knew there, and they showed up with these girls. One of them rode horses and wanted to be a rodeo queen. The next thing I know, I'm in the Jacuzzi with everyone, wearing my cowboy hat and drinking Budweiser. Mike had been doing some business on the phone, and he walked in with his beer in his hand, looked at me in the Jacuzzi, and said, 'I think this is going to turn out to be a good relationship. The two of us are going to go places together.'"

And they have. From Churchill to Dubai, they've flown their horses around the world and have been kind enough to bring me along for the ride.

Bobby likes to tell the story of the Monsignor who followed Cavonnier's rise and fall. On Derby Day, the horse's owners, the Robert Walter family, had attempted to curry a little favor with the big Handicapper in the Sky by bringing in a Monsignor to bless Cavonnier. After the horse lost by a nostril to the Lukas horse, Baffert wondered aloud whether the priest had gone to the wrong paddock. He assured the trainer his aim had been true, and his prayers precise.

Come the Preakness, the Monsignor worked harder, gathering Baffert, jockey Chris McCarron and everyone else related to the animal for a pre-race prayer. He sweated and strained and did his best to clear the phone line to his boss. Alas, he was disconnected.

Cavonnier ran fourth.

Now, at this point I would have suggested Baffert move up in weight class to a Bishop, but come the Belmont Stakes the Monsignor appeared once more. This time, he brought a large crucifix for McCarron to carry with him. Mounts are weighed to the ounce, of course, so there was no place to put the cross. Baffert politely passed along that information.

At the Belmont, Cavonnier pulled up lame, and for a moment it appeared the animal was in real trouble. Fortunately it was only a strain.

"A short while later," Bobby writes, "McCarron came back to see how the horse was doing, and we all got to talking about the Monsignor. My good friend Brad McKenzie, who my mother calls the fifth and nicest Baffert brother, says 'I think we need to send the Monsignor to the Lukas camp. He's killing us.'

"One thing about Monsignors, they will go to the window."

Truer words were never spoken. Not only will the Monsignors go to the window and place a bet, but so will most of the rest of us. Which brings me to a final word or two about the future of this horse business. As always, as my man David Brinkley used to say, "Everyone is entitled to my opinion."

Thoroughbred racing today is a clash of traditions with the old Kentucky money bumping up against upstart millionaires and Middle Eastern billionaires. For the outsider, those traditions can seem a little silly and even quaint, but for those in the middle of Bluegrass Country, those traditions are well known and generally respected.

Mrs. C.V. "Sonny" Whitney's annual Derby party was one of those quiet, dignified, deadly dull affairs that has been lost to the ages, replaced by Anita Madden's party. Mrs. Sonny Whitney used to give the No. 1 party. It brought the top-of-the-line people until Anita started giving her party at the Hamburg place right before the Derby at the exact same time and night that Mrs. C.V. Whitney was giving her party. Anita's party was so much more fun. The spread was unbelievable. It had two bands. It wasn't just a bunch of old people who were thoroughly impressed with their own upbringing.

Anita would bring the college boys, hire the football team to walk around like Greek Gods in nothing but shorts. She was just doing a very women's lib-type thing.

Year One she just collided with Mrs. Whitney and everybody talked about it. In Year Two, all the guys would go to Mrs. Whitney's, then slip over to Anita's party because it would go on virtually all night. Then Year Three, it got a little more lopsided. After five years, Anita closed down Mrs. Whitney. She had to stop having her party.

Then Mike Sloan came in and bought it for Circus Circus, which is now called Mandalay Resort Group. A master of marketing with an interest in gaining entrée into the inside world of thoroughbred racing, Mike paid Anita $200,000 for her party. Mike wanted to get involved in the horse business with Bill Bennett's money.

Anita is not only charming, but she's part of a grand tradition of thoroughbred breeding in Kentucky. Her husband, Preston Madden, runs Hamburg Farms, which was started by his paternal grandfather, John Madden, in 1898. Around racing, John Madden was known as the "Wizard of Turf," and in his time he coaxed and conjured some of the greatest horses on record, including the first Triple Crown winner, Sir Barton.

Preston and Anita took over a broken-down Hamburg as a couple of kids and returned it to its past glory, producing big winners along the way.

The Derby is definitely a place to see a horse race, but it's also a place to be seen. It's a stage for the wealthy who are only celebrities because of the status their money provides them. And there are the celebrities, those like Steven Spielberg and Rick Dees, who have a genuine interest in horses and the country, and those who are the "flavor of the month" in Hollywood or the movie business and think they simply must be seen at the Derby. It's a paradise for the paparazzi and a gold mine for the gossip columnists.

In recent years I've had the pleasure of taking in the Derby at Madeline Paulson's table. As I like to say, I'd marry Madeline in a minute, but she refuses to sign the pre-nuptial agreement! She has many assets, but her beauty and personality are her two greatest attributes. I'd hang out with her if she was plain as cornbread. The fact that she's wealthy and knows how to enjoy life only makes her more fun.

Madeline owns horses and is comfortable in the world of the thoroughbreds. Her table attracts a steady parade of celebrities and heavy hitters in the horse world, as evidenced by the 2003 Derby when we dined with Tim Allen and his wife and Rick Dees and his wife, along with gentlemen from Ireland who appeared to own half the island. At the adjacent table sat Phyllis George, who's as lovely inside as she is in the mirror, soap opera queen Susan Lucci, and the effervescent Ivana Trump.

Now, I don't know how much those ladies like the races, but they sure had a parade of studs prancing by them throughout the day.

Frankly, I prefer the company of my circle of friends, like banking executive and former Vandy basketball opponent George "Duke" Davis, and his wife, Irene. And there's my Florida accountant, Harry Murray, who never fails to bring stone crab and Cuban cigars with him from back home.

And you never know who'll slip past security. Take John Y. Brown, for instance. If ever there was a man Kentuckians were too slow to distrust, it's John Y. I tried to do business with him years ago, but the man was incapable of driving a straight nail. So when I see him I still have to remind myself that this too shall pass and my day will improve. Perhaps the only redeemable thing John ever did was father two children with Phyllis. Those kids are handsome young people for whom I have warm feelings.

But at the Derby I couldn't resist needling their daddy.

"Are you sure you had something to do with those kids?" I shouted at him from across the room.

John Y. Brown must have a strain of tent preacher in him because the guy just never quits trying to win souls over to his side. Whether it's the dark side is open to debate. His high-rolling forays into Las Vegas and on the big-league sports betting circuit are well known, and he has a reputation as a fast play, slow pay man. He owes the Hall-of-Fame poker player Chip Reese a million dollars. He owes other institutions. He's a compulsive gambler who bets millions, but shops for a five-cent line.

People get bothered by the new money and the strange faces coming in and taking over the game, but the truth is these new players on the thoroughbred breeding and racing scene are just passing through. The lifestyle is expensive, horses live better than most rich men, and few families can dominate forever. As a nontraditionalist, I see the new money players as great for the state, for the most part.

Thoroughbred racing is at its best in my home state, but it belongs to the world. Over the years, I've seen it swing from Charlie Engelhart of South Africa, to the Japanese business millionaires in the 1980s, to the Irish, which is about where it is now, to the Arabs — whoever's got the money. It's been good for the thoroughbred industry. Case in point: The No. 1-selling yearling in Keeneland went for $10.4 million and never raced. What these sheiks will do is buy a horse, train him, and race him against another guy who's bought a horse and trained him. Head to head. For millions.

Bluegrass and thoroughbred country attracts some incredible people. *Blackhawk Down* producer Jerry Bruckheimer is one of them. While any man of means can own a racehorse, Bruckheimer decided to go one better and own a whole town. He purchased idyllic Bloomfield between Versailles and Louisville and is returning it to its former glory as a quintessential small town. Bloomfield is a place Norman Rockwell would have painted, and Bruckheimer has the money to do the job right. I said good for him and good for Kentucky.

Of course, not all the big races take place in the States. Thanks to my friendships with Mike Pegram and Bob Baffert, I've been able to view the highest of high-stakes races in Dubai that few outsiders have seen. When the princes and sheiks of that tiny Middle Eastern nation go head to head, the competition is fierce and the millions flow like water.

It was common as grocery shopping for them to buy a horse for two or three million and bet for two or three million.

Over the more than 50 years I've been a regular on the rail and in the best seats at the track, I've seen the popularity of the Sport of Kings rise and fall. I've come to the conclusion that the only things that will save this beautiful combination of man and horse are the very things that brought it to prominence in the first place: the return of glamour and style to the track, and gambling, gambling, gambling.

There was a time I thought that Las Vegas's days as a celebrity haven were near an end. In the early '80s, the town had gained a reputation as a care-worn place more fit for also-rans than young studs. One of the things that made Caesars so popular was its insistence on adding to the resort. A boxing event here, a hot headliner there. Caesars, in fact, was among the first major resorts to book top rock acts like the Eagles and Beach Boys for the showroom or a special outdoor theater. It kept the resort ahead of the competition for years until management got small-minded and tight with a buck.

So too it is with horse racing. The key in my humble opinion is to continue to add to the track: Make it the centerpiece of a resort complex; bring in the entertainment where possible; give people a reason to come back more than once during the meet.

And for heaven's sake let the adults with cash in their pockets play adult games. There's nothing more hypocritical than a bunch of racetrack owners getting together to lobby against the evils of gambling. If it weren't for the parimutuel betting system, the Sport of Kings would be just that — limited to a few kings and other assorted royalty.

At this time in our history, legalized and regulated gambling has never been considered more acceptable. Sure, there are problems associated with it, but for the most part it's considered a form of entertainment that has raised countless millions in taxes in states across the nation. A gambling/casino component, whether it comes in the form of video poker machines or, more logically, in the form of a full-scale casino-resort, makes great sense for many racetracks from Saratoga to Hollywood Park.

The simple addition of bingo halls to racetracks would no doubt turn around most of America's struggling tracks. For now, with few exceptions, the hypocrites rule. Come Dan's revolution, that will change.

The fact is, betting on the horses is an all-American pastime that should be cherished and celebrated, not hidden like some stepchild of shaky birthright. In other countries, it's common to see children standing in line to place their bets on the day's races. And so far as I'm aware, there's no hue and cry in, for instance, Ireland to outlaw wagering and "clean up" the sport.

One of these days people in high places ought to try not being hypocrites for a short time. It would make life easier for the rest of us who get our mail on the lower rungs of society's ladder.

Larry Merchant said it well, "Betting stimulates the caring glands. That's why there is so much caring at the racetrack."

Horse betting is also a challenge to the emotional makeup of a man.

"If you have one chink in your psychological armor," thoroughbred expert Andrew Beyer once wrote, "playing the horses will bring it out."

He's right, of course, but that's the beauty of the exercise. As with so many things in this life, the key is not to lose your sense of humor even if you're losing your money at the track.

If you've dropped a few bets, remember what W.C. Fields once said: "Horse sense is a good judgment which keeps horses from betting on people."

13
Chapter

In This Corner

*M*y love affair with the fight game started early and came into bloom in Las Vegas at Caesars Palace.

Over the years, I have met some of the greatest pugilists of the century and have watched ringside at many of the great fights. They were things of brutal, bloody beauty.

But as with most things in my life, my first memory of the sweet science is traceable to my Kentucky youth and stars my father. I met a thousand champs, contenders and pretenders in Las Vegas, but I learned the importance of the fight game as a social event at an early age.

Daddy was away with important business in Washington at the United States Senate, and we were in Kentucky gathered around the radio preparing to listen to a championship fight from Chicago. My brother and I were boxing fans and mother was hovering within listening distance when the voice of Don Dunphy, the great fight announcer, came on. Before introducing the great Sugar Ray Robinson and his latest victim, Dunphy took a moment to announce the presence in the ring of "the senator from the Commonwealth of Kentucky, the honorable Albert B 'Happy' Chandler."

So much for that important business in Washington. Father, who was a close friend of Jack Dempsey and a hall of fame's worth of other pugilists, had taken the train from Washington to Chicago for the fight.

"God damn it, Happy," Mother bellowed. She was no heavyweight, but at that moment she was capable of felling a 100-foot oak with her bare hands.

Daddy rarely missed a major sporting event and circulated with uncommon alacrity among the swells, politicians, sportsmen, and Murder Inc. types. He kept a table in the Cub Room at Sherman Billingsly's Stork Club. He was so popular with Billingsly that the elder statesman of the New York social scene was glad to see me when I introduced myself years later during one of many visits to the city. Billingsly immediately took a shine to me and wouldn't give me a check, all in deference to my father. I was gregarious and outgoing, sort of like Happy Chandler on training wheels. Although, admittedly, my spending habits were more like my mother's. My daddy always said he married a spending agent.

It was at the Stork Club that my daddy was holding court with a variety of characters that included Damon Runyon and Jack Dempsey, when his foot began to feel unusually warm.

Dempsey was known for his incredible toughness, but in person he was really something of a prankster. While daddy was looking the other direction, Dempsey slipped a match between the sole and upper part of his shoe. Once the hot foot got going it was hard to extinguish, and Happy was so mad he drew back with a closed fist and intended to strike the physically fit former heavyweight champion of the world.

A surprised Dempsey looked at him, and in an instant Daddy thought better of his actions. Discretion being the better part of valor — and the safer part as well.

(A similar epiphany happened to me one afternoon at Arlington racetrack with Paul Hornung and Ron Kramer, the all-pro tight end with the Green Bay Packers. We were there with our wives and

Kramer had drunk a dozen martinis and had twelve more on the assembly line ready to go. Kramer was a huge mountain of muscle. He was adequately served and quite possibly over-served.

Well, he looked over and saw how attractive my wife was and began to make advances toward her. She was beautiful, had been the University of Kentucky homecoming queen, and was a member of Kappa Kappa Gamma Society, which was the leading sorority on campus in those days.

"You are gorgeous," he kept saying. "What in the world are you married to him for?" Then he turned his drunken gaze on me. "Look at those blues eyes," he said to me. "Are you gay?"

Hornung chimed in, "You don't have to take that, Dan. Smack him in the mouth."

Easy for him to say. Kramer was an all-pro tight end. This guy, as drunk as he was, could have mopped up Arlington Racetrack with me.

I said to Paul, "I'm not mad yet." (And I wasn't going to get mad, either.)

Las Vegas had long been a fight town, but Caesars put the activity on the map. Some of my first recollections of the place are of all the ex-prizefighters, many of them aging mob fighters, who found steady work in their retirement at Caesars and other resorts.

We had guys working for us who were former contenders and bust-out fighters who'd probably thrown fights — or had been on the receiving end of a fix. In those days there was a big connection between the casino and the boys in New York. A bag was sent that direction regularly, and people like Fat Tony Salerno were rumored to own a piece of the joint. So when their fighters could no longer perform, they sent them out to Vegas to the casinos. The boxers could always work the Big 6 wheel or stand around and look tough enough to eat a side of raw meat.

One of my favorites was Ralph Dupas, who actually dealt "21" and could barely shuffle from the dealer's break room to the table. They must have not stopped a fight, or several, soon enough, for Ralph appeared to have a couple of puzzle pieces missing. One night Ralph was on the floor dealing when he stopped his shuffle and listened to the discussion at the next table. He called over the floorman and said, "Those people are talking about me."

The floorman went to the next table and listened as the customers spoke nothing but Chinese. He reported this fact to Ralph, who would have none of it.

"Well, I hear them," he said. "And I know what they're saying. If they stay after me, they're going to have to answer right now."

With that he spread the cards on the table, stopped the game, walked to the next table and punched out one of the Chinamen. Boom. It was over. Security was called and eventually the proper arrangement was made so no one pressed charges, but Ralph remained sure that he heard them being critical of him.

The marriage of boxing and the casino is ideal, and we ought to hope it lives happily ever after, because the boxing crowd knows how to spend money at the tables. Which, after the commissions have had their say and the promoters have taken their cut and the public has weighed in with its opinion, is the entire point of the exercise. The bottom line isn't whether the fight was entertaining, whether Larry Holmes was the greatest heavyweight of all time or even whether that ear-biting Mike Tyson ought to be allowed to fight again on the Strip. The bottom line is what crosses the green felt and ends up in the casinos' coffers.

Boxing and casino go together because a big event brings out the heavy-laden jewelry crowd, the show-your-disposable-income crowd, the party-till-dawn crowd. It brings in a betting crowd more than just about anything.

Boxing is, after all, the age-old way of settling who's the better man. The last man standing is the better man, and I think there's something about our human nature, whether or not we want to admit it, that attracts us to the scent of that action. A little blood, a little sweat, a little vice. I don't know if it's good for you, but it works wonders on the circulation. I have seen 80-year-old men walking with spring in their step accompanied by their handsome "nieces." I have seen guys who work paycheck to paycheck dress like a million bucks come fight night.

And Vegas will always be the natural host, the fight capital. At least I hope so. With events centers such as those at the MGM Grand, Mandalay Bay, and, if the show is big enough, the Thomas & Mack Center, the venues await the greatest matches in the world.

If I live to be 100 I'll never understand why Caesars Palace, which had a world-renowned reputation for putting on the biggest fights in the business, allowed the competition a leg up. Although Caesars is still capable of great things in this area, it will take someone special to compete with the new big boys on the block.

Where would Las Vegas be without Muhammad Ali?

I first met Cassius Clay when he was on his way to a Golden Gloves championship in Louisville. He was willowy and lightning quick and moved at a speed that made his opponents appear to be wading through hip-deep mud. It was easy to tell he was special, but who knew how special in those days?

My dad told me to say hello and introduce myself and wish him well and so I did. "You tell the governor I'm fighting my heart out."

And he did. He always put on a good show, and a group of Louisville businessmen took an interest in him and helped him turn pro until a few years later, when the Muslims took him away and he became Muhammad Ali.

To meet him in his youth and watch him in his prime made playing host to the bitter end of his career all the harder to take. But Caesars knew the public's taste, and the public went wild over the Muhammad Ali-Larry Holmes fight.

Before becoming "The Greatest," Ali was known in some circles as the Louisville Lip. He was better known throughout the world than

Elvis and had been a one-man savior of boxing who helped bring the racket kicking and screaming out of the dark ages when the heavyweight division was run by Frankie Carbo and Blinky Palermo. Love him or hate him, everyone knew Ali.

On the contrary, relatively few outside the world of boxing and the city of Easton, Pennsylvania, knew Larry Holmes. Holmes was so plain he had no nickname. Why, he didn't even have a middle name as far as I remember. He had been Ali's sparring partner at one time and I know for a fact loved the man like a mentor and uncle. He was a dedicated, plain-spoken kid who knew what it was like to struggle. He'd dropped out of school early and worked at a car wash before turning to boxing.

That October night in 1981, Holmes cleaned up on his hero and was truly sorry to put such a hurting on the man.

Caesars, meanwhile, was putting a similar hurting on the customers at the tables. What is lost to many memory banks is that the seven days leading up to Holmes-Ali were the most lucrative in the history of the casino business and were responsible for creating the career of the gifted gaming executive Bill Wortman. The event was in reality a Wortman production. People underestimated the fact that Holmes-Ali was considered a battle of allegiances even within the black community.

Ali was easy to love and impossible to ignore. Holmes was ready to ring in a change of the guard and that wasn't endearing him to the masses. Years later, when he was a great champion, Holmes would continue to struggle with that reputation. The man who replaces a legend is rarely admired. And replace him he did, pummeling Ali from the opening bell and at one point pleading with the referee to stop the fight so he wouldn't have to knock out the once-great heavyweight. Larry was a simple man, but he was all right in my book.

It was an atmosphere where the blacks came with every bit of finery and every bit of cash that they could come with. They dressed to the nines. You would have thought they were going to see a vision.

To the rest of the country it was just a big fight, but to them I think it represented a lot more.

🐎

Don King took to me right away because of my father. He knew what my dad had done for Jackie Robinson, and that made me someone who was all right with Don. Don is a complex man and a lot negative has been said, some with justification, about him. But no one with a lick of sense can doubt his incredible impact on boxing and, in that way, Las Vegas. His shows have been wild and somewhat notorious, but, man, have they been good for the town. It's difficult to be a moralist in Las Vegas, and I have never been much good at moralizing.

🐎

In New York in the early 1960s I watched a guy on television do a touching piece on Jimmy Piersall. It was Howard Cosell. "People wonder about Jimmy Piersall," Howard said in his distinctive tone. "In my mind, Jimmy Piersall must wonder about people."

I liked the line and, in keeping with my father's method of introducing myself, I called Howard and did just that. I made sure that I was meeting people who I thought were going to loom larger than at the time I met them. Howard became a pal as much as he was capable of becoming. We would have dinner often when he came to town for a big fight, and I was always good company for Howard because I knew that all he wanted from our friendship was an audience. It was awfully easy to have dinner with Howard, but you had to be prepared to listen. (The same is true with Dick Vitale, who is a great guy but is definitely a Prime Time Player when it comes to filling the conversation.)

I remember one time at Caesars Don Klosterman was having dinner with Howard and saw Frank Gifford at a nearby table. Don said, "Frank, come over and help us listen to Howard." Giff just smiled. He had his fill of Howard in the announcer's booth during those "Monday Night Football" broadcasts.

🐎

Roberto Duran was a one-of-a-kind guy who gave the Panamanian people a hero to worship and was a favorite of Central and South American high-rollers. So naturally "Hands of Stone" was also popular with the folks at Caesars and Las Vegas generally. What a warrior. He was the classic example of a gladiator you just knew had no quit in him.

Until, of course, the day an out-of-shape and ill-prepared Duran quit against Sugar Ray Leonard in Montreal in the infamous "No Mas" fight.

His follow-up fight brought him to Caesars, where I nearly literally ran into him as I was leaving the Coliseum convention area. Who was approaching me coming the other way but the great Duran. I moved to the left, and he moved that way. Then I moved to the right, and he moved to the right. As he drew just out of arm's length he raised his hands playfully as if to pop me. I was just about to turn to Jell-O when he grinned. Thankfully, I refrained from saying "No mas."

Although Las Vegas, thanks in large part to Larry Holmes, became known as the world's heavyweight headquarters, it was the middleweights who put on the best shows. Think of the magnitude of a time in boxing history when Marvelous Marvin Hagler, Ray Leonard, and one of my favorites, Thomas "Hitman" Hearns, as well as Duran, took on each other. They were amazing spectacles.

I remember the Hitman's early days; he was an amazing marketing tool. Talk about a knockout. Any time he came out to Las Vegas in the early days he would empty out Detroit. We did phenomenally well with Detroit players. It's something to think about when you consider that, these days, some Las Vegas casino giants have opened gambling resorts in the heart of the Motor City.

One of the men most responsible for putting together great boxing spectacles was neither Don King nor Bob Arum, but Bob

Halloran, a fellow I helped bring out to Las Vegas from Miami, where we'd known each other well as bachelors back when I had the tennis concession at Walter Troutman's Jockey Club. Jimmy Conners and I were roommates and Halloran was the sports director of Channel 4, the CBS affiliate. Bob eventually went to New York, but he was between jobs when I heard from him. At the time, we had a guy who definitely needed help with entertainment and promotions after the retirement of Sid Gathrid. Gathrid had been best pals with Jerry Weintraub, the producer of *Vegas Vacation* and many more, and learned the hard way that his charm was at least substantially related to his ability to give RFB and other services to people. After Sid was out, he told me Weintraub wouldn't return his phone call.

Over the years I've learned just how charming I really am. I have a number of dear friends, but I have learned that how palatable you are to the public is in direct proportion to how much you can do for an individual. That's the power of the pencil at a major Las Vegas resort.

My daddy used to say, "You owe it to yourself to be successful, because if you're not, you're going to be stuck with your real friends — and they're not as entertaining as the phonies."

On the subject of real friends, my man Jake Scott had some words to the wise. Jake had been an all-pro defensive back with the Miami Dolphins and was an earthy fellow with a great sense of humor. Jake said he learned who his real friends were after he'd broken both his hands. He said, "When you go to the bathroom with your hands in casts, you learn who your real friends are."

Bob Halloran called me and told me he'd been fired at CBS, but I told him not to worry about it, that we had a crying need for him to come out and become the sports and entertainment director. The top spot was a juice spot, but we needed the kind of help that Bob could provide. He was an exceptional talent who took the lead and helped create a lot of fights. When people like Bob came into this business, the smiles he saw were somewhat less than genuine. I know exactly how he felt.

A mountain has been spoken about dangerous Mike Tyson's life inside and outside the ring. Between the ropes, he's gone from the youngest heavyweight champion in the world to an entertaining heavyweight of diminished skills but an enormous following. Tyson is a cult figure.

Outside the ring, he's a certifiable mess. He's admitted to committing armed robberies as a boy on the street in Brownsville, Brooklyn, and in an oft-told life story he was raised from reform school by the late, great fight trainer Cus D'Amato, the man who guided Floyd Patterson to the heavyweight title. When Tyson first fought in Las Vegas against a game journeyman named Alfonzo Ratliff, it was clear he had something special. He was Joe Frazier with more power and lateral movement. But he was also a time bomb.

Tyson sandwiched his heavyweight success with a rape conviction of beauty pageant contestant Desiree Washington, did three years, and reappeared from the penitentiary stranger than ever. He'd supposedly converted to Islam, but that religious experience didn't stop him from keeping long hours at the Las Vegas topless cabarets, especially Cheetahs. He was a five-alarm fire waiting to happen.

Then his behavior inside the ring got erratic, culminating in the infamous ear-biting incident, with Evander Holyfield as his victim.

Call it a tragedy, call it a shame. But don't call it a reason to keep Tyson from fighting in Las Vegas.

The boxing commission's stance on Tyson reflects a growing trend in Nevada gaming, namely the need to sanitize everything to fit someone else's perception of what we need to look and act like. The casino floors were once lined with men who were born and raised in the rackets, but in order to impress on the world how clean we were, we drove them into retirement. And I think that's a shame. A lot of these men were given second chances in life and were making the most of it.

The same is true for boxing, and Tyson is the perfect example. Let's agree that his actions against Holyfield and in his personal life were the most egregious in the sport. So why not accept that as a truth and understand that Tyson isn't unique, only a reflection of a side of boxing we'd rather not acknowledge?

Honestly, why should Las Vegas look at this guy as anything more than a cash cow for the casinos and community? That's what he is and has always been. The question we should be asking is, "What does it mean to the coffers of the machine that drives this economy we all enjoy?"

Don't get me wrong. I don't condone Tyson's actions. But here's how I'd make sure it didn't happen again. Have Iron Mike sign an ironclad contract that states if he commits fouls that end in disqualification, he forfeits his multimillion-dollar purse. At minimum, it would bring $10 million or $12 million into the state economy each fight, and it might actually serve to modify the wild man's behavior.

Forget the Harvard psychiatrists and lofty analysis: Put the ball in Mike's court and let the games begin!

Cut through the hypocrisy a minute and tell me, what do you really think boxing is? Legalized assault and battery. Regulated attempted murder. With due respect to my old friend George Foreman, you're not going to get candidates to the Billy Graham Crusade from the ranks of the heavyweight division. Candidates for sainthood are not coming from the Kronk Gym and Gold's Gym and Tocco's Gym. I don't think a guy should bite the ears, but I'm more concerned about fight fans who carry weapons into the stadium than a low blow in the ring. I advocate metal detectors throughout the new arenas, but don't hold back the warriors in the ring.

Vegas missed the Tyson-Lennox Lewis fight, which wound up going to Memphis and cost our casinos and community upward of $100 million. I'd hate to see us out of false pride or pretense miss such an opportunity in the future.

Some people blame boxing's problems on Don King, and that reminds me of a story I heard Cliff Perlman tell about the man. Here's how important King was in Perlman's mind: "If Don King fills the Coliseum and wants us to build him a bigger one, we'll build it. If Don King fills that one and wants a bigger one, we'll build it. If Don King fills the whole world, we'll find him a bigger one and build it." Perlman would give Don King anything he wanted because he understood Don's importance to the marketing of the casino and of the whole damn city.

14

The Great Joe Louis

*N*ext to Ali and Holmes, the most important heavyweight to grace this city of big fights never threw a punch in the ring here. His name was Joseph Louis Barrow, and he was the most celebrated greeter in the city's history.

It was obvious even to a neophyte like me that Joe's omnipresence around Caesars Palace was part of some kind of retirement plan courtesy of his friends Billy Weinberger and Ash Resnick, but folks who believed he was just a Joe Palooka charity case had their facts wrong.

The casino bosses commonly provided jobs for retired prizefighters. Joey Maxim, Paddy DeMarco, and Joey Giambra are just three of countless examples. But they were mere mortals, guys who'd once been at the top of their sport and ended up in Vegas working for wages.

People loved Joe Louis. They were excited like kids at Christmas just to meet him and be near him, and he seldom disappointed them by delivering for what must have been the millionth time stories of his great fights against Schmeling, Baer, Walcott, Ezzard Charles, and Marciano when he was well past his prime.

Watching him there in the Cafe Roma coffee shop or throwing a few chips around the green-felt tables, it might have been easy for some to forget that Joe had been one of the century's great icons. Not just of boxing or sport, but one the entire world took notice of. He had come to symbolize hope for black America in the days before Jackie Robinson broke the color line in Major League Baseball. A lot of folks believed, and I think there's great truth in it, that without Joe Louis there might not have been a Jackie Robinson, at least not for many years to come. And without Jackie, how long would it have taken for a Rev. Martin Luther King Jr. to gain the political ground and public sentiment that made him such a great leader?

No, for my money, Joe Louis could sit and visit or throw around the house's money or do nothing at all and still be all right in my book.

"Call me a greeter," Joe used to say. "I go round talk to people about the hotel, go to golf tournaments and that sort of thing. Other day, the president was talking to Ash and he say, 'When you find out what Joe does, you tell me.'"

Ash Resnick and Billy Weinberger were right. Ash and Billy were responsible for bringing people like Joe and Johnny Weissmuller to Caesars.

It was hard to describe his job because certainly not everyone could do it. Then again, I've tried for more than a quarter century to figure out the precise duties of the casino host, but have found the list would fill an Oxford Dictionary.

All you had to do was watch tourists who had been around in Joe's glory years meet the man the world called "The Brown Bomber" to know that what Joe did was allow strangers just a little access to their youth. He was a Hall of Famer's Hall of Famer, and his millions of fans knew it long after the press grew cynical about the casino's motives.

Joe had done it all — and not all of it praiseworthy. He was a man with feet of clay like the rest of us.

In Las Vegas, few may remember that Joe ran for a time with Sonny Liston before his death in 1970. Joe had managed to conceal a heroin habit that ravaged his body and nearly destroyed his mind. Joe gladly appeared in the trial of Teamsters President Jimmy Hoffa. Not as a witness, but as a celebrity who was glad to show his affection for the labor leader before an older jury that likely idolized the former champ. Remember, financially speaking, Caesars was a Teamsters creation, and Joe had been an icon in Hoffa's Detroit.

Joe Louis Barrow had fathered some kids out of wedlock and his wonderful wife, Martha, had gone the extra mile to make sure they were cared for. (To this day Martha's girlfriend, Lauretta Holmes, takes care of one disabled daughter now approaching 30). Martha had watched out for Joe after the IRS had ruined his finances and nearly destroyed the man.

Joe used to reply to inquiring minds thus, "Who was my toughest opponent? The IRS."

And he was right. The tax man has a better record than Louis and Marciano combined. Joe had lost a main event to the IRS. It made me feel better about losing my own undercard bout with the same opponent.

Whatever his shortcomings, Joe Louis was a great man and a great American. And it made me proud to be part of his last great tribute. Ash and the gang at Caesars, with a little help from Frank Sinatra, staged a tribute to Joe on November 9, 1978, in the showroom. There were nearly 2,000 of the biggest names in sports there, and Sinatra was on hand to officiate.

At one point, Muhammad Ali, who as a younger man had listened to Joe's teasing about who was the better fighter, stood at the dais and criticized Joe for not being more of an activist voice in the black community. The great handicapper Bob Martin shouted at him to pipe down. This was a lot of hogwash, of course. Joe was a man of his time. He was born a sharecropper's son in Alabama in the time of Jim Crow, for crissakes. As a Kentucky boy who knew plenty about race relations and what it was like to watch the action on the front lines of baseball's historic integration, I knew Ali was being too hard on Joe. My old friend Bob Martin, the Babe Ruth of sports handicappers, rose in the audience and scolded Ali. Bob was a great man and the world of sports betting would be nothing without him, but that might have been his shining moment.

Ali is a friend and was an ally when my father was under attack in Kentucky for an off-color remark. But he, too, was a man of his generation. And the trouble with big-promotion spectacles like boxing is, the hype is often biting and sarcastic. I heard that Ali and Joe buried the hatchet not long after that night, and it's a good thing, for they were both pillars not only of the boxing community, but in the coliseum of civil rights.

Joe did more than help save boxing. Joe helped lift his people and by doing so helped the whole nation. I was proud to know him.

Before his burial at Arlington National Cemetery, Joe's body was placed in state at the Caesars Palace Sports Pavilion with a military honor guard watching over him. The pavilion was really not much more than an enormous Quonset hut, but it was the site of some of the biggest fights of the century.

Some members of the press, especially those from out of town who looked down on Las Vegas, were appalled at the thought that the great fighter would be put on display one last time. They also sniffed at Joe spending his final years as a greeter at a casino. Perhaps they would rather have had the man, who was flat broke and suffered from mental problems and narcotics addiction, beg on the street or live somewhere high on a hill. Well, Joe was a survivor.

The fact is, Joe was at home at Caesars Palace. He was as happy as a man with his personal mileage could be. Exploitation is in the eye of the beholder, and complicated men like Ash Resnick took advantage of Joe, but they also placed him on a pedestal — right where he wanted to be.

Enough of this solemnity. I want to tell you a funny story about Joe Louis's final knockout. It was a special one because it came from beyond the grave. According to the *Ring* record book, Joe's final KO of an opponent came June 15, 1951, in New York against a journeyman named Lee Savold.

But I remember one that came much, much later.

After his death, as was befitting his status as a great champion, a grand marble statue of Joe was placed outside the sports book. (The ironies of its placement given Joe's sorry history as a gambler and sucker are too numerous to mention.) This was no simple marble bust. This was a larger-than-life-sized sculpture of Joe in his fighting prime. Joe is depicted in battling pose with his powerful right hand cocked for action and his left jab extended. But this marble Joe weighs slightly more than the man. The statue tips the scales at 4,500 pounds and stands seven feet six. It was sculpted out of solid marble by the hands of the artists at the House of Aldo e gualtiero Rebechi in Pietrosanto, Italy. It is a popular place for photo opportunities for tourists, especially during big fight weekends.

And for the record, although the great Joe Louis lost just three of 66 bouts, "The Immortal Joe Louis" statue is undefeated.

My man Vinny Magliulo, who ran the Caesars sports book, likes to tell the story of the big fight weekend in which the Joe Louis statue provided a little knockout action of its own. You'll recognize Vinny when you see him because he's the spitting image of Robert De Niro and as funny as Jerry Seinfeld.

Well, on this big fight weekend the Louis statue is getting plenty of use as a fantastic site for photo opportunities. Fans line up next to the replica of the champ and the flashes go off.

Some fans get animated and pretend to spar with the champ. One in particular decides he's ready for the main event and begins to bob and weave under the outstretched rock-solid jab of the great Brown Bomber. Says Vinny, "About the third or fourth bob and weave, the guy goes into a crouch, then stands straight up."

And smashes the top of his head against the granite glove of Joe Louis. He drops like a sack of coal, and his photo-snapping friend begins to count him out. When he gets to 10, he realizes his would-be pugilist buddy isn't joking. Security is called and eventually that piss-poor pug is revived, but in my personal record book it's one more knockout for my man the great Joe Louis, God rest his soul.

15

Chapter

Joe Willie Played the Field

I learned early in life that the best way to enjoy football is as a fan from a safe distance — not as a player on the field.

As a high school athlete, I excelled in several sports and went on to play three sports at the University of Kentucky, but I knew the difference between mere athletic exercise and all-out war. My dad had an intense interest in football, and in my college years Paul "Bear" Bryant was the coach at the University of Kentucky. He called my dad Skipper, and naturally I was pressured to go out for the football team. I played on the whipping boy squad for Rupp, so I was familiar with lung-breaking practices, but they were nothing compared with what I saw on the practice field as the guest of Coach Bryant.

Bryant appeared to have one outstanding rule: Make it off the field on your own steam. If you can't, something had better be seriously wrong with you. Simple heat exhaustion didn't count. Ankle sprain? Nope. Muscle pull? Keep guessing. From my observation, a severed arm barely qualified as an injury with the coach.

If a fight broke out on the practice field, Bryant let the combatants duke it out until they got tired of fighting. He never forgot that football was, above all, a contact sport.

Like Rupp, Bryant didn't believe you were building character until you were getting into shape to the point of absolute exhaustion. That's when they started driving you. We threw up a lot at Adolph's practices.

Then the day came that Bryant asked me if I wanted to go out, that he thought I could be a defensive back. But I took one look at his practices, saw the way the players lined up and hit each other, and I respectfully declined. I decided to stick with basketball, baseball, and tennis. Basketball was rough in college, but college football was really rough. There was no way to malinger and loaf, not even for a minute, or the Bear would find you.

All these years later, I regret not being one of his boys. Through the decades I've met many of his former players and all of them speak highly of that tough taskmaster. Unlike Rupp, who discarded you the moment he felt you couldn't be of further use and went so far as to drive you away, Bryant cared for his boys and remembered them long after they left the field of battle.

One of those old Kentucky players is my friend, former Baltimore Colts standout and quintessential football animal Lou Michaels. In the gridiron animal kingdom, Lou was the ultimate carnivore. Tough doesn't begin to describe the man. But like many athletes, I'll delicately say that school studies were not the highest priority with Lou. We took several courses together.

Lou is the only man I ever saw get away with turning in a typewritten mid-term exam taken in class!

The instructor said, "That's funny. I didn't hear a typewriter."

Lou sat next to some of the smartest students at the University of Kentucky and had the test scores to prove it.

Lou wasn't shy about asking to challenge a fellow's honor, and he was downright aggressive after a little vodka. In summer training camp, Lou had a run-in with teammate Alec Hawkins. A buddy of Hawkins warned him to stay away from Lou Michaels when he'd been at the fermented potato peelings, and Hawk ducked out of the gathering and went back to his dorm room and wisely locked the door.

A few hours later, he hears a knock. It was trouble come for a visit.

"It's Lou Michaels," Lou says.

"Lou, what are you doing?"

"Well, open the door. I'm gonna kick your ass."

"Wait a minute, Lou," Hawkins said. "You want me to unlock the door so you can kick my ass?"

"Yeah."

"Lou, I don't think I want to do that."

"Come on, Hawk! Unlock the door!"

Instead, Hawk called coach Shula, who came to the dorm and returned Lou to his own room.

It wasn't long after I ran into Joe Willie Namath in Las Vegas that I realized the man's life and personality were full of ironies.

As gifted as he was as a quarterback with the New York Jets, I knew he didn't complete every pass on the field. But by my count, he did complete every pass off the field. In those days at Caesars Palace, Joe was simply the most sought-after man in the USA.

Joe's knees were notoriously injured, but those who saw the scores of women get next to him might have bet another of his body parts would have worn out first.

Frankly, I've never had a problem with too many beautiful women thinking I was their fantasy man. But even among the most prolific players in all professional sports Joe was special.

And you know?

The fact that heads turned and people whispered everywhere he went didn't inflate his ego in the least. He made time for people, wasn't rude even to the drunks and jerks who sometimes approached him at inopportune times, like when he was in the middle of a blackjack game or a steak dinner. Joe and Las Vegas were a perfect fit. I only wish one of the powers-that-be would have handed him his own casino. It would have been hugely successful.

Fact is, the casino bosses have made a countless fortune playing on the celebrity of guys like Joe. In exchange, he's been treated to the best the house could offer, but when you add it up it's a pittance compared to the players he's attracted and the atmosphere he's helped to create.

Joe's name is synonymous with great sports predictions and weighty upsets. Namath startled the football fraternity with his hip fashion and unabashed bachelor status, and he floored the old guard in January 1969 when he was quoted in the press predicting a Jets victory.

But my story with Joe begins several years earlier when he was a star quarterback at the University of Alabama playing for our old family friend, the irrepressible Paul "Bear" Bryant. Joe was a great quarterback, but he was an even nicer person who possessed a kind of charisma that combined the country boy and the city kid. It didn't hurt that he was a handsome lad whom the girls swooned over.

Joe was precisely the sort of fellow who Brooklyn-born David "Sonny" Werblin, himself a former football player at Rutgers, figured could make the newly designed American Football League a going concern. Sonny had been a band boy for Guy Lombardo, and was a professional "rainmaker." Sonny and Taft Schreiber had been among the first top executives for the Music Corporation of America, better known by its initials MCA.

In the late 1950s, Sonny had been largely responsible for placing a whole slate of MCA shows on NBC, so he also knew the power of television and its future in the world of professional football. By the early 1960s, he'd branched out into professional sports by operating the Madison Square Garden Corporation and picking up twenty-three percent of the New York Titans, who later became the New York Jets. Sonny was the Jets' chief executive officer, but his marketing savvy was as important to the league as it was to the team.

Word was the Jets' team colors were green and white because they were Sonny's favorite — the color of money!

And if you want to make money, you have to have a product. And Joe Willie Namath had product written all over him.

That's why it was so important to make sure Joe signed with the league in 1965. Sonny was a man who, like his friend my dad, possessed a world of skill when it came to the powers of persuasion. But if there's one thing you learn in the casino racket, it's that nothing talks like Ben Franklin and his friends.

Dad and I were at the Orange Bowl, where Alabama was playing Texas, and Joe was at the center of the media spotlight. Joe would be frustrated in that final game of his college career after being stopped on four consecutive quarterback sneaks from the one-yard line by the great Texas defenseman and future NFL star Tommy Nobis, but the game did nothing to dim his rising star.

Coach Bryant introduced us to Joe and Sonny after the game at the Bal Moral Hotel in Bal Harbor, Florida. At the time, I had the tennis concession at the Jockey Club in Miami. It was clear that Joe's future, as long as he remained healthy, was about to be secured through his association with Sonny. When the deal was done, Joe signed what for that time was an incredible package — something along the lines of a $427,000 contract, including $150,000 of MCA stock, by then Sonny's former company.

It wasn't as if the National Football League was taking the AFL's advances lying down. Sonny was busy paying more than $600,000 for Namath and John Huarte, and that act was a shot across the bow of the NFL. The AFL's founding fathers, those Texas oil millionaires Lamar Hunt and K.S. "Bud" Adams, formed the league in 1959 and played the first game in 1960. But the AFL was going nowhere without a product that set it apart from the four-decade-old senior circuit. Joe was that product.

Joe was the number one pick in college in that important year of the AFL's ascent, and I'd argue that it was the glamour he brought to the game (thanks in part to the marketing genius of Sonny) that saved football from becoming too much of a drag for television viewers. In no time, everyone knew Broadway Joe Namath.

Someday, maybe the NFL players will get together to thank him for making them all millionaires. Without the bidding war started by his talent and charisma — by the mid-1960s the Green Bay Packers had spent one million dollars for Donny Anderson and Jimmy Grabowski and players were suddenly receiving six-figure signing bonuses — those NFL players would still be working on the docks to offset their incomes.

I'll even argue that it was Joe's popularity and his incredible upset of the heavily favored Baltimore Colts in Super Bowl III in Miami that went a long way toward cementing the championship game's place with American sports fans. Joe's Jets raised the Super Bowl from big game to international event.

The Jets, with flashy Joe Namath, weren't supposed to have a chance against the Baltimore Colts, who had Earl Morrall and an aging-but-dangerous future Hall-of-Famer in Johnny Unitas, a pair of hard-core traditionalists who still wore crew cuts. The Jets were 17-point underdogs, and most writers in the national sports press gave them less than no chance of beating the Colts. Oddly enough, handicapper Bob Martin, who would go on to become the most famous and respected sports numbers man in Las Vegas history, gave the Jets more than a fighting chance.

It was up to Joe to sell the game that most of the so-called experts thought was over before the coin toss. Well, he did not disappoint old Sonny Werblin.

When asked about the quality of play in the two leagues, he said, "There are at least four quarterbacks in our league who are better than Earl Morrall," rocking the sportswriters on their heels. "There's Daryle Lamonica, John Hadl, Bob Griese and myself. In fact, you put Babe Parilli with Baltimore, and Baltimore might be better. Babe throws better than Morrall."

Understand, Babe Parilli was an ancient mariner by professional football standards in 1969.

This was tantamount to sacrilege and blasphemy. Joe wasn't just putting down Morrall, he was laughing at the whole league. Morrall had been the NFL's leading passer that year.

Things went from bad to worse a few days later at a Ft. Lauderdale restaurant when Joe was overheard again talking up his team. This time, my old friend from the University of Kentucky, Lou Michaels, overheard him. Lou was the place-kicker and a defensive end for the Colts, and as ever he was ferociously loyal to his team. I've heard both men tell their sides of the story over the years, and to this day it's one of the great true tales in Super Bowl history.

"We're going to kick the hell out of you guys," Namath told a stunned Michaels, who could have eaten him for a snack.

A cleaned-up account of the incident by Murray Chass has Lou asking Joe, "Haven't you ever heard of the word modesty, Joseph?"

"We're going to beat you and pick you apart," Namath countered.

"If you fellows do, Joseph, I believe you are the man to do it. But it'll be kind of hard throwing out of a well and finding receivers."

Namath countered, "Don't worry about that. My blockers will give me plenty of time to do the job."

Feel free to sprinkle invective throughout those previous sentences.

Lou is the sort of man you want at your side in war. Joe is the kind of guy you want throwing the grenades (and finding the girls when it's time for a little R&R.) I respect both greatly, but if you were to ask me which one I would pick in the parking-lot fisticuffs that Michaels suggested at that point, I would have to make Lou the favorite. The man eats nails for breakfast.

"I'll knock your head off," Lou said, or words to that effect before Colts lineman Dan Sullivan stepped in to referee. Cooler heads prevailed.

So did the Jets, 16-7.

When I moved out to Las Vegas, Joe blew into town like a hurricane with fellow NFL players Ed Podolak, Ed Marinaro, and business manager Jimmy Walsh, Joe's friend from college and longtime business manager. Jimmy called me to make the arrangements, and when Broadway Joe came into the house, the place erupted. People were all over him for autographs. At that time, he outshined Elvis in the media spotlight and was every bit as big as Muhammad Ali.

And you know something? When the crowds thinned out and we were all having cocktails, Joe was just plain old Joe, the son of Hungarian immigrants who'd grown up in the Pennsylvania coal country. Of course, he was also the Broadway Joe who could pull off wearing white shoes on the playing field and a mink coat away from it. Joe is one-of-a-kind.

When it came time to honor my dad with banquets in Louisville and at Caesars at Lake Tahoe after his induction into Baseball's Hall of Fame, I asked Joe to act as emcee. He had plenty of experience with crowds and was a seasoned pro at the microphone after so many years with ABC-TV. With due respect to the departed Jimmy the Greek Snyder, at one point Joe was easily the best football prognosticator on television. I think he picked nearly a dozen Super Bowl winners in a row. You might recall that at one time he had his own talk show with Dick Schaap and even starred in his own sitcom, as well as making guest appearances on television and being featured on the big screen in *C.C. and Company*. Joe was multi-media and multi-talented. And he couldn't wait to come to help me when I needed him. That's a pal from the old school for you.

I would have been only too happy to have success change me, but all the adoration hadn't moved Joe off center one iota.

The only thing I've ever seen that dropkicked him was the breakup of his marriage. Joe was the world's most eligible bachelor, but when he got married and had children he took the duty seriously. In fact, those of us who count ourselves as his friends barely saw him for fourteen years while he worked in his primary roles as husband and father. He dropped out of sight for many years, and that was understandable. He had a couple of daughters and was proud of them and wanted nothing more in life than to see them grow up to be successful young women. For some reason, his wife busted up the marriage. When she cashed him in, it really hurt him. The breakup kept him from his kids. Maybe she thought she was missing something, that the grass was greener. My wife certainly suffered from that delusion. Women somehow think they're missing something, but, come on, where on Earth is a woman going to go to find a better looking, more humble and generous guy than Joe Namath? Nowhere I know. They just don't come in a higher caliber than Joe. And she goes and runs off with some yoga instructor. I'm obviously biased on this, but then I'm biased about all my friends. You know what Joni Mitchell says, Sometimes, "you don't know what you've got till it's gone."

When I was juggling girlfriends a certain predicament — the avoidance of a crime scene with myself as the bloodied victim — necessitated I ship one out of town before the other returned to find her in my company. At dinner one night at Nero's with Jimmy Orr and Ron Collier, I explained my situation. At the time, I had almost persuaded the girl to fly down to San Diego to spend some time with my pal Dickie Palmer, the University of Kentucky All-American who at that time played for the San Diego Chargers.

But then I got the bright idea that, since Joe was passing through town on his way to California anyway to his home in Beverly Hills, that the girlfriend might stay with him for a few days at his place in Truesdale Estates. He agreed, but immediately told the girl, "Don't think for one minute there's going to be anything between you and me."

Joe has a code about him with friends. Whereas most guys will be glad to intrude on another man's wife, much less a girlfriend, if you're a friend of Joe's, you're protected. You're exempt.

Which reminds me of the man who always wanted to meet Moses so he could ask him about that 9th Commandment. "How far down the block does it apply?"

The truth is, Joe's a very private person. These days, he plays a lot of golf and represents Mike Shustik's Vestin Mortgage Company. I see his face more on billboards and television commercials in Las Vegas than anywhere else.

That girlfriend is long gone, but I'll never forget the time he saved my neck — and the look in her eyes as she got set to travel with Joe.

Joe Namath was the most famous quarterback to come out of the University of Alabama. But I'd guess that Kenny "The Snake" Stabler was Bear Bryant's favorite. Ironically, his career as a signal-caller, which would take him to the Super Bowl with the Oakland Raiders, almost never happened. Bryant thought enough of his athletic ability to use him as a defensive back at Alabama while Steve Sloan was quarterbacking the ball club.

Kenny came from a tough upbringing with a dad who was rough and tough and had been mistreating his mother. Kenny had to leave school to go home to rescue her, and departing the team broke Bear Bryant's golden rule: The team comes first.

When he got back, Bear chewed him out, and Kenny quit. A promising career was in jeopardy.

A few days went by and Kenny returned, told the coach he'd been wrong to leave the team but couldn't let his mother suffer, and Bear let him back on the squad — right at the bottom with the scrubs and water boys. Instead of complaining, Kenny worked his way back and by opening day he was starting quarterback.

Adversity comes to every life. Kenny handled his responsibility. He didn't blink, and it made him stronger. It tempered his character into steel. From that point, Bear Bryant was a father figure to Kenny.

I thought I'd start with that story because the true character of Kenny Stabler almost always gets lost in the rock 'n' roll persona of the man. He liked to say, "There's nothing wrong with reading the playbook by the light of a jukebox."

He had a pocketful of jukebox money and then some by the time I met him at the Aladdin. I'd gone to work there after parting company with Caesars for the first time and was standing near the front desk when he walked in unannounced. No one recognized him despite the fact that he'd just guided the Raiders to a blowout victory over the Minnesota Vikings in Super Bowl XX.

I said, "Kenny 'The Snake' Stabler. I feel like giving you everything in my pocket because you sure won the money for me."

He told me he knew his team was going to win and over drinks he laughed about the game.

"I could go to work in a suit and tie," he said. "I had the biggest offensive line. When it comes to receivers, I've got the fifth-leading receiver on one side and on the other side I've got Cliff Branch, who can outrun all the cars in the parking lot. People talk about the quarterback, but I've got a ball club around me."

Upon close inspection, it was clear Stabler possessed a fierce competitiveness in his nature that helped him come out on top. He was fierce on the field and could be volatile off it. He wasn't shy about expressing himself physically when challenged. He wasn't allergic to contact.

A group of us were on the town having too much fun when I was approached by a guy who started giving me some static. A peace-loving man by nature, I had every intention of letting it pass.

Not Kenny.

He stepped up and started plowing in on him. Bam, bam, bam.

Before the guy knew what hit him, four of his friends ascended to assist him, and Talbert Todd and some others joined the chorus from our choir. The donnybrook ended quickly, and it wasn't the last Kenny would find in Las Vegas, but it taught me a couple of lessons. First, I'm a lover, not a fighter. And second, I'd rather wrestle a lion than mess with Kenny Stabler. He hits like a defensive back.

Chapter 16

Good Sports

*L*as Vegas has become the great second-best place to be any time there's a major sporting event. If you're not courtside at the Final Four, Las Vegas offers the next-best seat in the house. If you're without the big-time juice it takes to score good seats at the Super Bowl, Kentucky Derby, or Breeder's Cup, then it's Vegas or bust.

Truth is, Las Vegas is really the best place for sports fans. Why? First of all, it's painfully clear from the sky-high ticket prices of these events that corporate America has completely taken over the Super Bowl. It's nearly absconded with the Kentucky Derby and Final Four, too. Super Bowl ticket prices have gone from twenty and fifty dollars a seat to twenty-five hundred and five thousand with even higher prices on the scalping market. That's the cost of selling out to the corporate boys.

Second, Las Vegas just plain offers more fun for the buck than does New Orleans or Atlanta or whatever stadium the Super Bowl lands at. The rooms, food, and drinks are cheaper, and the pre- and post-game festivities are second to none.

Then there's the legalized sports betting. You name your action and you'll probably find a sports book willing to accept the challenge.

Although Congress loves to beat up the legal sports betting industry, it's a nearly scandal-free part of the casino. And even the critics and cynics acknowledge that the $5 billion a year wagered in Las Vegas is downright chump change compared with the $100 billion wagered illegally across the country.

Finally, fans who dream of rubbing elbows with professional sports stars have a field day in Las Vegas during the Super Bowl. A parade of talent from my man Paul Hornung to the latest quarterback sensation play host to parties for every pocketbook at Super Bowl time. It's an autograph-seeker's heaven.

It's no accident Las Vegas turns into a sports celebrity convention during major events. Gambling and sports have shared a controversial relationship since the days of ancient Rome. Players like Hornung and Namath broke real ground in the National Football League when they made little secret of their enjoyment of the action inside the casino.

After the original Super Bowl, Paul came to Las Vegas to be married and hopped over to Hawaii for his honeymoon. And don't think marketing types didn't appreciate it. Hornung gave Las Vegas countless dollars in free publicity in sports pages across the nation when he hit town and played gracious host to gamblers and fans from all over the country.

Next to playing the game itself, Kenny Stabler would love to come to Las Vegas for the Super Bowl parties. He and Jake Scott and Billy Kilmer and Eddie Podolak loved to come out and talk football and be with the fans. In fact, they'd get mildly upset if they were overlooked and not noticed.

Ed is the Polish Prince. He was nothing but a blue-collar hard worker. Like Pittsburgh's Rocky Bleier, Ed wasn't flashy, but get between him and the goal line and you're gonna get your pants pressed. Although he'd never get the credit he deserved — how many fullbacks ever do? — he was a fine player who for many years has held the league's single-game rushing record by gaining 350 yards in four quarters and two overtime periods. In the final overtime, Podolak ran the ball about 70 yards but Jan Stenerud missed the field goal and the Chiefs wound up losing to the Miami Dolphins. As far as I can tell, the players still hate Stenerud for it.

🐎

Then there are guys like Lee Majors and Nick Nolte, who dressed in funny hats and dark glasses in an effort not to be identified. Except, they were the only guys wearing funny hats and dark glasses, so they only called more attention to themselves.

Nick was always a good friend of Freddie Belitnikoff, who was our main man in the San Francisco marketing office of Caesars with Ron Collier. Fred was supposed to open doors for Ron, but he suffered from a short attention span after being contacted by Nolte about going to Hollywood and being in a movie. Nick cast Fred as a Russian killer. Fred still had his job with Caesars, but Ron ratted him out for not being at work.

Time takes its toll on all the party animals and all the ladies' men. Not even Jesse Owens could run full out nonstop, and the party circuit exacts a heavy price on its participants.

🐎

Nobody played off the field harder than Paul Hornung, the Golden Boy of the Green Bay Packers fame and a Kentucky native. In fact, I'd say Paul is among the three most popular athletes to come from my home state along with Ralph Beard and Wallace "WaWa" Jones. Paul is from Flaget High School in Louisville and was a Heisman Trophy winner at Notre Dame The Fighting Irish had a lousy team in 1956, and finished just 2-8, but Paul accounted for more than half the team's points.

He was an immediate star with the Packers, but was suspended in the 1963 season for betting on football games. (He helped lead the Packers to the NFL Championship in 1962.) Like so many players, and most team owners, Paul liked to gamble and had been friends with Abe Samuels, who owned a lumber company and a piece of the Tropicana in Las Vegas. It was an innocent relationship, of that I am thoroughly convinced. Paul would no more shave a game than he'd cut his own throat. He was a great competitor, but he and Alex Karras of the Detroit Lions were made examples of by Pete Rozelle.

After he retired, Paul went into business in Kentucky and maintained a relationship with Las Vegas by becoming a star attraction at high-roller golf tournaments. He remains a favorite among big gamblers, who seek him out to talk about those glory days on the gridiron. He's managed to keep himself in demand even to the present moment. He is so gracious with the public in general.

🐎

Come to think of it, so was O.J. Simpson.

No one will want to hear this, but O.J. Simpson was one of the classiest NFL stars to ever play Las Vegas. He was well-mannered, articulate, funny, and charming. He was smart with his money, had good contacts and made good investment choices. And he was the most exciting running back in the history of the sport. The guy simply had everything going for him. I considered him a friend, a guy I could call for a favor and one I would gladly do a favor for.

And so, naturally, it all fell apart when he was accused of killing his wife, Nicole Brown Simpson, and Ronald Goldman.

I did what you can count on a friend doing and surely what most of his friends did after the details of the grisly killings were made public.

I ran out on him and abandoned him.

Sorry, Juice. I draw the line at homicide.

🐎

I've never met a man with more honest character than Billy Kilmer. No human loves the racetrack and the racetrack's people more than Billy. Heaven to him is mingling with average guys on the ground floor at the racetrack, leaning on the rail and listening to the experts converse and solve all the world's problems.

Billy Kilmer led the Washington Redskins to their first Super Bowl in 1972. Although the Redskins lost, 14-7, to the Miami Dolphins, Billy carries the memory of climbing to the top of the game, a feat that has eluded so many great quarterbacks. Billy was an All-Pro that year, but people might not remember that he was hardly a young buck. He'd broken in back in 1961 with San Francisco. Billy was known as a tough field general whose biggest battle came in replacing Sonny Jurgensen, who was something of a legend around Washington.

Billy is one of my favorite people because he's just so damned honest when it comes to the realities of the relationship between gambling and professional football. He knows the gamblers built the sport from the sandlots to the stadiums, and unlike so many in his fraternity, he's not afraid to state his opinion.

Back in March 1983, when the United States Football League was in its infancy — and you'll recall it never lived to maturity — Billy was asked whether it had a chance. Sure, he said: You can bet on it, can't you?

"If somebody bets five dollars on a game, he's going to watch it on television," Billy told a reporter. And he knows of what he spoke. Billy for a short time in 1984 took over for Johnny Unitas as a spokesman for Mike Warren's hugely successful NFL sports service. The league, assembled by unwashed bookmakers and high-rolling gamblers, threw a fit. Commissioner Pete Rozelle got the vapors when Billy said, "I don't have any qualms about it. I've never been hypocritical in my life. The NFL was made strong by people betting all over the country. I don't care what Pete Rozelle says." Billy later went to work for Clint Murchison Jr., the founder of the Dallas Cowboys and a big gambler who also owned Nevada National Bank and created Trousdale Estates in Beverly Hills. Clint also owned the Del Mar racetrack for many years. Clint not only was a high roller, but he was close friends with J. Edgar Hoover and Richard Nixon. With friends like those, no one in the NFL dared utter a word about Clint's gambling. But let Billy Kilmer try to earn a living after his playing days had ended, and watch out. Here come the hypocrite police.

The duplicity on this issue never ends. Take my man Kenny Stabler. Anyone who watched him play a down of football knows he's one of the toughest, most competitive men to ever step on the field. He was Bear Bryant's favorite because he was brutally tough and wanted nothing more than to win.

Kenny was also a friend of an old bookmaker named Al Dudich. Al had been a knockaround guy, but he was harmless and Kenny knew it. Once word circulated that Stabler and Dudich knew each other, all hell broke loose down at hypocrite headquarters. There were a couple of newspaper and television exposes that muddied the waters without proving a damn thing, and Kenny had to defend himself. He also had to defend himself against Pete Rozelle, front man for a league that didn't mind its owners owning racetracks and gambling like fiends, but couldn't have a quarterback have a cup of coffee with a short-pockets bookmaker.

Kenny's a guy who wears his heart and habits on his sleeve. He's as honest as a country song, so of course no evidence was ever found that he'd gambled on his games or violated any law in any way. He sued for an apology and eventually was cleared by Rozelle.

Frank Gifford is known more today for his skills in the broadcast booth than on the football field, but in his day the game had no one better. I'm proud to call him a friend.

There's one thing I can say about Giff: The ladies loved him. Period. Here is a man who knew no foreign ports, if you know what I mean. It was alleged he had a beauty queen waiting for him in every town. When I first knew him, he was unmarried but seldom unattached.

Years later, Giff made headlines for what the press called a sex scandal. He'd met a stewardess and taken her back to his hotel room, which created a field day for the paparazzi and made his wife, Kathie Lee Gifford, America's wounded wife for a few weeks. Personally, I think the whole thing was good for her ratings.

I'd like to be able to muster a little outrage, but if there's one thing I've learned it's that men and women, if given an opportunity, will act like men and women.

I've been with Giff since the incident, which made him mad as hell, and it's safe to say it's not a topic of discussion in our circle. Fact is, if you're going to bait a trap that way, you're going to catch a lot of men.

⚘

One of my favorite football men was a general manager and all-around great guy named Don Klosterman. His life is an inspiration to those who think they have it rough.

Don was a promising ballplayer who starred at quarterback for Loyola of Los Angeles and could really light up the air. He was tough and known as a man who could really rally his troops. After college, he was a first-round draft choice of the Cleveland Browns but after a trade to the quarterback-rich Los Angeles Rams he signed a professional contract to play in Canada. His career nearly ended along with his life when he broke his back and injured his spine in a skiing accident.

Don was told he'd never walk again without plenty of assistance, but he didn't listen. Instead, he fought like a man possessed.

He once told his man Frank Gifford, "I began to live for each day alone. I stopped agonizing about yesterday or the future. I tell myself, 'Today I will work. Today I will get a little better.'" Don rejected the physicians' opinions when they told him he'd never leave his wheelchair. He refused to accept the bad news and worked his way back.

Eleven months later, he was walking again. It was a million-to-one shot, and he'd made it. In no time, despite his braces and cane, he was playing golf, too.

He wasn't through with football, either. Don managed to work his way into the front office of the San Diego Chargers, then assembled the talent that made the Kansas City Chiefs a great team. Along the way, he helped make the AFL a success. If they gave an award for courage, it would have Don Klosterman's name on it.

He used his inner drive and unbeatable personality to charm the best college talent to join the American Football League. He was so successful at getting veterans to cross over into the new league that at one point the pressure grew too great, and the NFL finally decided that a cooperative agreement was wise. When the leagues were finally joined as conferences, Klosterman should have received much of the credit.

🐎

It's strange what sticks with you, but I'll never forget the look of disappointment on my son's face when we were snubbed by coach Don Shula before the Super Bowl. Shula and I had been assistant coaches at the University of Kentucky after returning to pick up 12 credits to graduate after my stint in the Army. Shula was an apprentice under Blanton Collier when I was the assistant freshman basketball coach. Through the years I'd always assumed we were good friends, but I found out that a friend in need may be a pest indeed when we approached him in search of two Super Bowl tickets. It wasn't the money to pay for the tickets that we lacked; it was the tickets that were scarce.

I'd been telling Chan how close the coach and I were, really building myself up. I walked up and greeted coach Shula like the old friend I thought he was, then asked him where we could get a couple of tickets.

"It's a sellout," he said flatly.

"Well, I'm aware tickets are tough to come by," I said. "That's why I'm going to you."

"I don't know where to tell you to get any tickets," Shula said.

So much for how close we were. I was embarrassed and saw the look of disappointment in my son's eyes. I'd find some tickets in time for the game, but it taught me a lesson about friendship.

As we were walking out of the hotel, we ran into Lou Michaels. While we were visiting with him, he spied Burt Lancaster sitting in the lobby. The Super Bowl was such a big event that movie stars came to fawn over the players, and Lancaster got up and said, "Hey, Lou."

Always a joker, Lou snapped his fingers and feigned confusion as if he couldn't recall his name.

Then he offered, "You're Kirk Douglas, right?"

When former Atlanta Mayor Ivan Allen died in July of 2003, that city lost one of its great men and perhaps its greatest promoter. Allen loved Atlanta the way I love Versailles and have come to love Las Vegas. Allen is the man most responsible for opening the door to big-league sports in that city, and I'm proud to say I did my best to help him.

It was my idea to bring professional football to Atlanta, which I believed was more than ripe for it. I had access to the league and attempted to get Allen on board, but the city located so close to all those great college football programs appeared more interested in landing a big-league baseball team. Eventually, Charlie O. Finley, the flamboyant owner of the Oakland A's, talked Allen into backing a Major League Baseball team for Atlanta. My daddy had been the baseball commissioner, of course, but my juice was limited. In the end, I couldn't help Allen, but sports columnist Furman Bisher of the *Atlanta Journal-Constitution* was kind enough to recall that I was the first man to make a serious attempt to land a professional sports franchise in that city. Normally I'm late for everything but supper. For once, I was ahead of my time.

Chapter 17

A Bunker Mentality

*I*n Las Vegas, the green felt extends far beyond the casino floor. It stretches all the way to the city's great golf courses and tennis pavilions, for both of those sports have been part of the marketing of Las Vegas since the beginning of the modern era.

Attorney Louie Weiner once said his first big Las Vegas client, Benjamin Siegel, told him he planned to build a golf course as lavish as the Fabulous Flamingo. That was back in 1946 before Siegel's dream ran into big cost overruns. His plan to build the first championship golf course was cut short by rifle fire in June 1947, but four years later my man Moe Dalitz was in Las Vegas putting the finishing touches on the Desert Inn, which would host the Tournament of Champions for many years and establish the city as a playground for golfers of every handicap. (The tournament's first champ, Al Beselink, was an avid gambler.)

Golf has been a marketing tool ever since, and these days it's an even bigger part of the positioning of the casinos.

Las Vegas has been a popular spot on the professional golf circuit since the days of Moe's Tournament of Champions. In fact, increasingly golf fans are combining their love of the game with

Daddy's old friend Will Rogers once said, "It's hard to tell whether Americans have become such good liars because of golf or the income tax." And he was right on the money.

🐎

My man Lee Trevino was made for Las Vegas. Before he was a great pro, Lee was a great golf hustler. I'd be willing to bet he'd have made more money hustling golf here than in his incredible career on the PGA and Senior PGA tours. He learned golf from the bottom up and for many years was the game's best trick shot artist. He broke in as a caddie at one of the Dallas country clubs and was a natural showman. He'd tee off using a Coke bottle, play barefoot or with a putter and five iron, place a chair over the pin. In short, he did many of the things that gamblers and hustlers would do to make a buck and hone their skills.

He's also a bit eccentric on the course.

That is, if you call a guy who talks to his golf ball eccentric.

When Lee hits a shot, he gives it directions. I do the same thing when I hit the ball, but the conversation is limited to a string of epithets. But Lee will hit a ball and call out, "Be up, be up." One time he shouted directions only to have caddie, Willie Aitchison, respond, "Get down, get down."

Lee replied, "Leave it alone, Willie. Leave it alone."

Lee had been a poor boy who knew what it was like to struggle as a kid. But he had the gift of hustle in him and he took advantage of it and tempered that ability to handle the pressure that accompanies the money game.

After he'd made millions on the professional tour, he was asked how he handled the pressure. He had a great reply.

"Pressure is playing for ten dollars when you don't have a dime in your pocket."

The "White Shark," Greg Norman, concurs.

"When I was making 28 bucks a week, the only way I got to go out and play golf was through gambling," he told a writer. "It was a great catalyst for me, because I learned to play under pressure. There were times when I was playing that I couldn't afford to lose."

I've found myself in similar shape on many occasions, but unlike the pros, I managed to lose anyway.

That's the thing about golf. It's not always the best athlete who wins. Nor is it necessarily even the best fundamentally sound player who prevails in a head-to-head match. Often, it's the man who is capable of handling the pressure who takes the money. The fellow who doesn't choke is greatly valued on the country club circuit. Sometimes they'll surprise you.

Take Jimmy Girard, for instance. He's a mild-mannered bar and restaurant owner in Las Vegas, who, with his partner, Bob Harry, runs the successful Fellini's restaurants. Jimmy is too busy making money to play golf regularly these days, but there was a time he played more — and for high stakes. There were a good number of players in town capable of shooting lower scores than Jimmy. He wasn't quite a scratch golfer, if memory serves. But he was a go-to guy at the country club when a group of gamblers wanted to bet on a match. In short, Jimmy didn't choke.

And he was the closest thing to a match for Billy Walters, the Louisville native who'd come to Las Vegas seeking his fortune in the sports betting and casino gambling business but was known as one of the best golfers on the West Coast. The two men played rounds of golf for the kind of money that would make some PGA Tour veterans nervous.

It wasn't all their money, of course. There was a gaggle of gamblers betting on them just like ponies at the track.

Of course, no story of Las Vegas golf is complete without tipping a cap to the biggest gambler — and some would argue the greatest mark — in local history: Jimmy Chagra. Now, Jimmy was suspected by the authorities in those days of having amassed his fortune by trafficking in large amounts of illegal substances. In Las Vegas, all that mattered was that it was green and foldable, for to stand around and think twice about the origin of a man's bankroll is a sure way to drive yourself to distraction.

Jimmy loved to play golf and fancied himself quite a shooter. He was very good and had all that money to buoy his confidence. But there was a caddy shack full of players who were better, and they proved it to him regularly. No one was more successful than Billy Walters.

Here's the ironic thing about Jimmy Chagra and the law. If the government had been wise, it might have saved itself a ton of trouble prosecuting Chagra if it had instead just let him stay in Las Vegas for a few straight months. He lost so much money at the tables and on the golf course that he'd have gone bankrupt.

Another man who felt the sting of Billy Walters' swing was casino man Jack Binion. Jack and Billy are best friends now, and they got to know each other well on the golf course. Billy, as I recall, got to know Jack's wallet on a first-name basis, too. That sort of thing is bound to happen when you're playing golf for $10,000 a hole.

Funny thing is, instead of making them more distant, all that gambling and competition made them great friends. They remain close to this day.

There are many candidates for the title of biggest mark on a Las Vegas golf course, and my vote goes to the incredibly gifted and talented hotel man Jay Sarno. You know Jay as the man who created Caesars Palace and Circus Circus, but he wasn't satisfied with that important status. He also had to play golf for high stakes and, brother, was he susceptible to the hustle. He couldn't help himself and lost a fortune chasing the little white ball around the park.

One casino man I'd never want to tangle with on the golf course is my friend Gil Cohen. Gil is the son of Yale Cohen, the great gambling executive from the old school, and Gil is a marketing master around the green felt. But he's an even better player on green grass. To this day I don't know why he didn't join the PGA Tour. Maybe he was making too much money at the country club.

Of course, a good number of Las Vegas boys have grown up to make their mark as card-carrying professionals. Robert Gamez and Skip Kendall are two of many, and Chris Riley is another young man with great potential.

But I'd still give Billy Walters the nod in a head-to-head match with big bucks on the line.

These days, Billy has made the transition from the man to beat on the golf course to the developer who built it. He has amassed an impressive track record in a few short years of creating courses that stand out among some very good places. With its tropical island theme and Wolfgang Puck restaurant, Billy's Bali Hai near the Mandalay Bay is the only golf course on the Strip. Among several others, his Royal Links celebrates many of the greatest holes from courses in the British Open. If you can't fly across the pond, the next best thing is playing holes drawn directly from the Royal Lytham, Royal Troon, Royal Birkdale, Turnberry, and Old Course at St. Andrews. Billy has come a long way from Louisville.

Of course, the most mysterious and interesting golf course in Southern Nevada is Shadow Creek. Created by Steve Wynn for an estimated $48 million, it was his exclusive domain until Kirk Kerkorian bought Mirage Resorts. Now it's a slightly more accessible course — free if you're a high roller, but $1,000 a round if you're just curious — and still ranks among the country's best. It's an emerald island that sits on 320 acres north of downtown Las Vegas. The land cost just $3 million, but the desert became a forest after Wynn had 20,000 mature pine trees planted and added fallen needles to make the place appear established.

It defined corporate excess, but it was a helluva drawing card for Steve's Mirage. It gave him a leg up on the competition for nearly a decade when it came to providing an exclusive golf experience for high rollers and made his casinos millions in the process. It also fit Steve's rather eccentric personality and caused writer Mark Ebner to opine, "'If Frederick the Great was a golfer, this course would be his,' one travel writer wrote. And Shadow Creek, as it is known, is the despot Wynn's and Wynn's alone. He is its only member, and it's said that he calls it his 'fuck you' golf course . . . Shadow Creek may be played only by Wynn's personally invited friends. The fact that there's rarely anyone playing at this top-ranked course may tell us something about Wynn's popularity." The writer was being too hard on Steve, but the point is that Shadow Creek made a mighty impression on the golf world. It was ranked among the top courses by more than one magazine, and I think he might have built it in partial response to not being admitted to the Riviera Country Club.

One thing about Steve: Anyone who challenges him is in for some competition. Like a lot of the great gamblers who came before him, he's smooth on the surface and tough as nails underneath.

In Las Vegas tournaments, golfers will stroll a course trailed by a gallery with folks extra motivated because they've placed large bets on the players that day. One time the singer Frankie Laine, a Las Vegas showroom stopper for many years, was sighted in the Tournament of Champions gallery keeping a close eye on Gene Littler, who was more than a little superstitious. Littler noticed Laine wore red pants the first two days of the tournament, when the golfer played superbly, but switched to a brown pair the third day, which had been a bad one for Littler. Instead of working a little more on his putting or short game, Littler figured the problem was the singer's pants.

He asked Laine to wear the red pants, and on the fourth day Littler was back in fine form.

Laine won his bet, too.

Peter Jacobsen is one of the best players on the PGA Tour and easily one of its funniest. He penned a book with my man, Las Vegas author Jack Sheehan, called *Buried Lies* that's about as honest a take on the world of professional golf as you'll find. Jacobsen is known as a man capable of imitating all the great players' swings. But what he has to say about the game itself is more than funny. It's insightful.

"Golf swings are like snowflakes," he says. "There are no two exactly alike. I try to emphasize how different they all are when I do my swing impersonations. When I do Lee Trevino, I line up way open, take the club back way outside, and drop it back to the inside. When I do Miller Barber, I make sure that the first thing that comes back is my right elbow, which flies out as far away from my body as I can get it. When I do Johnny Miller, I try to do an early set and cock the club as much as I can. These swings are as different from one another as they can be, but they belong to players who have all been tremendously successful on Tour. The point is, they all return to the impact zone in the same position."

Easy for him to say. My best golf is played seldom and less so, but over the years I've been treated to some amazing courses and even more colorful characters.

But Peter isn't just in it for the giggles. He's in it for the green. He is the sort of player who can do all the tricks and end up with the money because he's an incredibly sociable man. He's a people person, loaded with charm and ability. Charm and social grace will lure the sucker into position, and talent will annihilate him. If that makes a simple golf game sound like one of those nature shows where the unsuspecting gazelle is run to ground and pounced on by the cheetah, well, the similarities run more than skin deep.

🐎

Given the fact that so many gamblers and celebrities who visit Las Vegas are looking for a suitable tee time, it's only natural that your humble servant would have come in contact with plenty of jocks and stars. I've certainly met my share. Rick Pitino is my favorite.

Pitino is the brilliant coach of the University of Louisville who previously led the University of Kentucky to three Final Four appearances and one national championship and also coached the

New York Knicks and Boston Celtics in the NBA. If I got to choose an alternative life, I might just pick his. Now here is a man who travels first class and knows how to have fun. He's managed in a single lifetime to become not only championship coach and best-selling author, but a successful thoroughbred owner as well. After watching him hit a golf ball, I've come to believe there's nothing this man can't do.

He's taking a shot at eliminating homelessness by creating the Daniel Pitino Shelter. Named for his son, the shelter directly benefits from the Pitino Golf Classic, which is an annual sellout in Owensboro.

Then there's Rick Dees, the Los Angeles disc jockey who, through hard work, has carved out arguably the best gig in all of radio. His "Weekly Top 40" show is a huge success. He's won "The People's Choice Award" and has a star on Hollywood's Walk of Fame. Rick's morning show is as popular as Pepsi, and what I love about the guy is he's a good family man who hasn't resorted to the smut and trash that pours out of the mouths of the competition.

This is a guy who on a lark cut a comedy tune called "Disco Duck" and watched it climb to No. 1 in 1976. All things considered, Rick is a quintessential Los Angeles personality.

And unless he tells them, most of his millions of listeners never suspect that his show is coming from his home studio at Sweetbrier Farms in the middle of Kentucky.

He's also, to put it politely, golf obsessed. A team of doctors couldn't cure this boy of the malady. "Have clubs, will travel" ought to be his motto.

True to his nature, and like Pitino, Dees sponsors the Rick Dees Central Baptist Hospital Charity Golf Classic each year to benefit that center of healing.

Rick loves golf so much that he built a course on a slice of his central Kentucky paradise. That way after one of those particularly rough days that all golfers experience, he can talk to himself and curse the god of three putts in the privacy of his own ranch.

Being in a position at Caesars to help gamblers and celebrities in need of prime accommodations, I've met dozens of college and professional coaches from throughout the sports world in the off-season when they're most relaxed.

That's how I met Digger Phelps, the current TV basketball analyst who at that time was fresh from losing his coaching job at Notre Dame. Poor Digger couldn't win for losing in those days.

Digger met, wooed and won the hand of the daughter of the great composer Henry Mancini, while he was between jobs. Marrying into such a wealthy family certainly added to his self-esteem, and Digger took his bride shortly thereafter to Tokyo. The relationship became less than memorable after she ran off with a drummer in the band. That was the equivalent of a nuclear attack on Digger's already damaged ego. Apparently, he decided it was time for a life change, for he soon cleaned himself up and reinvented himself as a commentator, where his prejudices are never in question. He's unable to conceal his biases, and his likes and dislikes of his fellow coaches shine through.

Frankly, I prefer the real pros like my pals Al Michaels, Jim Nance, Billy Packer, and the Henny Youngman of the basketball world, my man Dick Vitale.

Al is a guy who loves to come to Vegas and is a historical customer of the Sands. He's an incredibly knowledgeable play-by-play guy and he knows his way around the green felt as well. I put Al and Jim Nance in the rare company of men the caliber of Vin Scully, one of my daddy's old associates, who thrive because they're so damn talented, know the game and so forth. But more than anything they have the sort of personality that engages the fan. They make friends with sports fans faster than you can say, "Do you believe in miracles?"

As a gambler, Al never plays beyond his means. Like that guy fans know from "Monday Night Football," he's never out of control. Sometimes he even brings his luck with him.

Jim Nance is definitely a Vegas guy. He's a guy that Vegas doesn't beat. His opinion is too strong. He is the only guy I know who predicted both of the last Super Bowls — prior to the start of the season.

Jim predicted Tampa Bay and Oakland in the Super Bowl, with Tampa Bay the winner. Talk about a long shot. I just hope he bet that future. He would have cleaned up.

As a broadcaster, Jim is like he just came out of the library. He is exactly what the earlier sportswriters were not. They were a slovenly bunch of guys who were frustrated, flunk-out editorial writers. Jim puts the story out, and he's an incredible reporter. And any guy who survived rooming with Freddie Couples has to possess something special. Anybody who comes across Jim and spends time with him is welded to him as a fan and friend. For my money, Jim can tell a story like nobody in the game today.

Let's switch ends of the country club for a minute from the links to the nets. I proudly take my share of the credit for helping to create the Caesars Palace Challenge Tennis match series that not only captured the attention of the nation and improved the image of the sport, but drew some of the world's biggest gamblers to Las Vegas in the 1970s at a time when the city was sorely in need of attractions.

Jimmy Connors, my old roommate from the Jockey Club days, emerged as an immediate star and we hired him at Caesars to help promote the enormously successful events.

Jimmy remains one of those amazing babe magnets I've always loved to travel with. I am not ashamed to say I have trolled in his wake. Just fishing in his vicinity paid off in keepers on many occasions.

Bobby Riggs is undoubtedly one of the greatest characters I've ever known. When I think of him, the words, "Get a net" come to mind. And I don't mean a tennis net.

Talk about a little crazy. "Never Bet Against This Man," *Sports Illustrated* enthused in a cover story about little Bobby. He was in his element with all that media attention, and he played it to the hilt. Riggs was something of an enigma who never stopped chattering. That nervous energy must have kept him going long after others his age had slowed down. Not to mention an ego. After being hit by the spotlight following his Battle of the Sexes match against Margaret Court, Bobby was asked by Mickey Rooney to play the lead role in his life story. They looked like brothers in those days. "I'll play it myself," he reportedly said.

Now that's cocky. But Bobby almost always backed his play.

He was a superior athlete in his day, but by Mother's Day 1973 people forgot that he'd won the Wimbledon singles, doubles and mixed doubles as well as the U.S. Open in one year. To most, he was a 55-year-old hustler who appeared to get great satisfaction from taunting feminists.

How crazy for the action was Bobby? After reaching the heights of the sport, he gave up tennis for golf because it was a better betting game. In his day he'd played against Titanic Thompson and had hustled everything from tennis and golf to ping-pong and gin rummy. To this day I'm surprised Caesars never hired him as an executive greeter.

"If I can't play for big money, I play for little money," Bobby once told Mike Wallace. "If I can't play for little money, I stay in bed that day."

Bobby was playing for small change on the seniors circuit when he came up with the idea to challenge the best woman player. Billy Jean King wasn't available to start, so he conned Margaret Court into a challenge match.

It was a spectacle covered by CBS Sports and every newspaper in America, and that was with the fact it was held on a court at

San Diego Estates. What if such matches, not merely the gimmicky "mixed singles" affairs, but real head-to-head challenges featuring the greatest players in the world, could be arranged in an infinitely more marketable place like Las Vegas?

18
Chapter

Casino Confidential

Chances are good you won't set foot in Las Vegas for more than a minute before seeing a big reason for its existence: the ubiquitous slot machine. McCarran International Airport, one of the busiest and best in the nation, has hundreds of slots purposely positioned to scratch the itch of those players who can't wait to go through baggage claim and catch a cab to their hotel. Who knows, maybe someday the cabs will have slots in the back seat. But until then, you'll have to make due with the fact that there are only about 250,000 slot machines to choose from in Southern Nevada casinos. That number does not include all the slots in convenience stores, bars, supermarkets and launderettes.

At times it must seem there's a slot for every man, woman and child who visits this amazing city, but the rules of engagement are clear: No one under 21 — not even pop star Britney Spears or NBA phenom LeBron James — is allowed to gamble or even linger in a gaming area. Exceptions were made back when I was a young pup in the business and dinosaurs walked the earth, but the rules are strictly enforced these days. In fact, not many years ago at Caesars Palace, a 19-year-old man relieved his father at the MegaBucks machine and hit a million-dollar jackpot, only to painfully discover later how costly a mistake he'd made. Casino surveillance cameras, and they are everywhere, had captured him feeding the progressive machine. (A progressive is a slot whose ultimate jackpots build based on the cumulative amount of dollars fed into them, and International Game Technology's MegaBucks machines are linked by the score to a common jackpot pool.) It was not a candidate for "America's Funniest Home Videos."

The jackpot was denied.

In fact, you'll occasionally hear of other cases in which jackpots are denied by the house for such rare occurrences as machine malfunctions. Even computerized slot, video poker and specialty machines go on the fritz once in a while. All I can tell you is, it isn't some corporate casino conspiracy to deprive you of your big score. Because the odds never change and the house — with exceptions we'll discuss — always has a distinct advantage, it's easy to get a little paranoid when a machine suddenly starts grinding you down or a dealer after a few hands starts draining your bankroll.

Knowledge is power, and in this chapter I'll impart a little of the knowledge and horse sense I've developed in three decades of watching fortunes rise and fall on the casino floor. If you're here to throw your money around and dream of wealth untold, or simply to enjoy the entertainment and dine in the gourmet restaurants, then you might not care to improve your odds at the blackjack table or steer clear of the exotic bets in the sports book. But if you want to get the most for your money in this town, you'll want to remember what the great gambler Gronvelt says in Mario Puzo's *Fools Die*: "You have to live going with the percentage. Otherwise, life is not worthwhile. Always remember that. Everything you do in life, use percentage as your god."

That may sound a little extreme, but even if you don't embrace that motto, never forget that the house has done just that. Its actions on the casino floor are ruled by percentage. Over the course of time, chance or luck have very little to do with it.

After more than thirty years in the business, I've come to believe the gambling gene is as much a part of our human nature as breathing. It manifests itself in many ways, but it finds expression in the casino. My man Mario Puzo was right on when he once observed, "Gambling is a primitive religious instinct, peculiar to our species, that has existed since the beginning of recorded history in every society, from the most primitive to the most complex."

And the games aren't fixed. No matter what you've heard from your Uncle Louie back home, the games are so straight that chances are good one owner would surely rat out another owner if it was ever discovered that his games were crooked. It would be ruinous for the town's reputation as a place where a gambler can rely on square dice and unmarked cards.

Besides, it's the rules of the games that make them so strong. Math wasn't my best subject in school, but even I can figure the house percentage. I'll do the counting for you.

🐎

Take blackjack, for example. The house advantage is 5.5 percent if you know next to nothing about the game. But if you apply a few basics, that disadvantage diminishes to about 2 percent. From there, those fluent in the game's basic strategy can whittle the house edge to 0.8 percent. That's the importance of learning the rules.

Then there's the little wheel, roulette. With its spinning wheel, jingling ball the size of a pea and multicolored chips marking the bets of various players, it's a beautiful game and a veritable parade of activity for gamblers. It is not, however, much of a value. There is no roulette system that diminishes the house advantage. There are some big winners, and many big losers, on the game, but there's no reliable strategy that enables players to slice the odds in their favor. It's the game in which one strategy (based on something other than math) was to double a bet following a loss. It's sometimes called the Martingale Strategy, but the Lollipop Express is more like it. Around the casino, when a player says he's going to "double up to catch up," dealers must be sure not to break into smiles, for on the wheel the 5.26 percent house advantage doesn't change no matter how many times you play. Over the course of time, however, the casino's win from the customer is closer to 30 percent. And don't forget: The longer you play, the closer the house gets to keeping all the money.

🐎

To the uninitiated, the crap table is as confusing as the cockpit of a 767. It might be the most intimidating game in the casino next to getting up the courage to ask one of the showgirls to dinner. In reality, it's a simple game to play — as long as you steer clear of the number bets and the big 6 and big 8. As a rule of thumb, the numbers bets are for suckers and carry inferior odds, but betting on the Pass or Don't Pass lines, and approaching a table in a casino that offers players advantage odds (some clubs advertise "5 times odds" and above) you can reduce your disadvantage to 0.6 percent. That's not bad.

If you want to look like a seasoned pro at a craps table, approach it and place a wager on the Pass Line. If the shooter rolls a 7 or 11, you win. If he rolls a 2,3, or 12, you lose.

But what about the rest of the numbers?

Glad you asked.

If the shooter rolls a 4,5,6,8,9, or 10, he establishes what is known as his point.

If he rolls his point again, you win. If he rolls a 7, you lose. (The process is just the opposite if you play the Don't Pass Line. The odds, of course, remain the same.)

The craps layout is riddled with a lot of confusing proposition bets, but here's one of the best parts about the game: You shouldn't be playing those anyway. They're for the lollipop league with the house edge floating anywhere from 9.9 percent to 17 percent.

Once the shooter's point is established, back up your Pass Line bet with the available table odds. And don't forget to smile and say things like "Dice be nice" and "Baby needs a new pair of shoes."

Where do all the dice come from? Mostly, from the Paul-Son Dice Company of Las Vegas, the world's largest manufacturer of cubes and cards. Paul-Son estimates it produces more than one million pairs of dice each month to what even the toughest pit boss would admit is exacting specifications: 0.0002 of an inch — pretty close to a perfect square — to assure that one side doesn't come up more often than another.

While we're on the subject of what's square and legal, here's a bit of advice that might save you a little embarrassment. If you play craps for a while, you might notice that on occasion the dealer will change out the dice. Don't start shouting about the fix being in. It's standard operating procedure and perfectly legal. They can even switch the dice in the middle of a hand. Although luck merchants might think this is done to ruin the good fortune of a shooter, it's more often done to keep the dice brand new and to protect the game from anyone who might be contemplating switching legitimate cubes for the counterfeit kind.

Stories emanating from the craps tables are legion in Las Vegas. Tales of shooters holding the dice for up to two hours are not uncommon — although the average time is closer to two minutes. The Desert Inn once had a pair of dice on display that had made twenty-eight passes at the table, but the reason they were behind glass was because such a streak is extremely rare. Stories of long streaks have come from other casinos as well, but for some reason they seem to end after the twenty-eighth pass.

If you find yourself on a streak, respect the fact that such rolls don't come around often. Don Knepp tells of the time a shooter made twenty-eight straight passes at the table, but extracted only $750 from it.

"Little did he realize that such an occurrence was a million to one happening," Knepp wrote in *Las Vegas, the Entertainment Capital*. Had he rolled over every bet, the math would have been staggering. He would have won tens of millions of dollars.

Poker rooms are less pervasive in Las Vegas than they once were, but the city remains the ultimate Big Leagues for card players from around the world. The games themselves are varied, and I need not explain them in detail, for players already know and the rankest amateurs have no business taking a chair in the games.

Poker is not just a game. It's a subculture with a pantheon of legends and endless tales of high-stakes win and bad beat losses. Although today's poker circuit is riddled with high-dollar tournaments and heavy competition, its mecca remains Binion's Horseshoe Club downtown. Starting with patriarch Benny Binion, the family has taken great pride in holding the biggest games featuring the best players for the past half century. Today, the only competition for the Horseshoe Club's crown appears to be the Louisiana tournament conducted by my man Jack Binion.

Exposure on ESPN and a few feature films have created a resurgence of the sport among college kids and Friday night neighborhood players. And in their hearts every last one of them wants to come to Las Vegas to try their luck against the sharks and sharpies who circle those waters nightly.

To them I say good luck and don't forget to save enough cash for that long bus ride back to Boise.

There are some odd, interesting variations on traditional poker games that you'll no doubt notice on your way through the casino.

One is called Caribbean Stud, and it will remind you a little of the kind of cards sometimes played at the kitchen table back on the homestead.

After anteing up, you're dealt five cards. You're first decision is simple. If you think you can beat the dealer, you double the bet. If not, you fold and lose the initial bet.

If you decide to play the hand, the dealer turns over his cards. If he lacks at least a king and ace, his hand folds and you get you first bet back. If he has a suitable hand, then the best hand wins.

There's also a progressive element to the game that can be made with a side bet. It's not a great gamble, but it can be fun watching it build into a real pot.

🐎

Pai gao poker is played with a joker in the deck, so that might tell you what you need to know. The joker is wild, and so is the game.

The player receives seven cards, which are divided into a five-card hand and a two-card hand. Both hands are played against the dealer's hand. Win one hand, and it's a push. Your money is returned. Win both hands and you win your bet.

Sounds fair, doesn't it?

It is. Once you're familiar with the rules, the odds of you winning are identical to the dealer's. Does that sound like the house forgot something?

It didn't. If you win, you're charged a 5 percent commission.

Hey, nobody said life was fair.

🐎

Let It Ride is another version of poker adapted to the "21" table concept. It looks a little like five-card stud. Each player receives three cards. The dealer places two cards face down in front of himself.

In all, three equal bets are made, and players can retrieve two of the three bets. The third one always stays on the table. Players win with tens or better.

Like Caribbean Stud, Let It Ride also offers a progressive-style bonus payout as a side wager.

🐎

Then there's the casino game called War. It's based on the high-card-wins game kids are fascinated by when they're four years old, but lose interest in once they learn to read the sports page. It's a the fun of Las Vegas by taking in a tournament. The biggest of the bunch these days is the Las Vegas Invitational Invensys Classic at the Tournament Players Club at Summerlin. It's known for its big names, blistering low scores, and staggering prize money. In 2002, the winner, little-known Phil Tataurangi, was a first-time winner after shooting a 62 in the final round to take home a check for $900,000.

The PGA Champions Tour, formerly known as the Senior Tour, also makes a stop in Las Vegas, as does the LPGA. The tournaments change names and dates, but the golf is excellent.

There are few certainties in life, but here is one: In Las Vegas, despite its dramatic water shortage, there will always be enough water to keep the fountains flowing and the golf courses green. Golf is almost as much a part of the Vegas experience as gambling. And Benny Siegel himself knew that even the most devoted gamblers couldn't throw the dice without an occasional break. Gamblers seem to like golf, and the boys have always tried to be accommodating to their guests with fat wallets.

Resorts know golf is such an important component that they reserve hundreds of rounds at the valley's nearly four dozen courses, at times locking out locals but securing tee times for favored players.

With so many golf courses, so many gamblers and an unlimited flow of money, Las Vegas is a hustler's paradise. PGA veteran Dave Marr might have been thinking of Las Vegas when he warned about taking care not to fall prey to the sharks of the fairway.

"Never bet with anyone you meet on the first tee who has a deep suntan, a 1-iron in his bag, and squinty eyes."

That describes a fair number of Vegas golfers I've shot a round with. In Las Vegas, two ways to guarantee you won't get a straight answer is to ask a dancer if her tits are genuine and a country club golfer if that 20 handicap is accurate.

mediocre bet and seems sort of silly in a modern casino, but it's there for a couple of reasons.

It's easy to lose your sense of perspective in a gambling hall, but the truth is many visitors to Las Vegas are a bit awed and intimidated by the thought of approaching a blackjack table and placing a bet for fear of making fools of themselves. Forget that it's an unwarranted phobia, and that there isn't a person who's ever visited the city who hasn't experienced the same feeling. Fact is, some folks want to play, but aren't comfortable with "21" and would never dream of standing at the rail of a craps table shouting instructions to the dice.

For them, a game like War is perfect because it's simple and there's no book of instructions that goes with it. It's also not considered much of a bet, but that's true of a good many of the games in any gambling hall.

Baccarat and its diminutive cousin mini-baccarat are reasonable facsimiles of the French game "chemin de fer." In America it has been called "shimmy" and is sometimes called "the game of 9s" because the object is to draw cards adding to that number. On the Strip, it's considered a game for high rollers and is often played in exclusive-looking pit areas set off to the side of the main casino. But the truth is, it's one of the easiest games to play in the house.

There are only two combatants in baccarat: the player and the bank. Gamblers wager on the player's hand, the bank's hand, or on the possibility of a tie.

In baccarat, face cards are valued at zero and an ace counts as 1. The game is dealt with an eight-deck shoe, and hands adding to more than 10 are reduced to the remaining single digit. (For instance, if a 17 is drawn, the player's number is 7.)

Bet on the player, and you'll win even money. Bet on the bank, and you'll win even money minus a 5 percent commission.

From there, the game has very few rules: If his two-card total is from 0 to 5, the player draws a card. If the draw adds up to 6, 7, 8 or 9 (known as a "natural"), the player stands.

The bank draws if its two-card total is 0 to 2. The bank also draws if its two-card total adds up to 3 and the player's third card is not an 8. The bank also draws if its two-card total is 4 and the player's third card ranges from a deuce to a 7. The bank also must draw if its two-card total is 5 and the player's third card is a 4 through 7. The bank must draw again if its two cards add up to 6 and the player's third card is either a 6 or 7. The bank must stand if its draw is an 8 or a natural.

In baccarat, there's no real strategy. It's a matter of picking the side you think will win and betting on it. That's why the game is so attractive to high rollers: The house edge is almost flat, just 1.36 percent on a player's bet and 1.17 percent on a bank's bet.

My man Lyle Stuart is a veteran high roller who earned his millionaire status as a firebrand book publisher. He's authored several best sellers, one of them called *Lyle Stuart on Baccarat*. It's one of the most fun reads about the game and the international subculture that surrounds it. To hear Lyle tell it, you won't find a more interesting brand of character in the casino than the high rollers and hard-livers who frequent the baccarat tables.

"Baccarat is becoming more popular every day," Lyle writes. "In the 1960s when there were only a few tables in all of Las Vegas, I used to watch the Dostoevski-like shills who sat for hours turning over cards and waiting for the first 'real' player to take a seat.

"Two decades later I watched five tables working simultaneously in Caesars Palace — and half a dozen customers queued up, waiting for empty seats so they could play.

"There is more drama at a baccarat table than almost any other place you can name. I used to watch an Oriental whom the dealers called 'Mr.T.' I found him at the tables on at least one out of every two visits I made to Las Vegas.

"He dropped *millions* of dollars. Literally.

"I recall the time a couple years ago when the purple chips ($5,000) flowed through his hands like mineral oil.

"'That makes a million, Mr. T,' the dealer said one evening.

"The next morning I happened to be at the table struggling to recover my four- or five-thousand-dollar loss, when he sat down again.

"'Give me two hundred,' he said.

"'Did he win his million back?' I surreptitiously inquired of the dealer who sat at my right.

"No,' he said, shaking his head. 'This is the start of *another* million!'

"He lost the second one before I left the table."

Long years at the tables have tempered Lyle's philosophy about the game. He offers no foolproof secrets, just a reality check for players.

"The fact that you're holding the shoe doesn't change the face of a single card in it," he says. "(God has not taken time out from counting the proceeds in that Big Collection Plate in the Sky to look down and turn that queen of spades into a nine of clubs just because you once won Brownie points as a Boy Scout. Don't believe in 'the power of prayer.' Even if every human on Earth got down on his or her knees and prayed for a nine of clubs as the next card, the queen of spades would still come up the queen of spades.)

"Greed can be your undoing. It has often been mine. When you're ahead, take your winnings and run. Don't try to win the whole casino in one sitting. (You wouldn't know what to do with it anyway.)

"Always remember that baccarat is a 'heads or tails' game. Don't lose your head. Else you'll have a tale that shouldn't be told!"

Obviously, baccarat is a game that ignites real passion in its practitioners.

Those itching to try baccarat should probably weigh in on the mini-baccarat table, which allows small wagers and allows gamblers to touch the cards in blackjack style.

Chapter 19

The Sporting Crowd

Cards are grand, dice are dandy, but my heart belongs to the sports book. Some of my best friends are sports bettors, especially those who let me borrow money.

Seriously, though, I love to bet on sporting events, thoroughbred derbies, and political races, and have done so since childhood. And I'm not alone. Nationally, the experts in such matters believe up to $80 billion is bet on sports illegally each year. In Nevada, the sports books are legal, regulated, and often the center of a beehive of activity and a whole lot of fun. (Although, you can't bet legally on the governor's or president's race at a local sports book, and the lines the books put up on the Academy Awards are strictly for public relations purposes.) If you can't get to the ballpark, boxing arena or racetrack, they're the next best thing and are preferred by legions of fans who like their sports action nonstop.

Sports books make their money several ways. They offer point spreads and money line wagers on ballgames, boxing events, horse and dog races, and even NASCAR spectacles.

When I came to Las Vegas, sports books weren't legal inside the casino. They stood on the Strip and downtown in separate buildings with names like the Churchill Downs, Rose Bowl, and the Derby.

They were outgrowths of the old Syndicate racing wire services that used to provide thoroughbred information to the West Coast just after World War II and were operated by guys with colorful nicknames and even more colorful pasts.

Today, they're high-tech affairs that bear a closer resemblance to one of those video superstores than the cigar smoke-fogged sports parlors of old. Although they take up plenty of square footage and aren't as profitable as an endless bank of slot machines, they provide big-time customer service and in most resorts are respected components of the casino that generate more than $1 billion in play annually statewide.

Although the rules continue to be tightened by the Gaming Control Board, and the threat of outlawing college sports betting is an annual spectacle in Congress, the sports book continues to thrive. Some even offer phone accounts for in-state players with a minimum bet of $50 and a few hundred on deposit at the casino. There's no credit granted in Las Vegas sports books.

They're also some of the friendliest places in the casino. After all, most folks who wouldn't dream of approaching a craps table and don't know "chemin de fer" from Sonny and Cher have a favorite ball team.

The house takes its percentage by extracting a vigorish, or "vig" for short, for handling the bet. It's usually $1 for every $10 wagered. (If you win, you get your vig back, by the way.)

At some casinos, sports books have become as convenient as your neighborhood McDonald's with reserved parking lots for regular customers and even drive-through windows. That shouldn't be too surprising, given the fact that there's even a drive-through wedding chapel in Las Vegas.

One of the most popular ways to bet is with the parlay card. It enables the player to mark combinations of teams at increased odds. They're some of the most fun, but undoubtedly the worst bets in the sports book. The house edge on parlay cards is about 25 percent.

But that's still better than taking a shot in the dark on some of those Internet sports betting websites. I think there's a big future for gambling on the Internet, but at present the activity is too controversial to be relied on by players. First, the activity is illegal. Second, the credibility of many of the websites is highly suspect.

For my money, the Las Vegas sports books are the only sure bet for a sports bettor.

⋙

It should be remembered that most people who play aren't necessarily looking for the best statistical gamble. Gambling is about risk taking, and one man's sucker bet is often another man's big play of the day. Given that reality, the craps table retains 20 percent on average — and every last dime if you play long enough.

Then there are the games for those folks who could care less about the odds, but just want to have some fun. The Big Wheel, also called the Wheel of Fortune (Wheel of Misfortune is more like it), is one of those holdovers from gambling's carnival era that's fun to watch but wicked to bet on. It's a great game if you're tired of sitting and want to stand for a few minutes. Beyond improving your circulation, it's not much of a bet. Play a buck and see for yourself.

Keno is just the opposite. It's the game you play if you're tired of standing and want to rest. At many casinos, you'll find keno boards blinking from the walls of the coffee shop and a small area that resembles a cross between a courtroom and a classroom called a keno lounge set off on the edge of the table game area.

Keno is like bingo for loners, but for many people it's a fun gambling diversion with a history that's been traced to ancient Chinese empires.

The house edge in keno is 30 percent on an average, eight-spot ticket. Compare that with blackjack, and you'll see why even the most sophisticated casinos still keep the keno boards lighted.

There's very little positive that can be said about keno. I'm not the superstitious type, but some would say even when you win it brings you bad luck.

There was a player who hit an eight-spot ticket — as rare a feat for the average guy as finding a white rhino in your driveway — for $12,000. Instead of quitting and immediately taking his luck to Wall Street, where the real gamblers are, he sat and played and hit another eight-spot ticket for $12,000 using the same numbers. This is not only exceedingly rare, but it's guaranteed to generate an investigation by the keno manager, casino manager, hotel security, Gaming Control Board and IRS. Nobody, flat nobody, wins back-to-back eight-spots using the same numbers.

But the player had done just that. And it appeared he had done it legitimately.

He didn't have much time to celebrate his big victory over the long odds, though. Perhaps it was the shock of winning anything of value in the keno lounge, but the man suffered a massive heart attack and fell over stiff.

Sports radio talk show host Lee Pete has said of the game, "In case of an earthquake, go to a keno lounge. To my knowledge, nothing has ever been hit in one."

Back when I started, slot machines were genuine one-armed bandits with three reels and limited jackpots. Players put nickels, quarters and even silver dollars in the machines — the now-deceased Little Caesar's Casino was known for its penny slots — and pulled the handle. Play was only slightly improved by a button that enabled them to spin the wheels more frequently.

The microchip caused a revolution in America and had no less than that effect on the casino racket. Once slots were computerized, they grew slicker along with the technology. What was once an activity worthy of Pavlov's dog began to melt into the realm of the video game. Screens got bigger and sharper, and the computer enabled the manufacturer to use his imagination. And believe me, slot machine manufacturers have unlimited creativity when it comes to ways of extracting the coin of the realm from the pockets of the people.

Somewhere along the way, slots stopped being the exclusive purview of the wives and girlfriends of card and dice players. In Benny Siegel's day, I'm told, a self-respecting Joe wouldn't have been caught dead waltzing one of the one-armed bandits. They were for Josephines only.

Now the rules have changed.

The rules, however, still heavily favor the house.

If you're going to play slots, there's a smart way and a simple way. The smart way is, go directly to the slot cage and ask the attendant for an application to sign up for the resort's slot club. Fill out the form and ask if the entry means you'll get immediate discounts on "RFB," which stands for Room, Food, and Beverage." By using the initials, you'll be telling the jaded casino worker that you didn't just fall off the turnip truck, that you're a real player and a customer worthy of the available perquisites. Once you sign up, you'll receive a plastic slot club card, which resembles a credit card.

Corporate casinos today are wrenched down tighter than a drum when it comes to passing out comps. What I gave away in a day to marginal customers at Caesars twenty-five years ago would probably get me fired immediately in one of today's Gaming Inc. megaresorts. I'm not talking about complimentary privileges ("comps" is the accepted term) for high rollers; they've always received whatever their hearts desire. For our purposes in this chapter, I'm talking about average players with bankrolls of a couple hundred bucks over a long weekend. Although they rarely know it, their legions make up the heart and soul of the casino machine. It's time the low-rollers got a little r-e-s-p-e-c-t, and if you play slots, the only way you'll get the Aretha Franklin treatment is by joining a slot club and learning its rules. They're not all created equal, but the best way to cut through the fine print is to ask for examples of how much play it will take before you receive the goodies, which usually range from souvenirs to meals in the coffee shop, but can turn into showroom tickets, room upgrades and a whole lot more.

Want the painful truth?

For all but a few math brains who swear they can make money playing them, slots and video poker machines are simply forms of entertainment, ways of passing the time. If you enjoy playing them, and Lord knows there's an unlimited variety of machines these days, you need to remember that they're not built with the odds in your favor. They might appear to "get hot," but in reality they are controlled by computer functions that generate random numbers. The odds are against you, and chances are good that eventually your bucket of quarters will disappear, but damned it if isn't exciting when you win a little.

If you're going to get serious about slot play, you'll probably want to try some of the locals casinos and neighborhood bars, which generally offer superior pay schedules and are much freer with the whiskey and chicken wings. (The "pay schedule," by the way, is the chart usually located near the top of the machine that indicates the percentages it will pay for various jackpots. If you want to learn more about this, check out any book by Bob Dancer.)

By now, you're a card-carrying slot club member with full privileges. Just remember: Not all machines are created equally and don't forget to tip the cocktail waitress after she delivers that free drink.

Here's a tip that will save you that dollar and then some: When it comes to playing the video poker slots, always read the labels. On the glass there will be a payout chart that will tell you what you'll win depending on the hand you draw. Make sure you're getting the best value by checking to see the high-end payouts. Read a few machines and do a little simple math, and you'll find that some machines pay up to 10 percent more than others for the same hand drawn and number of coins bet.

One of the biggest developments in the evolution of the slot machine has been the growth of high-end play. I know that sounds strange, given the lowly slot's history as a nickel-eater, but it's true. For those players with a little more jingle in their jeans, there are machines that accept coins and tokens ranging up to $500. Their pay schedules are nothing special, nor is their technology. They're just bigger toys for bigger boys.

Unlike their diminutive cousins, big slot players receive royal treatment. In fact, some of the biggest gamblers in America today are the folks at the high-roller slots. They receive access to private jets and stay in the best suites in the house. They get a lot more than respect.

On the other end of the scale, nickel slot players are the Rodney Dangerfield of gamblers — but not for the reason you might imagine. You might think it's because they play nickels. It's not the nickel, it's the machine. Dollar in and dollar out, those machines are some of the most lucrative percentage earners in the casino. While a quarter machine might grab a few cents of every slot dollar processed, the nickel machines' average take is 15 percent. That's one of the highest percentages in the house.

Of course, there's no measuring the amount of fun all those nickel slot players have as they run those countless coins through the machines. In fact, I'll wager the nickel slot area has more satisfied customers than most in the house for that very reason: it's fun and only five cents.

Now, a few words about tipping. The Las Vegas casino industry is built on thousands of service worker jobs that range from maids and porters to waiters and dealers. Most rely in part on tips to help pay the rent, and traditionally the "tokes," as they are called by locals, have been more than good at the best clubs in town.

But gone are the days when dealers pocketed their tip money without the obligation of paying Uncle Sam. Tip income is heavily regulated today, and increasingly casinos cut checks to dealers after the pool of tokes has been equally divided among the folks working the floor. In other words, the world of Vegas tipping has gone mainstream.

Although there are plenty of thumbnail tipping guides, I've always told my customers to give whatever makes them feel good. There's nothing worse than having a dealer chip hustle a player or make him feel guilty for not coughing up a little cash. With that said, it's customary to tip a dealer who is especially cordial or who is present at the scene of a winning streak.

When it comes to tippers, my man Kerry Packer is the Michael Jordan of the activity. He's been known to tip millions on trips to Las Vegas.

In the restaurants, the standard tipping customs apply: 15-17 percent for acceptable service, more if the waiter is especially professional. I always like to make sure the bus help gets a little something extra for keeping the coffee cup filled.

By local custom, bellhops receive a buck or more per bag. A maid at an average joint gets a buck a day, sometimes more, for keeping your room spotless. Cocktail waitresses are zooked (another word for tip used by casino folks) at least a buck or two for delivering a drink to the table, and the valet parking attendants are getting two bucks and more these days for delivering your ride free of dents with your seat in its proper position and your favorite radio station unmolested.

Time was, a key job in a Las Vegas showroom was one of the most lucrative positions in town. I'd swear the captains and maitre d's made more money than some plastic surgeons. The custom of tipping $10, $20 or more to a maitre d' to ensure improved seating in the showroom has largely been phased out in the corporate era. Some of it still exists, and if you're dissatisfied with your seating, you can always ask straight up whether you can improve your position or whether the room is sold out. Don't be shy. Having a good time is the whole exercise of Las Vegas.

Now on to the tables.

For those not raised around cards, the casino floor can be as intimidating as ordering in a French restaurant. The terms and conditions of play are a foreign language to the uninitiated. Just remember: 36 million people each year come to Las Vegas and most of them gamble in one form or another. If it took the Mensa set to play the games, there'd be no need for all those fancy fountains.

The most common card game on the casino floor is "21," or blackjack. It's a simple game, but if you learn to play it applying the Basic Strategy, you'll shrink the house odds from 5 percent down to 0.3 percent. That's almost a level playing field, and believe me, in the casino, a level playing field is hard to find. Scores of books have been written on blackjack and Basic Strategy, but I'll give you the Cliff's Notes version by saying that your object is to beat the dealer's hand without going above 21. The dealer, by the way, always shows you his first card, usually referred to as his "up" card. If the dealer draws 16 or less, he must take a card. You, on the other hand, don't have to do anything but sit there. If the dealer reaches 17, he must stand. (Actually, he's always standing. What "stand" means is to stop drawing more cards.)

Unless you have a head for counting cards, in which case this section is not for you anyway, always assume the dealer's hidden card is a 10. If his up card is a 6 or less, stand with the cards you're dealt unless there's no way drawing another will bust you. If his up card is a 7 or higher, hit until you match the assumed 17 or above. It won't always work, of course, but your odds are better if you do.

You can double down in blackjack, which means doubling your bet. But remember, after doubling the bet you may receive only one more card. Here's a hint: Always double down if you're dealt two 10s and the dealer's up card is a 9. Beyond that, leave the doubling down to the players who carry an abundance of lucky rabbits' feet.

You're also allowed to split pairs in blackjack. If you draw a pair of 4s, 5s or 10s, don't worry about it. But if you draw a brace of aces or 8s, tell the dealer you'd like to split them. You'll then be playing two hands (and betting twice as much) at a mathematical edge.

The rules of blackjack, like the rules of war, include a provision for giving up called "surrender." Surrender is simple, really. If the dealer has an ace showing and you sense he's drawn a blackjack, you request surrender and forfeit half your bet.

You can also buy insurance, which enables you to keep half your bet if you're beaten by the dealer at the end of the hand. It's a good idea to request insurance if you've been dealt a blackjack and the dealer's up card is an ace. That way, you'll be paid even if the end result is a push (that's casino for a tie.)

As for the gimmick rules that some casinos offer, try them at your own risk. Most favor the house, and some tilt the true odds dramatically in the dealer's favor.

What about learning to count cards? I get asked this one on a regular basis by folks who obviously don't know your humble servant. Why, I can barely count to 52, much less remember the cards that have come and gone in a game that can include as many as six decks shuffled up and dealt out of a shoe (that's casino for the box those cards are held in). Card counting is not illegal, but it is frowned upon by the casino if the player happens to be very good at it. It's legal for the casino to ask that player to leave the premises, and I've never seen one win an appeal on the grounds of mistaken identity.

Card counting is featured in half the gambling movies ever made. Truth is, there are groups of players who have such a keen understanding of the game that they earn substantial livings playing it. But it's also true that many of those same players go broke during a hard-luck streak. It's the nature of the ebb and flow of the game. The odds are consistent, but those cards do the damndest things.

Bottom line? Unless you're possessed of a gifted mind and superior memory, don't sweat the aces. Just minimize your mistakes, split those aces, and have a good time.

That's the point of coming to Las Vegas, isn't it?

🐎

Now, a few words about getting yours in Las Vegas.

By all means do!

In Las Vegas, it's all about the green. Those who have it are smarter, more handsome, and wittier conversationalists than the cast of "Friends." And friends are never in short supply for the fat of wallet.

That's true in most places, I suppose, but nowhere is it more applicable than Las Vegas. I'll say this for the town: At least we're honest about our intentions.

Anywhere else in the world you must determine for yourself how much your money is really worth in a society. How much it will buy. How much influence you have. How impressed the local coterie will be by your bank account.

In Las Vegas, there's little mystery. If you've got the green, good things come your way. I'll see to it personally.

Those good things are most often referred to as "comps," which is short for complimentaries. Comps range from a free drink and a pack of cigarettes to the best suite in the house, free airfare on the company jet, and tickets to the Kentucky Derby secured by your humble servant from the Bluegrass State.

But only if you rate. Never forget, the casino is business disguised as pleasure.

Traditionally, there are two basic ways to rate a player. That assumes that the player isn't tight with management, in which case the rules might be made to bend like one of the contortionists in *Mystere*. But for the most part, there are a couple of basic ways to determine a player's depth at the tables.

The first method is to apply the theoretical time played, the amount of money played, and how much, given the house advantage, the casino should earn. The theoretical is popular with corporations because it applies math and accounting in an attempt to take the risk out of the equation.

It's also a way for the accountants to calculate how much in comps a player deserves. Guys like me have sometimes been known to give a merely good player the high-roller treatment, and some of the wonks in management can't stand that. How dare I hand out an extra lobster tail or filet mignon or front-row seat to a concert to an only "pretty good" customer. Forget the fact that I might just be watering the crops to get them to grow, that I might be making a friend who will come back in six months and drop a bundle at our house instead of the shop down the street.

I have always believed in the long-term strength of the hands-on method. Not the theoretical win or loss, but the actual play of the gambler. How much did he win or lose? How deep are his pockets? How far is he capable of going? Is he here with one-time money, or is there a wellspring of disposable income?

All these questions, in my estimation, need to be answered before the casino starts pulling out the calculators and charging a player for a bottle of beer. Nowadays, the computer boys are more concerned with the theoretical than the actual, but if a guy actually loses money, that's what's most impressive to me and the older hands.

If there's one thing experience in the casino business teaches you, it's to hang on to those people who are good judges of character and possess accurate opinions when it comes to judging players. Benny Binion was perhaps the best of the first-generation Las Vegas operators in this regard. He was known as a generous guy who was quick with the comps, but he was a far better judge of character than people might give him credit for.

And he wasn't afraid to share information. He knew that eventually the money would come his way. Unfortunately, the corporate structure doesn't allow for much camaraderie. It's a shame and it's changed the character of the business for worse, I believe.

The problem is, the accountants rule the roost. There's so little freedom to make an individual call on the character of a player that it's taken a lot of the fun out of the game. And, eventually, the players feel that chill.

The accountants want to know a theoretical number, and that number determines how much I am allowed to issue in comps. As a rule of thumb, casinos are willing to return at least 25 percent to the player in the form of room, food, and beverage or other perquisites. That number rises to 40 percent in some clubs and does not include the occasional discounts for high rollers who gamble millions but sometimes will get 10 percent to 20 percent shaved off their losses.

But take a moment to think about it: If the casino is willing to return to customers about 33 percent of their expected loss in the form of comps and casino services, why in the world would you be shy about asking for your fair share?

The simple answer is: You shouldn't.

So if you plan to gamble in one place, immediately ask someone at floorperson level or above what it will take to become rated as a player. More simply stated: How much and for how long do I have to gamble to be comped?

Finally, here's my shorthand version of getting your best gambling value in Las Vegas.

First, use those casino coupons available in many of the clubs. If you're going to gamble, it only makes good horse sense to place that 2-for-1 coupon on the line with your own hard-earned cash. Second, find a single-deck blackjack game and pick up a book on Basic Strategy play. At the very least, memorize those few rules I gave you earlier in this chapter. Make a line bet using the full odds the house allows. Bet a little baccarat and enjoy those nearly flat odds.

Don't be shy about joining a slot club even if you're only going to play for a weekend. You'll not only build points, but you'll wind up on a mailing list and will probably receive periodical discounts on rooms and entertainment. If you play more than a few bucks, ask your dealer about getting rated. A couple of well-placed comps can really smooth out the aches of a bad beat at the tables, and in today's corporate game if you don't ask, chances are good you won't get.

And while my bosses will hate me telling you this, for heaven's sake steer clear of the keno lounge. While you're at it, skip the Big Wheel. Pass on those twelve-team parlay cards unless you're in it for a lark. Don't bet the tie in baccarat. And never take insurance in blackjack.

That one paragraph ought to save you a day's pay. Use it to make a few smart wagers, and you'll make the most of your vacation in my favorite city.

Epilogue

Lord, Give Me One More Derby

Sometimes late at night, after the last of the visitors has left the cabin in Versailles, I sit back with a little Johnnie Walker Red and a good cigar and think about how my life might have turned out if things had gone just a little differently way back when. But then I sip a little, smoke a little, and laugh to myself. Oh, what an incredible ride it's been.

I have loved a good woman. I have known the joy of children, and the sorrow of losing my boy Chan far too soon.

I have gone from the governor's mansion to the penthouse of the greatest casinos the world has ever known. Along the way I've made my share of friends and acquaintances from all walks of life. I have enjoyed their company, the good times, and the laughter. I have made a little money, lost a little more, but have come to the conclusion that money is nothing without friends and family.

Having the love of my daughter, Erin, is everything to me. And although I don't always show it, I love her and am proud of her. Knowing that Happy Cornell and her mama Dolores think of me and smile makes my heart glad.

Somewhere along the way, my life changed. I think it has something to do with the nature of the casino marketing business that a man one day wakes up and finds himself playing the facilitator. By its nature the job can play tricks on your definition of friendship. Experience has taught me that I have a lot more friends when I have the power of the pen at a major casino, where on my word I can arrange for everything from a penthouse suite and gourmet meal to a first-class trip to the Super Bowl or World Series. Not only that, but I can open the door to millions of dollars in customer credit.

But it's when I've been between jobs that I've discovered who my real friends are. Dick Crane is incomparable. Through thick and thicker, he never left my side. To have one such friend in a lifetime is more than a man can ask for.

I have been fortunate when it comes to allies. Bill Wortman has been one of the great ones. Dan Ayala, Bob Baffert, Dave Hanlon, Tom Wiesner, Voss Boreta, Duke Davis, Mike Pegram, Bill Walters, and Brian Greenspun are a few I call friend. I'm thankful that Dan Gilboy takes such good care of our Erin.

If I had a prayer, it would be "Lord, give me one more Derby, one more chance to hear 'My Old Kentucky Home,' to watch them Run for the Roses, to go to the window with a winner, and to hear the voices of friends as we cheer each other's victories and laugh off the also-rans."

I'd like to be able to tell you that I was like Sinatra when it came to having only a few regrets in life, and those too few to mention. But my greatest heartache occurred May 20, 1993, when my wonderful son, Chan, accidentally shot himself. He was just thirty years old.

He'd been drinking and partying and had had an argument with his girlfriend, but what happened was a mistake, an accident. We all make them, and to my unrelenting regret his mistake cost him his life.

There are so many things I should have done, but there is nothing I can do to change the past. I'd trade everything for an opportunity to set it right with my boy. I only hope all will be well when we meet again.

When my race is run, whether I find the winner's circle or finish out of the money, more than anything I want us Chandlers to be a team again, the way things should have been before I took that road west and found the limitless neon of Las Vegas.

So, Lord, give me one more Derby, one more chance to watch them run, then I'll gladly return forever to my old Kentucky home.

Afterword

In Praise of Dan the Bluegrass Man

By John L. Smith and friends

Dan Chandler died of a heart attack on April 27, 2004, at his cabin in Versailles, just four days before the 130th running of the Kentucky Derby.

Mourners jammed his funeral service to capacity. Men wept openly. Louisville basketball coach Rick Pitino, attorney Dick Crane, and Dan's nephew, Congressman Ben Chandler, delivered eulogies as varied in tone and tenor as the man whose wild, colorful life they attempted to describe. The funeral procession for Happy Chandler's wayward son stretched for several blocks.

Although his friends and family knew of his ailing health, weight problems and hard living, they were still shocked to hear of Dan's death. To a person they had difficulty imagining how a man with Dan's unrelenting zest for life could be gone so suddenly from their midst.

Dan's death came at a time that the manuscript for this book was in the editing process. I was immediately reminded of the moment I decided to write a book based on our conversations.

We'd just arrived at Churchill Downs for the 2002 Run for the Roses, and as usual Dan had secured the best seats in the house. He ambled into the celebrity-scented air of the fourth floor in a canary-yellow sport coat big enough for his bear-sized frame, the smoke of a Cuban cigar following him like a vapor trail.

He was a one-man movable feast, Dan was, and the Kentucky Derby was his Paris in the bluegrass.

"My man," he boomed in that unmistakable Kentucky drawl as politicians, TV personalities, former beauty queens, and a contingent of retired National Football League stars rose to greet him. From Paul Hornung to Phyllis George, everyone knew Dan. He drew much more attention than Kentucky Governor Paul Patton, who stood a few feet away as anonymously as a busboy.

Chandler hadn't been elected to any office, hadn't played sports competitively since his days at the University of Kentucky, where he lettered in baseball and tennis and played basketball for the legendary Adolph Rupp.

In fact, Dan had hung his hat in Las Vegas as a casino host for decades and was known for his amazing employment track record at Caesars Palace. At last count, he was hired and fired seven times.

Over the years, the high-roller host occasionally butted heads with the Gaming Control Board, but muddled through and kept on grinning. Dan was irrepressible.

And he loved to laugh about the millions he didn't make as one of the world's worst businessmen.

When it came to being the life of the party, big Dan had no peers. Happy Chandler's wayward son was in a Hall of Fame of one.

When it came to meeting and greeting, Dan was all-world. He got that from his daddy, the late Kentucky political icon and former Major League Baseball commissioner Albert B. "Happy" Chandler. Everywhere we went that week, Dan ran into not just one friend, but dozens. He didn't merely acknowledge a person's presence, he roared his salutation like Foghorn Leghorn.

That year, Dan's namesake thoroughbred, the Mike Pegram-owned Danthebluegrassman, was a late scratch with a muscle strain at the 2002 Kentucky Derby. Although I know it hurt his heart to hear the bad news on Derby morning, he didn't flinch and instead added it to his repertoire of self-deprecating one-liners. After all, Dan knew a thing or two about a bum leg. He battled horribly painful circulatory and blood maladies in recent years.

"He was very ill," Dan's sister-in-law, Toss Chandler, said through her tears after learning of his death. "We just thought he could conquer anything."

So did I.

On that first Saturday in May 2002, Dan's man Bob Baffert took War Emblem to victory in the Derby. It was a win that placed the trainer on top of the thoroughbred racing world.

Baffert eschewed the international limelight the next day and drove out to Versailles to Dan's near-famous after-Derby fried chicken picnic. Celebrities from the horseracing world mixed with politicians and plain folks. They filled his big cabin, poured out across the lawn, and lived a little bit larger because of their man, Dan.

The whiskey was prime, the chicken sublime, but they really came to hear Dan work the crowd like a cross between a revival preacher and Don Rickles. He could build up a man's character and playfully assassinate it as fast as any nightclub comic.

Everyone I met that day hung on each word of Dan's homespun soliloquies, which usually began with, "It's like my daddy said . . ."

His daddy invariably said something that rang as true as a church bell and was side-splittingly funny.

Dan was 70 when his big heart gave out, and he packed a world of hard living into those years.

In future Derbies, they'll play "My Old Kentucky Home" and run for the roses just as in years past, but the party won't be the same without the original Dan the Bluegrass Man.

From *Las Vegas Sun* Editor Brian Greenspun: "Dan Chandler used to say that he was just like his father, without the accomplishments.

"For all of his friends — and the really good ones numbered in the hundreds — that was just Dan talking because his accomplishments were legend. And they all had to do with being a friend.

"Dan was the youngest son of another legend. Albert Benjamin "Happy" Chandler did all there was to do in one man's lifetime. He was governor of Kentucky from 1935 to 1939, a position that cemented Dan's future as the son of one of the great icons of the Bluegrass State. He spent a lifetime trying to live up to his name. And, as if the top political spot in what his daddy called "the promised land" was not enough, Happy Chandler laid claim to the earthshaking moment in sports history.

"Dan's father succeeded the tough-minded and immovable Kenesaw Mountain Landis as the commissioner of baseball and in 1947 did what no other man dared to do. He stood up to 15 major league owners and supported the head of the Brooklyn Dodgers, Branch Rickey, when he signed the first black player in major league history. When Chandler said yes to Jackie Robinson, when most of baseball and a lot of the country — especially the part from where Chandler came — were saying no, he changed forever the face of professional sports and made himself a hero for generations yet unborn.

"Living up to that kind of legend was no easy task and my friend Dan would be the first to admit it. He was also the first to embrace that legacy, which forever made him a favorite son of Kentucky. Of course, being a favorite son did not always mean he was in good favor. Dan had an indefatigable gift of gab and an unquenchable thirst for living life not only to the edge, but also many times over it.

"For him, there was only one place that could handle his love of this great life. Las Vegas. So this is where he made his home. It gave him the freedom to be the warm and caring man that he was as well as the opportunity to bridge the miles between his considerable number of gambling buddies in Kentucky and his duck-to-water job of hosting them in the mecca called Vegas. Dan was a natural.

"Dan was laid to rest not far from the scene of his favorite sporting event. A sporting event, I might add, that is the favorite for millions of people the world over. We have all heard a lot about the Kentucky Derby, but unless you had the pleasure of Dan's company when the Sport of Kings strutted its royal stuff at Churchill Downs, you had, as the man says, 'never seen anything yet.'

"Whether it was staying in his daddy's cabin in Versailles, visiting the incredible horse country of Lexington, or taking that short ride to the Derby aboard the governor's train, there was nothing like it and no way to do it without Dan Chandler's blessing and divine-like intervention. Just ask Claudine Williams and former strike force lawyer, Richard Crane.

"Dan died in his sleep in that cabin he loved so much just a few days before the Kentucky Derby. The first weekend in May was always a high point in the life of 'the man' from Kentucky. Dan's life had some very low points, too.

"The lowest time in my friend Dan's life was when his son, Joseph Daniel Chandler Jr., died 11 years ago. It was the kind of tragedy from which most parents never recover and I daresay Dan had his moments. The coroner ruled the death a suicide although Dan and some renowned experts knew differently. Sure, his son had his share of demons but nobody sets out to kill himself by playing Russian Roulette. That's when you put one bullet in a six-shooter and spin the cartridge. Not knowing where the live bullet is, you pull the trigger. You have an 85 percent chance of survival!

"It is stupid and it is downright crazy and you have to be nuts to play that game. OK, Dan knew his son was troubled — he was not of sober mind — but he also knew he never would have taken his own life. The coroner didn't agree, and as much as Dan tried to get an impartial judge to consider the facts, an intractable district attorney would not allow the case to be heard, thereby not giving a father the satisfaction of knowing he tried. It was inhuman and it ate at Dan for as long as he lived.

"I heard of Dan's death from one of his longtime friends, Dick Traweek, who called to tell me the sad news. He was already on his way to the Bel Air Country Club in Los Angeles — where Dan was the only nonmember member, as near as I could tell — to move the American flag to half-mast. Dan could tell the best stories at the drop of a hat and the guys at Bel Air loved his stuff, which made him a fixture at the round table of distinction. They will miss him there, too. Heck, guys everywhere loved to be holed up with The Man when he was on a roll. Which was almost all the time.

"I don't know how and if Dan ever came to grips with the giant shadow his father cast his way and I am pretty sure his son's death haunted him to the end. But I do know that a whole lot of us lost a man we can never replace, a man of many accomplishments. Chief among those accomplishments was his stubborn loyalty to those he called friends. As is often the case, he was a better friend to most of us than we were to him.

"And I also know this. Right now Dan Chandler is back with the man called Happy, telling him how he kept the legend alive. And Dan is also with his son, learning the truth and finally, putting that tragedy to rest. All is right in Dan's world.

"You might say our friend, Dan, is Happy now."

From former federal prosecutor Jim Ritchie: "My Man! The world's not going to be the same since we can't hear that from our friend Dan. We all have our Dan Chandler stories.

"I was at the Mirage. We were hosting the president's re-election fund-raising campaign in Las Vegas. I persuaded Dan to come to the reception with me. The biggest personality we had here, of course, was the president. But we had David Murdoch, who was the president's finance chairman for his re-election. David was surrounded by several female lieutenants with their clipboards listening to his every word taking down all his important notes. I approached Mr. Murdoch and introduced myself and said I'd like you to meet my guest, my good friend Dan Chandler.

"Dan said, 'Murdoch? I go to Bel Air a lot. There's a Murdoch who has a home there.' Mr. Murdoch swelled in his importance and said, 'Four homes. Young man, to show you what a great country this is, I started with a pick and a shovel and with my bare hands I created a financial empire. There's just nothing one can't do in this country.' And he began to wax poetic about all of his accomplishments.

"Chandler was silent until he said, 'Mr. Murdoch, I understand that you've ascended to all these financial heights in your success. But I was born in the Governor's Mansion in Kentucky and from that height we must have passed somewhere along the way.'

"We know how animals have unconditional love. Danny had unconditional friendship. He did not know how not to be your friend. We all loved him."

From casino executive Claudine Williams: "There are so many things that are sweet and cherished in my heart about Dan. And there are so many funny things.

"I remember Murray Ginnis once said, 'Do you know how to make Dan Chandler really happy? Let him comp everybody in the state of Kentucky for room, food, and beverage.'

"I was in his office at Caesars one day and Dan was going through his mail and throwing letters away. I said, 'Dan, that was your light bill.' Dan said, 'They'll send more.'

"There were twelve or fourteen of us at dinner in Kentucky the night before the race. And Dan had always said, 'I'm going to marry Claudine. And I'm going to retire. I won't have to work anymore.' And we were about nine-thirds drunk. At the end of the night, Kenny Sullivan said, 'Dan, what happened? I thought you were going to marry Claudine.' And Dan said, 'She wouldn't sign the pre-nup.'"

From casino executive Dave Hanlon: "When Caesars executive Harry Wald walked into the casino's barber shop and saw Dan getting a haircut in the afternoon he said 'Chandler, I can't believe you're getting your haircut on company time.'

"And Dan said, 'General, it grew on company time.'

"Dan taught me the definition of a friend in Las Vegas. He said, 'It's a guy who stabs you in the front.'

"Dan really did have the ability to love everybody. He was never, ever jealous of his friends. No matter what their success was, he was always thrilled for them."

From Los Angeles real estate investor Dick Traweek: "Dan was a man among men — the greatest casino host Las Vegas ever had. He had great humor and a warm personality for greeting everyone.

"Dan just admired his father. He started most of his stories, 'My daddy said . . .' "My favorite is the one he used to tell about leaving home. He'd ask his dad for $10 to go somewhere and said his dad would give him $20 and say 'go twice as far.'"

From Las Vegas political consultant Sig Rogich: "Dan was a Damon Runyon character with a Southern heritage — very bright, very likeable, a good friend to a lot of people."

From Cache Creek Casino executive Kent Donithan: "Dan was an incredible individual. He had a tremendous impact in my life as a friend and colleague. Unfortunately, in the world we live in today, there are not the characters in this industry that there once were. Dan was a great character who taught me a lot about the industry and life itself.

"And he was so funny. Dan once said, 'If you have any character at all, you won't go very far in this business.' When we'd run across an executive who was in over his head, Dan would say, 'Kent, that guy couldn't get a job pumping gas in Arizona.'

"Dan had a magnetic personality. He was an incredible guy, but his life in a lot of ways was shortened by the death of his son. Dan was haunted by the death of his son. He definitely felt a lot of remorse.

"At his funeral, Dick Crane said, 'Dan was a gift. He was a gift that we received.' And Dick was right."

From golf course developer and gambler Billy Walters: "He was an unbelievable guy, one of a kind. No exaggeration. There are a thousand colorful stories about Dan Chandler."

At a ceremonial supper with Chandler, the dining room was packed with golf and entertainment celebrities.

Walters said, "The room was filled with very important people. But there wasn't anyone there who didn't know Dan, and there was no one there who knew more people than he did."

From Debbie Munch, a longtime public relations official at Caesars Palace: "He rubbed elbows with some of this country's most powerful characters. He knew how to take care of every customer, and he will be missed."

From Las Vegas realtor Marti Scholl: "Dan was like a brother to me.

"When I first met him, he let me stay at his place while he was out of town. How could you not have a sense of humor about Dan? Either that or you couldn't be friends with him.

"I don't know how many times his phone, water, and power were turned off because he forgot to pay the bill. And I don't know how many times he left it to me to help him get his phone, water, and power turned back on.

"Dan was totally irresponsible, but totally lovable. That's contradictory in my mind, but it's true. His irresponsibility was so unintentional. He said he'd do something and when he said it he meant it, but the thought was gone from his mind as soon as the words were spoken. In some ways Dan was so child-like. In other ways, he was so sophisticated. He knew everyone in the world of show business and sports. There are so many I couldn't name them.

"The whole world was there around Dan. I think they all loved him. I loved him."

From Mandalay Resorts Vice President Mike Sloan: "Dan was an intensely loyal person and a good friend. And he was a great character straight out of the old Las Vegas. I don't know anyone who didn't think he was a remarkable person — even if they were vexed by him on occasion."

From former federal prosecutor Dick Crane: "We've met one of the great characters in our lives. And we loved him."

Dan's Note on Sources

*T*his is my story and I'm sticking to it, but some of my memories are shared by others, and it's only fair that they get their due. Joe Namath once said, "I don't remember all the figures I'm quoting. I have to look them up. Hell, I don't even remember the point spread for most of the games." If it's good enough for Joe, then it's good enough for me.

Astor, Gerald. *"…And a Credit to his Race": The Hard Life and Times of Joselph Louis Barrow aka Joe Louis.* 1974. Saturday Review Press. New York.

Baffert, Bob, with Steve Haskin. Baffert: Dirt Road to the Derby. 1999. The Blood-Horse Inc. Lexington, Ky.

Bak, Richard. *Joe Louis: The Great Black Hope.* 1996. Taylor publishing. Dallas.

Castleman, Deke. *Las Vegas.* 1996. Fodor's Compass American Guides. Oakland, Calif.

Chandler, Albert B. with Vance Trimble. *Heroes, Plain Folks, and Skunks: The Life and Times of Happy Chandler.* 1989. Bonus Books. Chicago.

Chandler. "Happy Chandler on the Road to the Hall of Fame." Prepared with the assistance of John P. Holway. March 14, 1982. The *New York Times.*

Cosell, Howard with Peter Bonventre. *I Never Played the Game.* 1985. William Morrow and Company. New York.

Gifford, Frank with Charles Mangel. *Gifford on Courage.* 1976 Bantam Books. New York.

Hollander, Zander, Editor. *Great Moments in Pro Football.* 1969. Random House. New York.

Jacobsen, Peter with Jack Sheehan. *Buried Lies: True Tales and Tall Stories from the PGA Tour.* 1993. G.P. Putnam's Sons. New York.

Kessler, Ronald. *The Richaest Man in the World: The Story of Adnan Khashoggi.* 1986. Warner Books. New York.

Land, Barbara and Land, Myrick. *A Short History of Las Vegas.* University of Nevada Press. Reno. 1999.

Lasorda, Tommy and David Fisher. *The Artful Dodger.* 1985 Avon Books. New York.

Liebman, Glenn. *Golf Shorts.* 1995. Contemporary Books. Chicago.

Lyons, Paul, editor. *The Quotable Gambler.* 1999 Lyons Press. New York.

Moldea, Dan. *Dark Victory: Ronald Reagan, MCA, and the Mob.* 1987. Viking Penguin. New York.

_____. *Interference: How Organized Crime Influences Professional Football.* 1989 Morrow. New York.

Munchkin, Richard W. *Gambling Wizards: Conversations with the World's Greatest Gamblers.* 2002 Huntington Press. Las Vegas, Nevada.

Namath, Joe Willie with Dick Schaap. *I Can't Wait Until Tomorrow . . . 'Cause I Get Better-Looking Every Day.* 1969. Random House. New York.

Nelli, Burt. *The Winning Tradition.* University of Kentucky Press. Lexington, Kentucky. 1998.

Puzo, Mario. *Inside Las Vegas.* Charter Books. New York. 1977.

Rice, Russell. *Adolph Rupp: Kentucky's Basketball Baron.* Sagamore Publishing. 1994.

Robinson, Jackie. *I Never Had It Made.* The Ecco Press. Hopewell, New Jersey. 1995.

Shoemaker, Bill and Barney Nagler. *Shoemaker: America's Greatest Jockey.* 1988 Doubleday. New York.

Smith, John L. *Running Scared: The Life and Treacherous Times of Las Vegas Casino King Steve Wynn.* 1995. Barricade Books. New York.

_____. *No Limit: The Rise and Fall of Bob Stupak and Las Vegas' Stratosphere Tower.* 1997. Huntington Press. Las Vegas.

_____. *Access Las Vegas,* Fourth Edition. 1997. Access Press/HarperCollins. New York.

Stevens, Gary, with Mervyn Kaufman. *The Perfect Ride.* 2002. Citadel Press/Kensington Publishing Corp. New York.

Stuart, Lyle. *Lyle Stuart on Baccarat.* 1982. Lyle Stuart Inc. Seacaucus, New Jersey.

Sugar, Bert Randolph, with Cornell Richardson. *Horse Sense: An Inside Look at the Sport of Kings.* 2003. John Wiley & Sons. New York.

Vinson, Barney. *Las Vegas Behind the Tables 2.* 1991. Gollehon Books. Grand Rapids, Mich.

_____. *Ask Barney: An Insider's Guide to Las Vegas.* 2002 Bonus Books. Chicago.

Wade, Don. *"And Then Arnie Told Chi Chi..."* 1993. Contemporary Books. Chicago.

Weatherford, Mike. *Cult Vegas: The Weirdest! The Wildest! The Swingin'est Town on Earth! 2001.* Huntington Press. Las Vegas.

Wilson, Earl. *Sinatra: An Unauthorized Biography.* 1976. Macmillan. New York.

Index

G

Gale, Jackie 106

Gathrid, Sid 94, 159

Gaughan, John "Jackie" 56, 69

Gaughan, Michael 69

Gennis, Murray 79–80, 117

George, Phyllis 145

Giambra, Joey 163

Giancana, Sam 75, 96

Gifford, Frank 186–187

Gilboy, Dan 5, 230

Girard, Jimmy 194

Glick, Allen 91

Gluck, Henry 78, 82

Goldstein, Butch 90

Gomes, Dennis 120

Goodman, Oscar 87, 91, 112

Gordon, Jerry 94

Gormet, Edye 105

Greenspun, Brian 230, 235

Griffith, R.E. 51

Grober, Bert "Wingy" 75–76, 109, 113, 127

Grossman, Melvin 57

Groza, Alex 29

H

Hagen, Cliff 30–31

Hagler, Marvin 158

Halloran, Bob 158–159

Hanlon, Dave 230, 239–240

Hanson, Dave 81

Harrah, Bill 50

Harry, Bob 194

Hawkins, Alec 172

Hearns, Thomas "Hitman" 158

Henley, Don 102

Henry, Pat 98

Herbst, Jerry 69

Hilton, Barron 67

Holmes, Larry 154, 156, 158, 163

Holmes, Lauretta 163

Hoover, J. Edgar 20

Hope, Bob 20, 36–37

Hornung, Paul 106, 152, 182–183

Houssels, J. Kell 56

Hughes, Howard R. 60–64, 65

Hull, Thomas 51

I

Irwin, Barry 135

J

Jackson, Travis 24

Jergensen, Sonny 98

K

Kashiwagi, Akio "The Warrior" 119–121

Katzenberg, Jeffrey 77–78

Kefauver, Estes 54

Kempton, Bill 44

Kennedy, Ethel 42

Kennedy, John F. 37–39

Kennedy, Joseph 37–38

Kennedy, Robert 39–40, 57

Kerkorian, Kerkor "Kirk" 64–70, 132

Khashoggi, Adnan 123–124

Kilmer, Billy 98, 106, 182, 184–186

Kim, "Mr. Kim" 114

King, Billy Jean 202

King, Don 157, 162